New Beginnings: Annabelle's Story

New Beginnings: Annabelle's Story

By

Charlotte Parker Caminos

New Beginnings: Annabelle's Story
First Edition

LEDGE MEDIA
WHERE THE LEADING MEET THE EDGE

Published by:
LedgeMedia
P.O. Box 230054
Encinitas, CA 92023
www.LedgeMedia.net
info@ledgemedia.net
Phone: 833-533-4363

ISBN: 978-1-944891-87-9
Library of Congress: 2023921854

Dedication

To my beautiful grandmother, Margaret, who I thank for the inspiration to write and the gift of love she gave to me.

Table of Contents

Chapter One The Passage 1

Chapter Two The Landing 16

Chapter Three Bayonne 29

Chapter Four Budapest 48

Chapter Five Alfredo's New York 64

Chapter Six The Wedding 87

Chapter Seven After the Wedding 97

Chapter Eight New Beginnings 103

Chapter Nine Trouble in Paradise 127

Chapter Ten The Engagement 141

Chapter Eleven Christina 158

Chapter Twelve Miklos 173

Chapter Thirteen What Next? 186

Chapter Fourteen A Surprise for All 192

Chapter Fifteen A Lot to Think About 199

Chapter Sixteen A Day to Remember 209

Chapter Seventeen Another Confusing Day 216

Chapter Eighteen Finally, The Wedding 223

Chapter Nineteen Settling In 229

Chapter Twenty Next Steps 243

Chapter Twenty-One Life Begins 250

Chapter Twenty-Two What to Expect..260

Chapter Twenty-Three One Family 275

Chapter Twenty-Four Best Laid Plans 279

Epilogue 282

About the Author..286

CHAPTER ONE: THE PASSAGE

Annabelle clutched the side of the railing and reread the letter she had studied so many times before, while preparing for this journey.

My Dearest Annabelle,

Naturally, you can use my name as a means of gaining entrance into the United States. We will support you in your emigration process. However, you must understand that Rowena and I have no room for you or your child to stay with us on any kind of permanent basis. But we will certainly help you for the first fifteen days you are here and we will come to pick you up at Ellis Island.

To answer your questions about Ellis Island...We came through before the new facilities were built, so I hope you will have a much better time of it. The experience for us was dreadful. We were treated much like animals without regard to our feelings or to our comfort. There were thieves all around us and we found it impossible to rely on anyone for the correct advice, even the so-called officials. We learned of other immigrants who had money stolen from them as they were not given the proper exchange rate for their funds.

The surroundings were dark and dreary and we were literally herded into lines for inspection, just like cattle. That was not as bad as what happened next. When we got to the exchange counters, we had the most trouble because they gave us less than what our money was worth.

Grandmother, fortunately, had warned us of the dangers as I am now trying to do for you, and so we were aware of the correct rate of exchange when we arrived and were able to argue for them to correct the mistake. I suggest that you remember these dangers and learn all you can before disembarking. Do not depend on any other human being for your welfare and that of your child.

We came before the fire at Ellis Island in 1897, and we were pushed all together into the large two-storied building. There were many windows and many drafts too. The two towers reached to the sky and I first felt like there was a warm welcome from this country when I gazed at them. But the officials we encountered did not make us feel the same way. The walls of the interior were a kind of drab brown, but we had shelter and a place to eat.

We were able to go to the ticket sellers on the second floor to buy our passage to New York. Many other people were stranded. One man was left with almost no money after the exchangers took his currency and replaced it with only three American dollars.

When he realized that he had been cheated there was no one to help him and he was not able to defend himself, unlike us. Even going to those in charge did not make a difference. He demanded a hearing but he got nowhere. It was fortunate for him that he had family living in New York who could come and meet him, because they threatened him with deportation if no one was meeting him.

Keep your person clean and that of the child. They will separate you if they see a problem and the young one could be caged alone, without you, for further examination. Be sure that your hands and face are free of rashes and do not exhibit any nervous behavior. I would not want to see you detained for weeks or even longer.

I wish you were not traveling alone, but rest assured that I will meet you when you arrive, as I promised.

Lovingly,
Your cousin, Janos

Annabelle tucked the letter back into her bodice and slipped along the deck, searching for Magyar, the palm reader. She found the old woman huddled against the freezing winds in the corner behind stacks of coiled ropes. She had her head buried beneath the woolen blanket that was wrapped tightly around her body; only her babushka was recognizable. Her face was reddened from the wind whipping around them.

"Magyar, Magyar, wake up. It's Annabelle. I need your help."

Taking a few coins from her secret hiding place, she tried to tempt the fortune-teller.

Magyar lifted her head only slightly; there were not enough coins to awaken her.

Remembering Janos' words, she hesitated a moment. Then she reached deeply into her pocket and displayed another two coins. Magyar's eyes opened slightly, then a little wider. She pretended to be too tired, but Annabelle knew her well enough to know that this was a way of masking her interest.

"Annabelle, my dearest. What is it that you want?"

"Magyar, I cannot sleep thinking about the landing. Please read my palm and tell me the future."

"But Annabelle, I have already done this for you."

"Well, then, do it again and find something new to add."

"All right, my dear, sit down beside me." Annabelle hurried to find a cushion before she could change her mind. Scurrying back as quickly as possible, she settled in next to the gypsy so that she could extend her arm in comfort. In the background, the dull hum of the emigrants' voices made Annabelle sigh in annoyance. And she never noticed the handsome man staring at her and hiding himself from her view.

Magyar went on without any discomfort. Clicking her tongue in her mouth, she focused on the lines in Annabelle's palm. Annabelle stared too, but, try as she might, she could never see anything special there.

Magyar ran her fingers lightly over Annabelle's palm. "I see, she whispered, "that you have a very long life line." Annabelle squirmed. "But, alas, it is a broken one. I can tell that you will have a major illness or an accident. Do not worry, my dear, for you will recover, but you will be very sick...close to death."

Magyar paused for a moment; she seemed to be searching the crooked lines for the right answers. Annabelle's heart skipped a beat as she prayed that the gypsy would find the future she wanted to hear about. She squirmed impatiently. Magyar continued, "You will have many children, at least five with the same man. There will, however, be seven in all; one child will not live. I can also see that you will be meeting a new gentleman soon."

Now Annabelle started to pay attention. She had not heard this part before. The wind was blowing so hard that Annabelle had to lean forward to hear her better. She knew she could not get the gypsy to repeat herself, so she had to listen very carefully.

"He will be very important in your life. He has traveled with you in other lives; he is your soulmate. It will not be long for you now, Annabelle. You will marry him."

"What will he look like, Magyar? How will I know him?"

"You will know him at once; you will feel it. Now, Annabelle, that is all. I am tired."

Abruptly it was all over. Annabelle watched her pull her head back into the blanket. She turned in frustration, bumping into a young man beside her. His laughing eyes told her that he had been amused by the gypsy's palm reading. Angrily, Annabelle straightened her back, shot her nose into the air and stomped away.

Alfredo turned away from the woman and watched her make her way across the crowded deck. He smiled at her youth and her beauty, wondering what had brought her to this ship and where she would be going, once she reached the United States. Idly, he retired once again into his thoughts. He paced the deck, feeling the wooden surface through his thin shoe leather. He realized he had lost track of time; when he noticed that the sun had set in the sky, his stomach reminded him that he had not eaten. He wondered if he should pay a visit to the palm reader as the strange girl had done. His mind wandered to the young woman he had watched so intently. Though he could not understand their conversation, he could sense the intensity of the exchange.

He had to admit that this woman was attractive, in an unusual sort of way. He would not call her beautiful. She was intense. Yes, that was it. Her green eyes suggested depths of emotion. He found himself wanting to know more about her. He decided he would meet her before the ship landed and make an opportunity to talk to her. It would be too bad if he should lose track of such an alluring female.

Suddenly he reeled from the force of an unexpected blow. Regaining his balance, he saw a frail-looking child scrambling frantically away.

"*Ciao, bambina! Aspetta!*" he yelled.

But the child continued to run, disappearing into the darkness. He wondered what could have frightened her. Shrugging his shoulders, he decided to find something to eat. He was much hungrier than he had first thought. Shuffling along, his head hung low, he was deep in thought. He reached into his threadbare pockets to finger the few coins left. He drifted into a dreamy state, feeling how he could not wait until they got to Ellis Island. He had such plans.

When he arrived at the dining area, most of the people had already left. He chose a quiet place in the corner where he would be safe from the prattling of Lucia. She would never find him here, he hoped. But, within five minutes Lucia had entered the room. "Alfredo, I'm so happy you are here. I have been looking all over the ship for you."

Alfredo winced but responded politely, "Lucia, would you like to join me?" She had already seated herself before he finished speaking.

"How nice of you," she replied coyly.

Alfredo knew she would have joined him, invited or not.

"Did you hear about the excitement on deck?" she continued.

Uninterestedly, he murmured, "What excitement?"

"A young woman has lost her child somewhere on the ship."

"How could anyone lose a child? Surely you exaggerate."

Lucia ignored his comment and continued. "The little girl was playing under the stairway with her doll. The mother was talking to some friends a short distance away when, suddenly, the child began to scream and run off. The mother tried chasing her, but it was dusk and the child was too fast. She was unable to catch her."

"Lucia, the child will find her way back to the mother. You wait and see."

"Alfredo, you don't understand. It's getting cold up there and it's dark. The child could fall overboard; the mother is beside herself. A search party has been organized to help the woman. It feels like everyone is busy looking for the little girl." She lowered her voice and tucked her arm in Alfredo's, drawing closer to him. "Wouldn't you like to help? We could search together."

"All right, Lucia. As soon as I finish eating I'll join the others. Is the mother from Naples too?"

"No. They say she's from Hungary and only about 18 years old."

"And the father of the child?"

Lucia put her head down, feigning shyness. "There is no father of the child, if you know what I mean."

Pushing his plate aside, Alfredo rose in annoyance. He did not feel like doing anything tonight and Lucia was wearing him out with her hint of gossip.

Reluctantly he followed her, noting her tiny form and well-shaped bosom. Her rosy cheeks made her attractive, but she talked too much for him. He thought she could drive a man crazy. Why couldn't he be happy with her? It would make everyone else content, including his own parents who had tried to convince him that this would be a good marriage for him and for the family. That was the reason they persuaded Lucia's parents to bring her to the United States now, since Alfredo was moving there. The families thought, "What better time to encourage the culmination of their life-long relationship in marriage!" He shook his head in anger, as if to dislodge this prospect of his future. Why did he have to be subject to an arranged marriage? He wanted to direct his own life, not continually take orders, first from his parents and now, it seemed, from Lucia. When he reached the doorway, he stooped to clear the entrance. In doing so, he brushed against Lucia's sweet-scented hair. Its fragrance and sheen had a disturbing effect on him; he could feel the heat rushing through his body. His excitement grew in spite of his feelings about her. He became angrier, this time at himself. He would not permit himself to be so easily influenced. To cover his feelings, he snapped, "Lucia, go a little faster, I would like to get some sleep tonight."

When they reached the deck, they could see that people were gathered in groups, all excitedly conversing in their native tongues.

There were emigrants from different countries. Alfredo searched for his fellow countrymen, knowing that he could learn the facts from them. Spotting them on the other side of the deck, he approached and rapidly joined in their conversation. The excitement was catching, and he was anxious to become involved. He almost forgot about Lucia until he felt her tug on his sleeve.

"Alfredo, no one has searched below deck. Why don't we do that?"

Admitting to himself that she was right, he decided to follow her once again. Yet, he resented the fact that she was the one who had thought to search on the lower levels. He knew how unpleasant it was in steerage and hated to go into that area. He considered himself blessed to be traveling as a second-class passenger.

Annoyed with the situation, he began to admit how easy it was becoming for him to reject Lucia's advances. Was it really Lucia that he was rejecting or was he just railing against the pressures that both families were applying to him?

Rounding the corner, he stopped abruptly. There was the same young woman who had been with the palm reader. Her eyes were red and her spotless appearance was gone. Smudged hands gripped the corners of her apron, which were permanently pinched into a knot. Her dark blonde hair was cast in all directions while she tugged feverishly at one single curl. Her helplessness was in direct contrast to the secure and independent attitude she had displayed on deck. Alfredo felt his breath catch in his throat; he was overcome with concern.

What was happening to him, he wondered? Suddenly he wanted to go to her and draw her into his arms. Yet, he didn't even know her. He felt sorry that he had been laughing at her when she was talking to the gypsy. Why was he feeling so confused? It was frustrating.

What was wrong with him? She was not even what he had been taught to admire in a woman. He mentally compared her to Lucia who was very much like his own mother. No wonder his father had sought out so many mistresses. Like Lucia, his mother was boring, always the same, a simpering woman, bland, like unbuttered bread. Yet he did love his mother, so why couldn't he love Lucia?

Lucia grabbed his hand and pulled him toward the stairway. Her only hope of capturing his attention was to distract him from the others. If not, he would fall into conversation that would probably continue for hours. Alfredo loved to talk, but not to Lucia, and she knew it.

He turned in exasperation toward her. "I'll be along in a few minutes; I want to question the mother."

He pushed his way towards Annabelle. Giovanni was on the sidelines, translating from Annabelle's broken English into Italian. Alfredo knew he could count on Giovanni to get every possible scrap of information from the woman; the man thrived on gossip. So Alfredo edged closer to his friend, cocking his head to hear better.

He suddenly sensed the presence of another man who was intently listening but who was discreetly keeping his distance, like he was hiding something. Alfredo felt the hairs on the back of his neck stand up straight. Instinctively, he recognized that this was a person to watch, someone he felt was not honest, even harmful to others.

Giovanni was relating, "The little girl, Paula, was playing behind the ship's ropes, near where the fortune teller was sitting. Her mother had just left the gypsy when she heard her child scream. She started towards the child, who suddenly began to run. No one has seen the child since then. The mother is frantic and blames herself for leaving the daughter she calls Paula, all alone."

"What does the child look like?" asked a voice from the crowd.

"She is very frail - only four years old. She is wearing a gray muslin dress with a flowered apron; her eyes are blue and her hair yellow."

Alfredo asked, "Does the mother have any idea what could have happened?"

Giovanni patiently spoke with Annabelle a few moments and then turned, "No, she does not know. Everyone here has been kind to the child. She cannot imagine what could have happened."

Barely able to draw his eyes away from Annabelle, Alfredo forced himself back through the crowd to Lucia's side.

"Let's go now," he barked at Lucia.

"Why do you act so angry?" she replied mildly. She continued reassuringly, "After this is all over, we will sit and rest. Just being together will make things go better." Alfredo recoiled from her touch, as she slipped her arm through his.

They began the laborious descent and the long search in the lower regions of the ship. It was dismal and tight, the air fetid from the smell of the people pressed together. Alfredo dragged Lucia from one dark corner to another, searching wherever he found an isolated spot that might hide a child. He turned over crates, moved discarded clothing and blankets, uncoiled ropes, looked under benches and behind doors, to no avail. There were so many people packed in the ship that Alfredo started to think they would never find the child until they landed. However, the thought of Annabelle so desolate and alone drove him to continue searching. There was something about that woman that made him want to help her, to take care of her. He was annoyed at himself for becoming so unnaturally involved, yet he could not help himself.

Lucia now began to tire and whine. Her clothes were dusty and smudged with the dirt and grease of the ship's steerage compartments, but she tried to persevere, and even Alfredo had to admit that her efforts were sincere. Finally, when it seemed totally hopeless, he escorted Lucia back to her section of the ship where her own people were huddled together.

"I will continue to search," he stated abruptly. She only shook her head in silent agreement. He left her to continue the search, poking and prodding wherever he spotted anything unusual or wherever he saw a child sleeping. Still he could not locate the child.

Finally, in desperation, he wove his way back through the masses of people to find Giovanni. Passing near the stairs, he noticed what looked like another pile of blankets. It was now so dark that he had to squint to see more clearly. Curled into a ball was a tiny child. This must be the missing girl. And when he moved closer, it seemed to him that this was the little girl who had run into him.

He studied her face; she appeared to be asleep. Yet, she was not moving, even a bit.

He touched her, but she did not seem to be breathing. He reached out to feel her face; it was cold as ice. He thought he felt a faint pulse. Rather than move her, he bounded up the stairs to find the mother.

Pushing through the crowds of people, he finally reached Annabelle, who sat silently behind the ropes where Paula had been playing. She had her arms folded close to her body and was rhythmically rocking back and forth. Someone had drawn a shawl around her shoulders, but Annabelle seemed unaware of anything. The tears were continually flowing down her face, and she clutched a battered corn husk doll in her fist.

No one was paying any attention to her. She seemed totally alone. Alfredo felt like everyone had given up. He thought, the child will probably die, and how can I tell the mother?

He whispered, "*Signora, Signora.*"

Annabelle showed no sign of recognition. Alfredo rested his hand on her arm and still she did not respond. He reached into his pocket, grasping the worn piece of handkerchief, he wiped the tears from her eyes. She turned her head slightly; he motioned for her to follow him.

She tried to stand, but she did not seem to be able to regain her balance. With his arm under hers, he guided her forward. A faint glimmer of hope showed on her face, as they made their way to the stairs. She was so unsteady on her feet that he was forced to practically carry her down the stairwell until they reached the bundle in the corner. He pointed out the child to the mother.

Annabelle fell to the floor and gathered her baby in her arms. She stroked the child's forehead, cooing in her ear. Alfredo stood nearby, feeling helpless. Overcome with emotion at the loss of a life so young, he shifted from one foot to another, trying to decide what to do next. Annabelle continued to rock back and forth while he silently watched her. After a while, he began to think that he was dreaming the whole event.

Exhaustion ensued and Alfredo sat listless on the stairs, waiting for Annabelle to make a movement or ask for help. He dozed while he waited.

When he awoke, the first hint of dawn brought him out of the stupor into which he had fallen. Startled that he had drifted off like that, he called himself to attention, only to note that the scene had not changed. He reached out to feel the child again. Now, there was no pulse, but Annabelle had not realized this. She still cuddled her child, as though nothing had happened.

He ran to find Giovanni who could, at least, speak to the mother. He knew that he would translate her broken English. Alfredo edged closer to his friend, straining to hear. Together, Alfredo and Giovanni, after talking, decided to get help from a crew member; all three returned to Annabelle. But the scene that followed would be imprinted in his memory forever and would haunt him; he repeatedly would find himself reliving it in nightmares.

Giovanni gently reached out to Annabelle, trying to get her attention. In her grief, she was not able to understand what he was telling her. She just gripped the tiny figure tighter to her bosom, refusing to be separated.

They called for the gypsy who came to provide solace. In her native tongue, she attempted to explain to Annabelle that her child had died.

But Annabelle kept shaking her head in disbelief, though the gypsy continued chanting. "Annabelle, you must let go. Paula is sleeping with the angels. Let me help you."

Finally, the crew assembled, grabbing Annabelle from behind, pried her arms open, examining the limp figure of the child. They discovered the marks on her arms and neck where she had been bitten. They said that it clearly was the rats. Unwilling to start a panic, they covered the small body with an old blanket and tied it with ropes. Annabelle began to fight, striking them and kicking them to regain a hold on her child. The deadly fear evident in her eyes made her wilder by the moment. From her throat came a horrifying moan; it caused everyone to shudder as they watched her crumple to the ground. Alfredo had never heard anything like this cry in his life. It made his skin crawl.

Alfredo witnessed the burial at sea and heard the prayers and chanting of the other emigrants. Annabelle heard nothing, remembered nothing. For three days she remained unconscious. Alfredo feared that the crew would take her for dead as well and throw her overboard.

Alfredo sat at her side, wanting to reassure her, wanting to offer warmth and comfort. He was afraid that she would also die, and though he could not understand why he felt that if that happened, a part of him would also die. He could not understand how he became so deeply involved. Yet he was unable to help himself.

Lucia kept her distance, sensing that if she said or did anything to provoke him, she would pay dearly. But she stayed nearby, hoping he might see her and ask her for help.

When everyone had given up, Alfredo continued to guard Annabelle. He was the one who saw her eyelids flutter; he was the one who brought her a morsel of food.

Two more days passed before Annabelle started moving about. The once beautiful young woman had disappeared. Her hair lacked luster; her eyes stared listlessly. Her sureness of stature was replaced by a bent and stricken form. With shoulders drooped and the new wrinkles in her face, she seemed ten years older. Yet, Alfredo stayed true, attaching himself to her side, remembering the alluring, fascinating woman he had seen before.

He knew he could do nothing but watch. When he heard the news that they would be at Ellis Island the next day, he feared for Annabelle and himself.

How would she ever get past the inspectors? He knew he would be the only one who could get her through the checkpoints. But why should he take responsibility for her? And would he ever see her again? He could not help but wonder what would happen to her. How could she have made such an impact on his soul? In his mind, he somehow knew that his life would never be the same again.

All this while two observers took note of Alfredo's movements: Lucia, who suppressed her jealousy for the sympathy she felt for this woman and the unknown man, who suspiciously hovered nearby, never speaking, but always looking with an unnatural interest. Annabelle never noticed him, but Alfredo kept him closely in his vision.

CHAPTER TWO: THE LANDING

The morning of the landing was gray and dismal. The emigrants were not affected by the weather, milling around the deck and watching the horizon to glimpse a sign of the Statue of Liberty, the symbol of their freedom and success. Alfredo stood with the others at the railing, but his mind was not on Ellis Island.

He was barely aware of the excitement filling the air. Voices were rising in a happy crescendo as people searched for their possessions and their family members. Those who had made new friendships were animatedly discussing the experiences they hoped to share in this wonderful country where they would soon live and prosper.

There was only one passenger not involved in the preparations of the day. Annabelle still sat in a lifeless position, forlorn and lost.

Alfredo started to worry that they would send her back to her country. He approached her very slowly. Nearby, the gypsy lingered, watching with interest.

He tried calling her name, but she did not answer him.

And so, looking around, he saw the gypsy and directed himself to her. He knew that she could speak Italian and could converse with both Annabelle and himself.

"Have her prepare herself for the landing."

The gypsy responded, "I have already spoken to her. She says she is ready."

Angrily, Alfredo snapped back, “She is ***not*** ready. Help her prepare herself. If they see her like this, they will send her back to her country. Make sure she combs her hair and straightens her clothing.”

Magyar flinched under his commands, “And you, young man, what is this to you?”

His face reddened. “I want to see her have a chance for happiness.”

“There is little chance for happiness for Annabelle.”

Again, anger welled up in his chest. “Everyone makes their own happiness. Do as I say.”

Begrudgingly, Magyar leaned over to Annabelle and, in a soothing, melodic tone, urged her to get ready. Annabelle looked up and, glancing at Alfredo’s worried face, slowly began to move about, gathering her things together. Alfredo turned to the railing, anxious to avoid Annabelle’s gaze. She was making him feel self-conscious.

He became aware of what, at first, was a slight humming sound. In minutes, it gathered in intensity until all the voices of all the emigrants joined together in the language of frenzied excitement. On the horizon was the Statue of Liberty. Standing majestic in the harbor, she invoked a glimmer of hope in Alfredo. Though he had heard a lot about the statue and imagined just what it would be like to see her for the first time, Alfredo could not explain the chills he felt running along his spine and the anxious anticipation that was welling up within him. His dreams came cascading back through his mind, the dreams he had woven over long months of preparation. He stared with disbelief at the symbol of his new life.

He felt Lucia behind him. “It is wonderful, isn’t it?” she asked.

“Yes, it is,” he replied. “Now take yourself back to the group you came with so you get through the investigators without a problem.”

“What about you?” Lucia inquired.

“I am going to see that this young woman gets safely ashore. After her experience losing her child, she is unable to comprehend or communicate.”

“If you must,” Lucia replied, turning her back on him and swiftly walking away.

He watched the other passengers shed silent tears, and his own heart skipped a beat. Slowly the ship moved along, and Alfredo could see the uplifted hand bearing the torch that would light their ways. He wondered where he would end up and if he would remember this moment for the rest of his life.

The ship became chaotic; people pressed themselves along the railings, cheering and shouting with abandon. More and more packed themselves against the metal restraints, boisterously pushing themselves forward. Alfredo felt himself getting crushed under the weight of those behind him. He was afraid the railings would give way, plunging them all into the harbor. He turned to find Annabelle, but he could barely make her out in the crowd behind him.

The ship inched its way until they neared Ellis Island. Anxiety seemed to take over, making the crowd suddenly quiet down. Anticipation hung in the air. Alfredo recalled the stories he had heard on the crossing about the inspections at Ellis Island. He remembered the experiences of those who had gone before them; he recalled the incidents of confusion and mistreatment. His anxiety heightened. Everything seemed magnified. He tried to calm himself. He remembered that he had meticulously planned that his own entry would be without consequence; his papers were in order; his relatives would be waiting for him. He pictured his sister Maria and her husband Luigi, laughing together. But, now he knew that it would not be a carefree experience. He felt an intense sense of responsibility for this helpless woman that he really knew nothing about. And no matter how hard he tried, he could not figure out why he felt so strongly about her.

He reviewed Luigi's words, "Alfredo, don't worry. Together we will work in my vegetable market until it is the largest and grandest in the City of New York. We will build our own empire in this great land of America. And it will be our achievement, together."

New York, the city with magic in its veins, mysterious and vast, a place where castles could be built without obstacles, where streets were paved with golden opportunities that were available to all, without exception. All you had to do was work hard. Alfredo knew he could do that. This was the land where he would build his fortune and his future. All he needed was a good woman by his side to help him, and children to bring him strength and continuance. Love was another story. Alfredo did not count on love; he had never seen married love or experienced it in his own family life; he did not believe it was real, only the imaginings of the impractical.

The ship jolted, bringing him back to the present. He heard the shouting of orders and was jarred into action. They were ready to disembark. The mass of people became more uncontrollable. First class passengers were taken first. He found Annabelle, waited with her, as out-of-the-way as possible, and watched these more well-to-do emigrants disembark with no difficulties. After a couple of hours, second class passengers were released into the City of New York. He understood that it would soon be time for the steerage passengers to move forward; they were being prepared by the ship's workers.

He found himself carried along by the movement of the other bodies pressing in around him. He started to feel frantic, unable to hold himself erect. His first thought was of Annabelle, almost helpless in her stupor. He inched his way towards her, fighting the energies of the crowd pushing against him. He felt the shock of pain as he began to get battered, a fist in the stomach, an elbow in his side, a heel on his instep. The electric, searing agony from a kick in his shins made him take a deep breath and halted him momentarily.

He reached for Annabelle, who was pushed apart from him, helplessly getting jostled along. Now he could barely see her through the crowd. People towered over her, and she was lost from his sight. Then, once again, he shoved himself forward, finally finding himself at her side. She had allowed herself to be mechanically driven along with the mass of people, not caring what happened, hardly able to stand on her feet, floating along with the milling horde, unaware of the throng, of Alfredo, of the landing.

Alfredo firmly grabbed her arm, so she could not slip away. He heard instructions being shouted, first in one language and then in another. The crowd continued surging forward, screaming in unison. He was carried to the gangway like a ragdoll, at the mercy of the moving surge of people with Annabelle at his side.

At the edge of the gangway stood the first inspector, who was critically looking over the emigrants as they approached the shore. Placing his foot on solid ground made Alfredo aware of the fact that he was also surprisingly unsteady. In spite of his self-control and his significant size, he could not control the sensation of drifting back and forth, as though he were still on the ship. He glanced at Annabelle; she had a blank expression on her face. He knew, with a sinking feeling that she would never respond to questioning; she was completely adrift in some world of her own making. At that moment, he decided what he would do.

Protectively placing his arm around her shoulders, he tried to present a picture of unity and contentment. He stood proudly and possessively next to the girl, trying to display a calm exterior, so the official in front of him had no idea how his stomach was churning.

Gratefully, he muttered a prayer under his breath as they passed through the first checkpoint. They were driven up a flight of stairs until they found themselves in the Great Hall. For most of them, this was the day of reckoning, the culmination of dreams. For Alfredo it was more magnificent than he could ever imagine. From here, he would start his new life.

Castles built in the air; dreams fashioned on fantasies woven by need. He glanced around the room, the largest he had ever seen. He knew they would interrogate him here. He knew he could be physically examined if they thought it necessary. He kept repeating to himself – over and over again, that only confidence would win him entry, and now he had to worry about Annabelle too.

The room itself was about 200 feet long and 100 feet wide. As the masses of people began to file in, the room seemed to shrink in size. Alfredo allowed himself to be led onto one of the ten long lines moving slowly towards the interrogators. Grabbing Annabelle, he pulled her along behind him. He saw those at the front of the lines being inspected for disease. He watched as hands, throat and eyes were checked. Some people had their shirts marked with colored chalk for purposes of segregating them. Undesirables would be carried back to Europe, only to face the grueling trip in reverse.

Waiting was tedious. It was a long and arduous process. He and Annabelle were put through inspections to ensure that they were not diseased or impoverished, that they were not criminals or undesirables. The line slowly inched forward.

Alfredo tried to distract himself from the tension he was experiencing. He was unable to converse with Annabelle, since they did not share a common language. So he tried to imagine his life with Maria and Luigi. Hard work and hearty meals, a purpose and a goal, and, oh yes, his health. His health was the most important factor. If he was well, he could always work. He turned his hands over to examine them; he was proud of what he saw. They showed calluses that spoke of intense labor. They had character, not the hands of a sheltered or coddled man. Rather, his hands could master things; they were a reflection of what he was.

In just another minute, they would be there. He glanced furtively at Annabelle so he would not betray his concern. Her face was passive; he decided it was a good thing.

The inspector looked at them routinely, as they advanced forward. He did not seem impressed one way or another with anyone. Next, they found themselves face to face with him.

"Are you with this woman?"

"*Si, Signore*."

"Do you speak English?"

Alfredo looked at him blankly. It was apparent that he did not understand.

The inspector called for an interpreter who then repeated the questions in Italian.

"Let me see your papers." Alfredo extended his hand without hesitation.

"And you, young lady?"

Alfredo poked her to prod her into action. Miraculously, she reached into her bag and produced her documents, although she understood nothing that was being asked.

The interpreter continued to question Alfredo, ignoring Annabelle, not realizing that she spoke a different language.

"What are you doing together? You boarded at different ports."

Alfredo spoke through the translator, "Our families have known each other for many years. My father was a professor in Budapest."

The translator painstakingly went back and forth with prying questions.

"Are you planning to marry?"

"In time," Alfredo responded, "after a suitable arrangement has been made." He felt his face reddening at voicing his inner thoughts, as if voicing them would make them true, Alfredo waited for the next question.

"Who is meeting you?"

Alfredo was surprised that the interrogator allowed him to speak for both of them. "We each have family members coming," he continued hesitantly.

"Well, move on. You both seem healthy enough." How could they be so lucky?

Either the inspector was blind or distracted or overtired, Alfredo thought, as he stole a look at Annabelle. She was the picture of death, pale and weak looking, hair tousled, clothing rumpled, and hands shaking. Alfredo knew the difference with Annabelle's condition; he had seen her beauty, had basked in her loveliness; he even had experienced her spunky personality.

But taking in the rest of the passengers, they all looked dirty and fatigued. A good bath and some rest seemed in order for everyone. Maybe she did look like all the others? Did he also look like that? He wondered.

The level of confusion made it that much more intimidating. The medical and legal questioning was overwhelming, as Alfredo watched people detained and moved into the Hearing Room, where they might be rejected. He cringed to think that almost 20% of the immigrants would never enter the United States and thanked God that he and Annabelle were not directed into this room. With the wooden benches holding those awaiting questioning, the room took on an air of threat. He could see one person after another standing at the Board of Inquiry, being examined in detail until the legal decision would come forth.

He said a prayer of thanksgiving as they moved along the second floor towards the ticket sellers stationed at the far end of the room.

Suddenly, he heard his name called and turned to see his sister running forward, her face lit up with joy. He grabbed her in his arms, swinging her around in circles until they were both dizzy. Laughing and crying at the same time, she kissed him soundly on the cheek.

"Alfredo, you look wonderful! The sea air must have agreed with you. You are the picture of health, though you don't smell so good."

He laughed, straightening his shoulders, proud of his robust and healthy appearance. He recognized then that he was in contrast to the thousands surrounding him, dressed in worn and tattered clothes.

"Well, that can be fixed," he smiled," with some good soap and water."

"And you, Maria. You are so beautiful!"

Maria pulled her husband Luigi towards Alfredo. "Luigi, this is my brother."

Luigi had held back, allowing his wife the chance to privately experience the pleasure of their reunion. Now he stepped forward, grasping Alfredo's hand in a crushing hold.

"We are so happy you have come to share this life with us," he offered.

“Thank you, Luigi. I am looking forward to going home with you.”

He had almost forgotten the fragile figure behind him. Turning quickly, he realized she was gone. He frantically looked around but could not see her.

“Maria,” he said, “there was a young woman here with me. I wanted to introduce her to you, but she is gone.”

“She is in the far corner. I saw her walk away. I think her family has come to get her. Anyway, Alfredo, I thought you would be traveling with Lucia.”

He was quickly angered. “Never mind, Lucia. She is with her own group of people. She has driven me crazy this whole trip. Always by my side, always wanting my attention....”

“That is why father had decided that she was the girl for you. She will make you a good wife.”

“I am not interested in marrying her.”

“I think you must be; her father and ours have made a pact. You will disgrace the family.”

“I will break the pact.”

“You cannot do that. It is not done,” Maria continued. “Lucia’s parents have already started making wedding preparations. We saw them only last week and they have been so excited to see their daughter and you too, Alfredo. They did not want to leave her in Italy with her grandmother, but they wanted to ensure her future, her future with you.”

“Not now. We can talk about all of this later,” Alfredo snapped.

He looked around distractedly. “*Uno momento*,” he said to Maria.

Spotting Annabelle, he took long strides towards her and her family. When he reached them, he bowed his head in greeting. They gazed at him in confusion; Annabelle made no sign of recognition of him.

Alfredo realized he could not communicate with them in their language. He spotted the gypsy and entreated her to help. She answered with a price. Pulling his precious funds from his pocket, he presented her with a coin and pulled her over to the group.

"Tell them I am pleased that they have come to get this girl," he directed.

With a look of disgust, Magyar translated his comment.

Alfredo listened to their response, trying to recognize a word or two so he could figure out what they were saying.

Magyar turned back to him, "They want to know why you are interested in her."

"Tell them first about the child," Alfredo ordered.

With annoyance, she turned back to Annabelle's family.

"The gentleman wants me to tell you that the child named Paula died on the journey." She pulled Janos out of the range of hearing. "It was a mysterious event and no one knows exactly what happened. The child was playing by her mother's side. I was there, too. Suddenly, Paula jumped up and ran away, screaming in panic. She disappeared so fast that no one could catch her. There were too many people on the deck. We could not find her, though we searched and searched for her. She was gone for hours. In the end, it was him that found her," pointing to Alfredo. "She was dead at the bottom of the stairs. Annabelle has not been right since it happened. She does not care about anyone or anything. This man has been helping her through the rest of the journey and through this interrogation process."

Janos interrupted, "Does she care about this man? What is his name?"

"He calls himself Alfredo Caruso. No, she does not care about him."

She glared at Alfredo as she continued, "He only cares about *her*."

Alfredo shifted nervously from one foot to the other, trying to understand what was going on. He continued to sneak looks at Annabelle, trying to see her expressions and if she was responding to the conversation that was going on.

At the same time, he knew he was keeping his sister and her husband waiting. He would have a lot of explaining to do on the way home. From the corner of his eye, he could see Maria, arms folded, tapping her toe impatiently. Luigi was trying to smooth her feelings. He would have to thank him later on.

Alfredo listened in frustration to the answers and questions going back and forth. When he thought there was a lull, he interjected, "Tell them I would like to inquire after Annabelle in the future. Try to get her address for me."

Magyar repeated his request while Janos tore a piece of paper from the brown bag he carried. Balancing the broken bag with their lunch spilling out, Janos dug in his pocket for the stub of a pencil to scribble the street name and numbers. Alfredo took it from him carefully, anxiously awaiting the information.

Alfredo realized that this was the first time he had actually looked at Janos. He was amazed to find himself dwarfed by this overpowering man. He had always thought of himself as powerful and large, but the blonde, blue-eyed Hungarian towered over him. Although Alfredo was more muscular, with a well-developed back and hands of steel, he suddenly felt insignificant. Pulling himself up to his full height, he puffed out his massive chest. He had spent so much time in exercise that others usually thought him intimidating. Tall for the average Italian, Alfredo assumed an aristocratic air as he stretched to his full 5 foot 11 inch frame.

Janos was also assessing his opponent. He strived to keep a silent presence, fighting back the undercurrents that Alfredo seemed to emit. He could not fathom the ulterior motive that this young Italian had. Annabelle had no wealth, and there were many more girls who were much prettier than she was. Anyone of them would have been glad for the attention of such an attractive man. But it was Janos' job to protect his family.

With his piercing blue eyes, he looked at Alfredo, as though to see into his very soul. Alfredo moved uncomfortably, shifting from one foot to another. When the silence continued, he bowed with exaggerated politeness and tipped his cap to Annabelle, turning on his heel.

Muttering a few words of thanks to Magyar, he began to cross the Great Hall to rejoin Maria and Luigi. He bore a passive expression on his face, but he was already calculating his next step. How could he learn English well enough to navigate in this land of opportunity? How could he find an excuse to reconnect with Annabelle with graciousness? And, if he was able to accomplish that, how could he communicate with her?

The obstacles seemed too numerous and overwhelming to him, so he put the whole thing out of his mind, vowing to find a way to succeed. Alfredo was used to succeeding; he always accomplished what he started out to do and would never accept a 'no' for an answer, and he would keep Lucia in her place. He promised himself that.

Annabelle, standing off to the side, was quietly considering this strange man who had befriended her. He entered her life so suddenly and was now just as suddenly leaving it. Only a fleeting moment of awareness and a tinge of sorrow crossed her mind before she turned her thoughts back to her lost child. It was a solitary spark of interest, and then she promptly forgot about Alfredo.

CHAPTER THREE: BAYONNE

Annabelle allowed herself to be pulled along by Janos and Rowena. She refused to speak to them, turning her head when they asked her all the tiring questions that relatives always want to know. She recalled how she had felt that day on the ship when the sun was high in the sky and Paula was hopping around on one foot and pulling at her skirts every few minutes. She wondered why that had seemed so tiring. She would give anything in the world to be interrupted just one more time by the precious child who, at times she now admitted to herself, had seemed like just too much of a responsibility.

Her mind was not kind to her. Just when she thought she had herself in control, another searing memory surged forth, and she began to feel the overwhelming weight in her chest, mounting until the pain started again. It came in surges. There was intensity and then an ebbing, a building up and a slowing down. The constant throbbing in her temples had taken its toll on her; she finally laid her head back in the carriage and closed her eyes.

Janos and Rowena were perplexed. They discussed Annabelle at some length while she slept.

"Nothing will be as we planned," the woman said.

"How is that, Rowena?"

"Well, we agreed that Annabelle and the child could stay with us a fortnight at the most. How can we turn her out now? She is unfit to care for herself, and we really cannot afford to take on any more responsibility."

"I will go to see her grandmother tomorrow."

"Janos, what can you be thinking? You know that her grandmother had decided that she would have nothing to do with Annabelle since the child was born."

"Grandmother has more compassion than that. She will never deny her now that she has suffered such a loss."

"I think you misjudge Grandmother. Once she has made up her mind to anything, no one and nothing can change it."

"Rowena, you remember my words; she will accept her now."

"I hope you are right."

"Trust me, my wife. I have managed to keep us safe and secure up until now. I will continue to handle our lives, so you will be happy."

"I wish I could be as sure of myself and our future as you are."

The couple lapsed into silence until only the clopping of the horses' hooves broke the stillness. Soon the rain began to fall lightly on the carriage and the night filled with mist. The journey seemed like it would never end.

"Janos, is it much further?"

"No, not at all. We are almost there."

They continued through the city until they reached Cherry Street. At the doorway, Janos stopped the team, jumped down and lifted Annabelle's trunk from its perch. He then lovingly reached for his wife, hesitating only a moment to kiss her gently on the cheek. He swept her to the ground and escorted her safely to the door. Annabelle was still sleeping.

Janos returned for his cousin, wondering quietly how he would be able to handle this broken and frail young woman. He had remembered Annabelle for her headstrong ways and her vivacious character. She was always in command of herself, in spite of difficulties. She never strayed from the path she had set. When she became pregnant with the child, she did not apologize, but accepted her situation with gladness, even when the gossiping women in the family judged her harshly. Janos respected that. If she had loved enough to conceive a child, she could love enough to raise it, even if she had to do it all alone.

And so, Janos was happy to have her in his home. He understood that Annabelle's mother was to blame for her plight. She had not made Annabelle feel loved; she had continually left her with relatives so she could engage in her own love affairs.

He tried to remember how many years Annabelle had lived with her own grandmother before her mother and latest husband had yanked her away from her grandmother and taken her back to Hungary. It had to have been at least six years.

Gently he shook Annabelle's shoulder, trying to wake her up. She did not respond.

"Wake up, Annabelle. We are home."

Still there was no response. His heart skipped a beat, as he momentarily feared that she had also died. That would be bad luck.

Now he climbed up into the carriage and placed his arms around her. She was slumped over, so he slowly lifted her to a sitting position.

Again he called her name. When she sighed, he breathed more easily, glad to know she was alive.

"Annabelle, please wake up," he insisted.

Her eyes fluttered open. He thought as he watched her come out of sleep that she must have been quite pretty at one time. It was difficult for him to recall the twelve-year old child, too lanky for her size, never seeming to be able to do or say the right things. He always thought of her as awkward, though assertive, the black sheep of the family, but he had been very fond of her back then.

Annabelle felt Janos' frustration. She could not seem to come out of this sleep that claimed her; she was grasping to reach the surface of consciousness. Grief had overtaken her, and she wanted to drown in it. It was too hard to breathe, too hard to have to remember the horrible events she had endured. She felt that she was under a mountain of rocks, and the air was too thin.

Finally, as she gasped, a slight moan escaped from her lips.

"Annabelle, everything is all right. You are here with me, Janos. Do you remember where you are?"

She was barely able to open her eyes. She tried to recognize the face before her; it was vaguely familiar. In a few minutes she would remember who this was. She knew him; he belonged to her.

Suddenly she thought she remembered. It was Franz, and she was back in Budapest. He would take her in his arms and make everything all better. This feeling would go away. It was just a bad dream. This pain and sadness could not be real.

She answered the voice, "Franz, I am awake. I will be fine and come with you."

Janos shook his head in disbelief. This was going to be much harder than he had expected. Maybe, he thought, she is just exhausted, and tomorrow she will be herself. After all, she had had a grueling journey and an unthinkable tragedy. He began to appreciate the help the Italian had given her.

He finally just lifted her in his arms and carried her into the small, cramped apartment. Rowena had made up the cot in the hallway, and he deposited her on it. There was no sense in trying to get her to eat.

"Let her sleep, Rowena. Tomorrow she will be more like herself. I will go and get her luggage from the carriage."

Rowena tiptoed around the apartment and tried to quietly prepare the dinner. She loved to make *kapusta* and was glad that she had some to heat over. The meal of stuffed cabbages topped with sauerkraut made her mouth water whenever she thought about it. She made it because Janos loved it. She would do anything to make him happy.

She lifted the lid of the pot and inhaled the enticing aromas. She was glad it did not make her feel sick to her stomach. Being pregnant was full of surprises. She pulled her shawl more tightly around her shoulders and sighed with contentment. She knew she was lucky to be in a place of warmth and love.

She wondered how Annabelle was able to sleep through the hearty smells coming from the simmering food. She quietly approached the cot where Annabelle was deeply asleep and where she continued to sleep through dinner.

Later, nestled in Janos' arms, Rowena again recalled her own good fortune. She had married the man she fell in love with; she had everything anyone could ever want – her own place, a baby on the way, a loving and attentive husband. She murmured a prayer of thanks and turned her head to gently kiss Janos' face. He was also sound asleep, tired, she was sure, from the stressful venture he had undergone today.

She listened to the sounds of the house and to the sounds coming from the street outside. It was strangely comforting.

She turned on her side and closed her eyes, but all she could think about was Annabelle, robbed of her child and cast alone in life's journey. If she did not have Janos, she would never even want to live. She could never survive alone, of that she was certain. She wondered if Annabelle was going to survive.

The next morning, the sun was shining brightly; it would be a good day, thought Rowena. She tidied up the small kitchen while she prepared the morning meal – good hearty sausages and dark bread with oatmeal. Just the kind of breakfast that Janos enjoyed! She wondered if Annabelle would join them, but there was no movement from the form on the cot. She knew that she, herself, would only be eating the dark bread. She felt queasy, as she did every morning. It does not matter, she thought. It is a blessing from God, and it will surely pass.

She again nervously glanced down the hallway at the cot and saw that Annabelle still had not stirred. She was asleep in the same position. She wondered when the last time was that Annabelle had actually been able to sleep in a real bed. She hoped she would awaken soon.

Otherwise, she would not know what to do about it and Janos would not be here to ask him.

Janos came into the room smelling of clean soap and manliness. He took her into his arms and caressed her hair, as he placed his lips ever so gently on hers. It was a warm beginning to the day for Rowena; her heart swelled with happiness. She could feel the heat flowing through her body as he continued to press against her. She made no effort to fight him; she adored him. She wrapped her arms around his neck and kissed him until she was breathless. They both began laughing at the thought that such a passionate moment could be happening in the presence of the sleeping Annabelle. Even their laughter did not awaken her.

"What shall I do with Annabelle today, Janos?"

"Do whatever it is that women do while their men are working."

"And what do you think that might be?"

"Taking naps and braiding hair", he laughed.

"Unlikely, my love, if you want clean clothes and dinner on the table when you return from work."

"I know the maid does those things", continuing their banter as he winked at her.

"Are you going to *Anyóka's* today?" Rowena asked, using the name Janos used for his grandmother. "How will you get there?"

"Yes, I am going to Bayonne. Please do not wait for me to have dinner. I will go to Cortland Street and get the Ferry to Jersey City. It is only about four and a half miles to *Anyóka's* from there, and I will eat something at *Anyóka's* house. I am planning to leave work early; I think the foreman will understand our problem."

Rowena wrinkled her brow. "I hope so since you also had to take time off yesterday. We really need this job and the money it brings, with the baby coming."

"Don't worry so, *szeretni*. It will be fine." She loved it when he called her 'sweetheart'.

He rose and put his cap on his head. Taking his overcoat in the other hand, he swept her off her feet and kissed her full on the lips again. Then he planted her on the floor and grabbed his lunch pail. She whispered nervously, "Please, Janos, she might wake up and see us kissing!"

"I think she has seen more than that, Rowena," he laughed. "Now be good and take care of Annabelle for me. I will settle this whole thing today." He chuckled as he strode past Annabelle and out the door.

Rowena had the feeling that Janos had met his match in Annabelle and that he probably would not be able to settle anything at all unless Annabelle agreed to do what he wanted. Would she consent to see her grandmother? Too many words had passed between them, and Annabelle's stubbornness might prevent her from seeing her grandmother.

Maybe the right solution was to find that young man from Ellis Island, what was his name – Alfredo? Maybe he would agree to take care of her; he had done that on the crossing. She immediately felt guilty and pushed the thought out of her mind. How could she be so insensitive, trying to find a way to get rid of this poor, unfortunate woman?

It was not that she didn't like Annabelle. She really didn't even know her. It was that she and Janos had just gotten this apartment and hadn't been married very long. They were so spontaneous with each other; she did not want to give that up so quickly. He was a good lover, gentle and exploring. He never rushed her, just let her savor the experience of loving him. She liked the way he stroked her breasts when she was falling asleep. She enjoyed having him study her body, and she liked touching him and seeing him like that. She stopped herself from thinking about this anymore. She knew her mother would not approve of such thoughts. She just couldn't help it. So, she kept these thoughts to herself, not even sharing them with Janos.

Annabelle spent most of the day silently staring out the window. She didn't respond to Rowena's efforts at friendship; she seemed to be existing in another world. Rowena had no idea what to do about this, so she busied herself with her regular household chores and with planning the evening's dinner. She offered Annabelle some lunch, but Annabelle just pushed the food around on her plate.

When Rowena had finally pulled out the scrub board and rolled up her sleeves, she heard the vegetable cart in the street. Pulling her purse from its hiding place and straightening her dress, she ran downstairs to make her daily purchases.

The street was crowded with other women carrying their baskets. As she selected her produce, she turned to chat with her neighbors. She really liked living on this street. She felt comfortable; she belonged with the many other families from Hungary; she felt happy and thought of home. For a moment, she hoped that Annabelle would come to like it too and settle here with someone nice. Then she remembered how she did not want to share Janos and took back the thought.

From the window, a face was staring through the sheer curtains, watching the activity below. Annabelle was confused. Where was she and who was she with? She could not really recall yesterday's events, but somehow, she was not afraid. She knew she was being helped by someone who loved her. She thought at first it was Franz, but she recognized that she was not home in Hungary, so it could not be Franz. He was in Budapest.

Then she remembered Janos and the beautiful woman who was his wife. Slowly it was coming back to her. She watched Rowena pay for her purchases and head back to the building. She looked so self-confident and secure. Annabelle wondered if she would ever feel that way again.

While the two women started to get acquainted, they exchanged stories. Janos, however, was trudging along the deserted lane to Grandmother Margaret's house. He had gotten a ride along the main road, so he only had to walk the final mile to reach her home. With the sun warming his back, he felt good rehearsing his story that he would share when he got to his destination.

He thought he might say, "*Anyóka*, I know you feel uncomfortable about Annabelle, but she has no one now. She needs you to care for her. Rowena and I cannot do it with a baby on the way. "

No, he thought, Grandmother might think he was trying to manipulate her. Instead, "I really do not have the resources to feed one more person and provide for their needs."

But then, it sounded like he was crying poverty and was not man enough to take on the responsibility. He cringed to think that someone might view him in that way.

In the end, it was not anything like he had planned. When he rounded the last bend in the road, he spotted the large, isolated house, set so far back from the road. In the front, he could see a figure bent over, working in the garden. He knew it was a man, but he was unsure about who it was. As he got closer, he realized it was Rudolf, grandmother's husband. How he had aged since he had last seen him!

He had gained weight, had gotten lots more white hair, but looked really content.

Janos had often wondered why someone would decide to marry in later years, but seeing Rudolf, he realized it had benefited him greatly. He only hoped it had improved his disposition, since he was normally a very grumpy man.

Rudolf turned as he approached. "Janos, is that you? We have not seen you for so many months. What brings you here today? I hope nothing bad has happened."

"I have come to see Grandmother Margaret. Where is she?"

Rudolf offered, "She has someone with her now. She is trying to help them. You already know about this and that she is a healer. Her clients always bring her food and gifts, but she never accepts money from them, even when they leave her after being healed."

Janos asks, "Rudolf, do you really believe she has this power to heal?"

"I can only tell you, Janos, that I have seen her do it again and again. I do not know how. I just accept what I see, even if it really is the person's own mind that is doing it."

"My mother always spoke of her with affection," said Janos, "and claimed that she could change the world for someone. She told me I should seek her out if I ever needed help, and I do right now."

"Let's go inside and wait for her," said Rudolf. As they approached the front door, the client was just leaving. "Margaret will be so surprised to see you, Janos."

Margaret opened the door for them as they got to it. "Janos," she said, "I expected you one hour ago. What took you so long?"

"How did you know I was coming?" he asked.

"I know many things that are happening, that have happened and that will happen. I also know why you have come. To relieve your mind, I want you to know that I will be happy to take Annabelle in and help her out. You should have just brought her with you. I would never turn her away. You should not doubt that I love her. I was angry that she did not use her head, but only followed her heart."

"Is there nothing I can tell you?" questioned Janos.

"I know about the baby dying. Annabelle has a burning hurt in her chest. It is not just losing her child, but also the rejection she experienced from her mother. And then there is the failure of her lover, Franz, to stand up for her. She needs the quiet and comfort of this countryside to find peace. Bring her here tomorrow and I will care for her."

Janos replied, "I am so grateful to you. I feared for her and for me and Rowena, that we would not be able to handle this. But I can't bring her until Sunday. I have missed too much work and cannot stay out another day for fear of losing my job."

"Do not be concerned. Your foreman likes you and understands the circumstances. But do not try to take advantage of his good graces. Come when you feel comfortable to make the trip. On Sunday, I will plan dinner for all of you."

Margaret pulled Janos to her, embracing him warmly. Janos gazed into her eyes and felt safe and sure that everything would be fine, just as his aunt was telling him. Her round body and face put forth a quiet, gentle peacefulness. He recalled, as a child, how he would beg to be able to stay with her. Now, as a man, that same feeling overcame him. He did not want to leave because she reminded him so much of his own mother.

Reluctantly, he kissed her goodbye and started on his way. All of the angst he suffered in thinking about this encounter was gone. He still couldn't get over that she knew everything – she knew that he was coming and even that Annabelle had suffered such a tragedy.

Rudolf stood on the porch watching the tall figure recede into the distance. He thought about how much he liked Janos and how that young man gave him a sense of pride. If he had been lucky enough to have a son, he would have wanted him to be like Janos.

Margaret stared in silence. She was pleased with both her husband and Janos. Things were beginning to work out. The only dreadful event was the death of the child. She knew it had been horrible, but she also knew Annabelle would soon share the information with her and that her sharing would give her some relief.

Margaret suddenly remembered when Annabelle was playing on the front lawn. She had turned six the day before. She was enchanted with the flowers in full bloom, their tantalizing fragrances and the many different colors she saw. Her mother had just told her that she was leaving her with her grandmother, if she wanted to stay. But she also could return to Hungary if she liked, though not right away. Annabelle wanted a real mother and father and said she would choose to join her mother and her new husband. But her mother told her it would be in the future; she would have to wait for the right time.

So many times when she was separated from her mother, Annabelle asked her grandmother why she could not live with her mother. Margaret remembered her saying, "Doesn't she love me? Doesn't she want me?"

Margaret had told her that her mother was attempting to make a new life and would send for her as soon as she was able. That day finally came much later on when Annabelle left Margaret with a smile on her face and tears in her eyes. At six, she had already experienced the cruelty of life, and now, as an adult, she was experiencing it again. The only hope for happiness for Annabelle was in her future. But Margaret knew that would not come easy, either.

Rowena had tried to get Annabelle to participate in the cooking. She finally convinced her to knead the dough for the bread they were going to bake. But Annabelle had that faraway look in her eyes and wasn't paying any attention to Rowena.

"Annabelle, are you listening to me?" There was no answer. Rowena tried again.

"Annabelle, I am speaking to you."

Annabelle blinked. “I am sorry, Rowena, I was thinking of my childhood and of my grandmother.”

“Annabelle, I want you to know that I am sorry about what has happened to you. And I will try to help you, if I can.”

Annabelle’s face softened, “Thank you, Rowena. I will be all right in time. I was just wondering if my grandmother will see me, since she had been so angry with me.”

Rowena asked carefully, “Do *you* want to see her?”

“Oh yes, very much so. I would like to be in touch with her and visit her. And yet, since I know how angry she was with me, I keep wondering if she will consent to see me.”

She continued, “When Janos comes home, I will ask him to help me make peace with my grandmother. She was such a big part of my childhood. I just wish she could have met Paula. Such a beautiful child!” The tears were streaming down her face.

The sun was just beginning to dim when Janos returned home. Rowena had completed her table setting; the simplicity of the meal was fortified by the warm country flavor of the atmosphere. There were fresh flowers on the table, filling the room with a light airy fragrance. Rowena had painstakingly set out her best, embroidered napkins, wanting the dinner to be an occasion, wanting to provide some limited happiness for Annabelle and to make Janos proud of her.

They rarely had people for dinner. Not only did their meager finances limit them, but they also had little time for company. Janos’ hours were long; he came home from work so tired that he frequently fell asleep right after his meals.

The sound of the doorknob turning sent Rowena into a frenzy of activity. The candles she had made for their Christmas dinner were now on the table, and she lit them quickly. Annabelle sat in the rocker, blankly watching Rowena as she sped around the small kitchen. She made no comments and did not seem to take any interest in what was going on. She had that faraway look that Rowena had seen throughout the day. She made no offer to help Rowena with the last-minute preparations. Rowena thought that strange.

Suddenly, Janos entered the room in a rush of enthusiasm.

"Rowena, where is Annabelle?" Annabelle said nothing.

"She's right here," Rowena replied, pointing in the direction of the darkened corner of the room where Annabelle sat, out of the rays of the sun.

Janos strode quickly to Annabelle, pulling her out of the chair and grasping her tightly in his arms. Rowena's eyes danced with resentment. She was accustomed to demanding all of Janos' attention, and certainly to getting his immediate attention upon his arrival home. He had gone directly to Annabelle, not even stopping to greet her.

Annabelle suddenly brightened up, "Janos, what is it? You seem so excited. What has happened?"

He marveled at her response, catching a flash of the old Annabelle. "I have been to see someone that you know well."

Her eyes lit up with hopefulness. "Did you see Grandmother today?"

"I did," he stated.

"Did she ask about me?"

"Ask about you? She wants you to come and stay with her until you begin to feel more like yourself."

"Can it be true?" Annabelle's eyes glazed over.

"It ***is*** true. I would not deceive you about this."

Annabelle dropped to her seat, limp and breathless. She stared fixedly at the ceiling, tears welling in her eyes and sliding down her cheeks.

Janos and Rowena, each in their own way, tried to disguise their embarrassment. Janos went to their sleeping quarters to clean up and Rowena busied herself with chopping the fresh vegetables for the salad, sending prayers of thankfulness at the thought that Annabelle would soon be leaving them.

But Annabelle's tears did not stop, and after a while the low sound of sobbing filled the room. Rowena blew out the candles, feeling that the evening was spoiled. She wondered how she could endure these outbursts even one more day. Janos, on the other hand, started humming an old Hungarian folk tune. The sound of his voice filled the apartment and somehow succeeded in quieting Annabelle.

A touch to her shoulder startled Rowena, and she gasped softly. Turning, she expected to see the massive figure of her husband, but instead faced Annabelle.

"Rowena, I am sorry for my behavior. I cannot help myself and I don't want to spoil your plans for dinner. Let me help you." She wiped her tears with the corner of her apron, an old habit that returned.

Rowena was frustrated beyond her limits. Was it the baby inside her or the situation? She could not decide. Yet, for Janos' sake, she could not betray her feelings. He would not have any patience if she were not gracious and accepting of his cousin.

Rowena turned back to her cooking and replied without looking at Annabelle.

"Can you please cut the bread for me? I will finish here."

By the time Janos returned to the room, looking more rested than he had in months, some of the festive atmosphere had returned. The three settled down to a quiet meal. Janos was too hungry to talk, but Rowena knew she had outdone herself. His face betrayed his enjoyment of the food she had prepared.

The goulash was just right. The meat was done to perfection, tender and seasoned as her mother had taught her. The vegetables made up the largest portion of the meal, succulent and cooked just enough. Janos sopped the gravy up with the freshly baked bread, not saying a word until he was satisfied. Rowena ate sparingly. She was fearful of losing her figure and not being able to regain it. And she was afraid that Janos would stop being attracted to her during her pregnancy.

Her body was beginning to betray the child she carried, so Rowena was becoming more and more self-conscious. She sat back, taking in the vision of Janos devouring his food, and caught her mind wandering to their last intimate moment. She dreamily thought about being in his arms, smelling his manly fragrance and floating in a kind of ecstasy that he so easily invoked in her. She did not even hear him speaking.

"Rowena, what is wrong with you?" he asked impatiently. "Do we have more butter?"

She regained her composure. "Of course, Janos, I will get it for you." She clumsily pushed away from the table and started for the worktable, where she had set out the extra food for the meal. She knocked over her chair in her rush to respond to his request. She did not feel very feminine tonight. Just when she wanted to be that much more appealing to him, she clucked her tongue in annoyance with herself.

"You seem to be upset. Has something happened that I should know about?" he asked.

"No, Janos. Everything is fine. I am just tired tonight."

To herself she thought, I do not want to have another woman staying in my house, and I want my husband all to myself, but I cannot share that feeling with him.

Rowena pressed her teeth tightly together and took a deep breath. Janos would never understand her feelings. There was no need to try to explain how she felt. He would only become annoyed with her and think she had failed him just when he needed her support.

He concentrated all his attention on Annabelle, savoring the experience of being with her again. They lapsed into conversation, talking about childhood memories, and Rowena felt even more left out. She quietly listened to them, resentment building.

"Annabelle, do you remember when I stayed with you and Aunt Margaret, and we chased butterflies in the field? You had a bottle to collect them, but could not catch them, as well as hold the bottle. I carried it for you and let you catch all of the butterflies, even the beautiful Monarch."

"I remember, and what about the day we dug up worms for fishing? I thought they were so interesting that I started to break them into pieces. You stopped me from doing that, but I could not understand why it mattered, since they were bait anyway."

On and on it went. One memory flowed after another until the sky was dark and the hour late. Rowena felt left out of everything. The queen of her household, she was suddenly forgotten. So she sat in the rocker in the corner, knitting a tiny sweater for the baby, feeling more and more rejected. She chided herself. Why couldn't she be glad for these joyful moments for her husband and Annabelle?

Why did this girl have to come out of nowhere to disrupt her life? Then the guilt came.

Please, God, she thought, please forgive my selfishness.

Later in her bed, snuggled next to her husband, she forgot her frustrations. She collapsed in his embrace. She closed her eyes and allowed herself to drift in the sweetness of their lovemaking. When she awoke, it was early morning, and the sun was just beginning to peek through the bedroom curtains.

Rowena turned on her side and caressed Janos' back. She hoped that her touch would awaken him and that she could experience the sudden arousal of his body. But he continued to sleep deeply. He did not feel the kisses planted on his neck, nor the light touch of her fingers on his belly. After a while, she closed her eyes and drifted back to sleep. She realized how much she did not like sharing him. She wondered how she would be able to share him with a baby. A little speck of doubt crept into her mind, but she pushed it away, resolutely. Somehow, she thought, I will make it all work out.

CHAPTER FOUR: BUDAPEST

Annabelle sat in the back of the carriage on the way to Grandmother's house and dreamed about Franz. She was hardly aware of Janos and Rowena, so absorbed was she in her own thoughts. She could hear them in the background, laughing and playing in the front seat of the carriage. In fact, they had also forgotten about her for the moment, because they were so taken with each other and their future plans. Expecting a new baby was exciting; she remembered how it felt.

Her mind drifted back to the day when she discovered that she was pregnant. At first, she feared telling Franz; she feared he would not want her anymore, that she would have complicated his life and compromised his reputation. After all, he was the Count.

She had gently knocked on the door of his study. When he saw that it was Annabelle, he turned with a smile and warmly invited her to join him. There was never enough time for them together and so they took stolen moments when they could find them. And she always felt that there were never enough "stolen moments."

She remembered how she had become involved with Franz. When her father died, Annabelle, who had commanded the admiration of the lower classes as a respected member of the Rakosi family, now found herself not only penniless but homeless as well.

Without her father to support and protect them, Annabelle and her mother suffered from her mother's mismanagement of the household.

Franz, as the Count in the village, heard about their situation and was the one, in this time of need, to suggest that he employ Annabelle until she became of age and could become independent, even married to a gentleman. Engaged as a servant on the estate, she found herself in a happy place.

Yet Fate had other plans for them. Annabelle saw Franz as a father figure and, at first, clung to him in her childish ways. But when the years had passed, the childishness had also disappeared. They fell in love, not suddenly, but slowly, so that neither one quite noticed it at first. She was attracted to Franz for so many reasons. The fifteen-year span between them was not important to her, and he never seemed to notice it either. When she walked into a room that Franz was working in, her heart automatically skipped a beat. She could feel the flush of excitement moving from her chest through her neck and onto her face. In fact, on more than one occasion, Franz asked her if she was all right because her face was so red. She laughed to herself. How she would love to once more feel that charge of excitement move through her body and warm her heart. She missed Franz in so many ways.

As for Franz, he became so entranced with her natural beauty and the maturity she demonstrated, that nothing else mattered to him. He told her, “You bring joy to my being, in the way you look, how you speak, how you treat me. You make me feel special; I love to see you walk into the room, so elegantly. You have your mother’s stature.” He realized that she had him mesmerized and he wanted to be with her always. Foolishly, he thought that it would all work out in the end, not believing that his own mother would be such a powerful force to keep them apart.

Gradually he pulled her into his life, first in small ways – paying her special favors: a rose from the gardens, a bottle of perfume that he spontaneously brought back from the village. There was even an atmosphere of intimacy that started to prevail between them, even when others were present. He would look at her from the corner of his eye, and she would lower her head demurely, thinking instead of the stolen kisses that they shared. His heart was touched by her, and he was determined to make her a more permanent part of his life. She showed so much enthusiasm about virtually everything that happened and everything he shared with her, that Franz found pleasure in just observing her and her reactions to things. And, surprisingly, he told her, "Annabelle, you have changed me from someone who had always looked at the negative side of things to a man who gravitates to the positive. You are good for me."

Soon, even Franz's mother started to notice what was happening. In time, she had a conversation with Franz about his future because she wanted to impress him with her level of displeasure.

"My dear son, you have no idea of what you are doing. I will not permit this infatuation to continue."

"But Mother, Annabelle, comes from a good family; her father was a respected landowner, and I want to marry her."

"Yes, all true, but he was not of the same caliber as you are. There is royalty in your blood; he was a commoner who made a good life. Annabelle is not a suitable match for you. I will *not* have it!"

Franz first thought that over time his mother would change her perspective, because she was just initially upset. However, that did not happen, no matter how kind and attentive Annabelle was to her. Then, when Annabelle became pregnant, Franz thought his mother would surely acquiesce, but he was wrong again, and he did not have the internal strength to stand up to her demands.

He decided to seek out his best friend, Miklos, to see if he had any advice to offer.

Miklos at first listened attentively to Franz's story, but quickly became bored with the "rags to riches" tale that Katrina claimed was behind Annabelle's interest in her son. He offered to visit Franz and see for himself what Annabelle was all about. Franz agreed to set up a singular dinner meeting for the three of them.

When Miklos arrived at Franz's home, he was immediately taken with Annabelle. He found her beauty overwhelming and felt that Franz really had a challenge to overcome, trying to convince his mother of her worth. For Miklos, if this was his situation, he would have no trouble accepting Annabelle. She had a proud and respected father, and Miklos knew that he himself never let anyone else dictate to him what he could or could not do.

He stated, "Franz, wait for your mother to calm down. I think that she will acquiesce over time. Annabelle is so sweet and loving. A mother could only wish the best for her child." Franz felt glad that he had such a faithful friend in Miklos, and he vowed to air his concerns with him as time went on. Yet, the more Franz talked about Annabelle, the more enamored Miklos became with Annabelle, and he began to have thoughts about how he would plan to cement his own relationship with her. He came to believe that Franz's mother would never agree to a union between her son and Annabelle.

It was clear to everyone that, over time, Katrina never would have agreed to accept Annabelle. Franz made it a habit of talking with Miklos every week, hoping that their relationship would give him the strength to stand up to his mother's demands. Miklos, instead, continued to entertain thoughts of Annabelle that fed his desires. He wanted to have her for himself. He promised himself he would wait it out and see just what would happen. He would take his time in planning his strategy. In the end, he vowed that he would succeed, because he now believed that Katrina would never change her mind. He was right.

Franz finally was obligated to submit to his mother's will and, sadly, was forced to share with Annabelle his mother's refusal to accept their marriage. She was disappointed, yet Annabelle was sure that time would bring a new solution. After all, Katrina Amillie was 84 years old. How much longer could she live? Annabelle loved Franz, so she could just wait. In fact, she was happy to wait, to be there for him wherever and whenever he needed her.

When he shared that same information with Miklos, his friend smiled to himself, deciding that he would step in when it was the right time. Surely, Annabelle would be his. Observing Katrina and hearing Franz's comments about his mother, Miklos was now sure that she would never relent. He felt he could save the day.

In the meantime, Annabelle and Franz continued to steal moments together, even when they knew that they could not control the passion between them. From this union, Paula was born. And Annabelle firmly believed that when Franz's mother saw her grandchild she would soften and become accepting of what Annabelle thought was inevitable, a union between her and Franz.

Now, remembering back to that time, Annabelle could not shut out the horrors of her realization that she was completely wrong. She recalled the shame she endured when she was expelled from the household. Leaving the mansion where she had felt so safe and secure was difficult, and the shame she felt overcame her.

She recalled how, in the end, she had to accept the living arrangement in the cottage that Franz secured for her, where he shared every afternoon with her, and where together they awaited the arrival of their child. Residing happily in that cottage after Paula was born, Annabelle even found herself becoming content with this arrangement. She told herself she just had to have patience. Eventually the marriage would come.

Annabelle loved the warmth and comfort this small home provided her. It was the first time she ever had anything exclusively of her own. She loved the décor, the furnishings, and the way things were arranged; she had no desire to change anything. It was a magical place for her. She anxiously awaited the sound of Franz's knock on the door, and the happiness he brought with him. She wanted for nothing else but his attention and loving caresses. Day by day, their love grew. Tenderness and attachment replaced the passions that had been a daily ritual.

However, when Katrina learned of her son's new arrangement, she set her mind to changing the course of Franz's life. She was determined to ensure that Franz and Annabelle would never legally marry. She successfully secured the hand of the daughter of a Count in the neighboring district. This marriage would only increase the Amillie landholdings by 1,000 acres; it was less land than she would have wanted, but Katrina considered this a satisfactory outcome and solidified the agreement without Franz's consent. She would squelch this illicit affair once and for all. And the troublesome Annabelle would have to disappear.

The rest of the story was more than Annabelle cared to recall. Franz accepted his mother's directives, if he wanted to retain his inheritance. Still, he assured Annabelle that she was the love of his life and that he would, nevertheless, take care of her, in spite of his mother's wishes.

He confided the outcome to Miklos, who learned that Franz was finally sending Annabelle to the United States, where she could reside with her grandmother. Katrina would no longer allow Franz to use the cottage to house Annabelle and the baby, so Franz had no other option.

Secretly, Miklos began to plot his own relocation to the United States. He had enough money to make it happen, and he felt he could rescue Annabelle when she reached her new lodgings and vowed to secure from Franz all the information he needed to make that happen.

Before his wedding took place, Franz gave Annabelle enough money to emigrate to the United States and promised that, once she got there, adequate funds would be awaiting her. She would be able to care for herself and his child until the time came when he could manage to extricate himself from the situation in which he was being placed. Then he would divorce and come to her in the United States. Together they could happily live as a family.

Sadly, Annabelle took their child and left. Both she and Franz wept, each vowing to the other that, if God permitted it, they would reunite...somehow, someday. In thinking back on it now, Annabelle realized that the "somehow, someday" would never happen and she now had to figure out a pathway for herself. She did have some funds, but not enough to last a lifetime. She could not survive alone, and now that Paula was gone, she felt certain that Franz would not feel that commitment to support her anymore. She reminded herself that she would have to let Franz know about what happened to Paula. She did not have a clear picture of what really happened to Paula. She wondered if Katrina had anything to do with her death. But then, how could she?

Annabelle got jolted back to reality when the carriage skidded to the side of the road, jarring everyone within and hitting some obstacle. While Janos jumped out to inspect the damages, cursing the driver who had cut him off and disappeared in the opposite direction, Rowena turned to face Annabelle.

"Are you all right?" she asked.

"Fine, and you?"

"I guess I am fine," replied Rowena, clutching her arms to her chest.

"You do look a little pale," Annabelle observed.

"I think it was because I was frightened that we might turn over."

"Well, we didn't," Annabelle snapped. She was impatient with women who were so easily frightened. "So now try to relax. Take a deep breath and try to remain calm. In a few minutes we will find out what harm has been done."

They sat in a strained silence until Janos hopped back into the carriage. Rowena was stunned by the change in Annabelle's demeanor. For her, this was just another reason not to like Annabelle. One moment she was placid and the next giving orders like a general. She felt they would never be able to get along, even though they were family.

"It's nothing," Janos barked. "I just wanted to be certain that the wheels are secure. We have a long way to go, so now we will continue as before." But it was clear that he was irritated. Surely nothing would be the same today. Too many difficult personalities.

The rocking motion of the carriage as it continued lured Annabelle back into her reverie. She now tried to remember just exactly what *Anyóka's* home looked like. The last time she had seen her grandmother was twelve years ago. If she closed her eyes, she was sure she would be able to see her clearly. She remembered the piercing green eyes that seemed to be able to look through you, to sense just what you were thinking. If Annabelle could gaze into them again, she knew she would feel a peacefulness that she had not experienced in so many months. Her grandmother had the ability to bring peace to all.

She reminded herself that her grandmother was really a faith healer; Annabelle had never believed in these magical events, and yet…she had seen….

Annabelle's own mother, Karola, had told Annabelle how *Anyóka* had been able to cure her of a mysterious malady. Karola said she had not been able to eat anything at all; nothing would stay down, not even water. Though Karola had seen several doctors, no one had questioned Karola in detail, and *Anyóka* finally concocted an herbal tea that Karola had to drink three times a day. After the first two days, the illness had disappeared. Karola wanted to know what she had given her, but according to Karola, *Anyóka* would never reveal it, not even to her own daughter.

Annabelle had thought that strange and decided that this was one of the things she would ask about, in time. But she also knew that her grandmother did not trust Karola and probably thought she would misuse information. Annabelle felt that it was sad that her grandmother felt unable to trust her own daughter. She thought a lot about her own mother and why that might be the case.

Annabelle remembered that Karola was majestic, the kind of woman that every man desired. She was tall and elegant with a graceful, lilting walk. When she inclined her head, it was in such a way that she could impress men with her presence. Anabelle remembered how she would gather men around her and bathe in their attentions. To these men, this seemed attractive. To Annabelle, it was affectation. It was difficult to get close to her mother; she was so distant all the time. Only interested in her own life, Karola spent little to no time interacting with Annabelle. She considered her a problematic responsibility, and if she could pawn her off on her own mother, life would be better. She manipulated the world to set the family circumstances the way she wanted them, in a manner convenient to Karola and Karola alone.

Annabelle finally dozed, and in her dreaming state, her mind went back once more to her mother. She felt the sadness she had endured because she could not feel love for Karola. She recognized her harshness and the wall she had erected between the two of them.

On the other hand, Annabelle had deeply loved her father and felt he loved her as well. She had given him unquestioning devotion, so losing him was devastating to her, especially at a young age. Karola had not given a thought to her dead husband, nor to Annabelle's welfare. She had continued to bask in the attentions of the men she met, making herself available to any and all for whatever she could get.

Annabelle recalled how Franz was the one who helped her cope with her father's death, and with the fact that her mother remarried three months after her father had passed. It was shocking. Annabelle just could not understand how her mother could even think about someone else. She shuddered at these memories. They flooded her mind, cascading through her memory, bringing up emotions that she had not experienced in a long time. Fear and uncertainty reigned within Annabelle. Suddenly she cried out in her dream, "Franz, where are you? Why can't you save me from this situation?"

Janos and Rowena turned to look at Annabelle. She surely was asleep, though she continued to mumble, talking through some problem with someone.

"She must be thinking about Franz," Janos conjectured.

"Why would she?" Rowena asked. "When he treated her so poorly!"

"Remember, Rowena, that he was the only one who took an interest in her and who treated her with any level of consideration or love. She was really a lost child- probably still is."

Rowena conceded, "I suppose, if you say so." Inside herself she felt the agitation growing as she listened to her husband defending the woman who had invaded their lives. She was never going to like her, no matter what Janos said.

Janos went on with his explanation, "Karola, Annabelle's mother, had always loved the exquisite and the lavish. Before Annabelle's father died, Karola led a life of contentment. Priding herself on her ability to entertain, she held many parties in the Great Hall of their estate. She was always careful to invite the government officials, feeling that, in this way, she could ensure her husband Rudy's position in their world and ensure herself of an active social life. Rudy rather enjoyed the quiet simple life, but tolerated Karola's parties because he loved her, and because he thought that Karola's behavior was typical of women in that phase and status of life. He could only see her through "rose-colored" glasses, admiring her beauty and strength."

"How could you know so much about this?" Rowena questioned.

"*Anyóka* told me. She explained how Annabelle's father prided himself on his honesty and his energy. He accepted his responsibility for his family without question, and never complained about the workload he had to endure. Every day he arose early to ride across his estate, inspect the land, confer with his workers about how they thought things could be improved, making sure they had all that was needed and assuring them of their importance to him. For a while everything was going fine, until Karola attached herself to Gyorgy Rajk."

"Who was that?" Rowena asked.

"Gyorgy Rajk was known by all to be politically influential and not too sympathetic with the needs of the peasants in anyone's employ. It was rumored that he had influenced Rudy to decrease the allotments that the peasants were receiving from the lands they cultivated. Annabelle was sure that this, of course, was not true. She knew her mother's influence on her father was the factor that caused changes."

"What happened to Rudy?" asked Rowena.

Janos continued, "Rudy had always felt that his men would know him well enough to realize that he would always be fair to them. So, he disregarded the unrest that was building. He felt that his workers would understand him by his actions. He never realized the impact that Karola's behavior had on his future. He was blind to her disloyalty because he loved her so deeply."

"Did she love him?"

"It is hard to say," Janos continued. "Meanwhile Karola persisted in planning her parties, making Gyorgy the focus as her favored guest, without regard to her husband's feelings. Rudy chose to ignore his wife's behavior, and as Karola chose to further cement her relationship with Gyorgy, Rudy continued to look the other way. Their servants were dismayed and made the local community aware of it, worrying about what would ultimately happen to them. It started to cause deep unrest that eventually led to an uprising."

"Did everyone realize that Karola could convince Rudy to do anything she wanted?"

"I guess they did. They saw that he adored her to the point that he turned his head from her indiscretions with Gyorgy. It had become so serious that Rudy himself became the object of suspicion; the peasants assumed that he would not treat them fairly anymore. They thought he no longer cared about the rights of those who lived on his land. And they distrusted Karola and saw what she was trying to do. They understood that her interests did not lie with their welfare. She was abrupt with them, unfair when problems arose and unkind to those who had any special needs that were out of the ordinary."

"Didn't Rudy understand what was happening around him?"

"No, he was so taken with making Karola happy that he ignored all the signs of trouble. When Rudy, encouraged by Karola, entered into an agreement with Gyorgy to have him manage the properties for him, the peasants panicked and discontent increased. Blinded by what Karola kept telling him, he disregarded the subtle signs of unrest. And Karola didn't care."

Meanwhile, while Janos and Rowena talked, Annabelle, in her dreams, felt she was reliving the past events. She did not hear the conversation between Janos and Rowena. She was dreaming and too deeply involved in her own thoughts.

She went back to the day her father died. She remembered how he had saddled his horse for his routine inspection of his properties. She and her mother were occupied with the running of the daily household activities and were involved in planning another of Karola's famed gatherings. They had loaned their carriage to a neighbor and sent their few trusted servants on errands for what was needed for the upcoming night's festivities, so it was unusual that they were unprotected at home.

They suddenly heard shouts and the sound of gunfire outside the manor. Fearful, they fled to the lower regions of the house, huddling together in the darkness of the dank, empty basement. They remained there until dark when they heard the ugly laughter and heavy footsteps recede. They now were less afraid, though they had no idea what had taken place; they trusted that Rudy would be back for them.

When silence had overcome the household for better than two hours, mother and daughter decided to venture outside. They were unprepared to find Rudy's crumpled and broken body on the front steps, crushed from the weight of the steel that had struck him. His head was smashed, and his fingernails had fragments of muslin under them, as though he had clung to his assailants until the end. This was Annabelle's last memory of her father. But Karola could only think of one thing and that was to send for Gyorgy. Though she tried, he did not come. Karola was devastated, not understanding or believing that the man she had admired might be behind the murder of her husband.

Janos continued with his tale, "Annabelle recalled how Franz was the one who came to their rescue on that night of terror, taking both her and her mother to his home and protecting them from further danger. Because he was the Count, people feared him. He told her that he was certain he could ensure their safety with him."

"Then what happened?" asked Rowena.

"As it turned out, Annabelle said she recalled that it was she, not Karola, who needed his protection. Because three months after Rudy's death, Karola managed to marry Gyorgy, who made it clear that he did not want Annabelle around. When Franz learned of this development, he offered to keep Annabelle on as part of his household staff. Her mother and Gyorgy were happy to abandon Annabelle at Franz's home. Gyorgy wanted no part of her."

"So, that is how she ended up in Franz's home," Rowena commented.

"Yes. That began her long association with Franz. Karola never inquired about her, never tried to see her and had no idea of her loneliness; her feeling of abandonment increased as time went on. When Karola learned of Annabelle's pregnancy, she told her daughter that she never wanted to see her again. Grandmother said it went like this."

Karola stated, "You have disgraced me and the memory of your father."

Rowena inserted her thought, "That was an interesting thing to say to Annabelle, given what Karola was doing with other men."

Janos continued, "Annabelle responded, 'But Mother, we love each other. It is only a matter of time and we will be wed. Franz has told me that he will make sure that everything works out for us." However, Karola was adamant. She continued to berate her daughter, "I do not care what you say. Do not speak to me and do not cross my doorstep again. To me, you are dead."

Rowena's eyes filled with tears as she imagined how a young girl like Annabelle, in that difficult situation, had no one to be there for her.

Janos said, "With nowhere to go, Annabelle put her mother out of her mind but continued to blossom in Franz's love. His love was the only thing she could be really certain of, the only thing she thought she could count on. Even when Katrina, Franz's mother, banished Annabelle. She accepted that decision with gracefulness because she believed that Franz would always be there for her. Grandmother told me that Katrina, Franz's mother, said, "You are a disgrace to my household. We have taken you in, sheltered you all these years, given you mercy and protection, and now you have betrayed us. Franz does not want you either. He only feels obligated to you."

"Annabelle told *Anyóka* that she bowed her head in acceptance and tried to explain her situation. She told her, 'Madam, I love your son and I will make him a good wife, if you would just give us your blessing.' But, instead Katrina threw her out of what had become her home.

Annabelle tried to apologize and offered to leave in the morning. But she was told to leave immediately."

Rowena started to soften towards Annabelle as Janos continued to explain.

"Franz, in response to his mother's outrage, had then sent her to the caretaker's cottage, and, in the morning, found her a dwelling of her own. She told *Anyóka* how much she had enjoyed that time with him. They had their privacy to express their love for each other with abandon. There were no accusing stares or sly comments to tolerate. Franz was too feared, too powerful for anyone to say anything about her."

"How did she manage through the pregnancy?" asked Rowena.

"I am told that Franz sent a servant to care for her needs in the last months before Paula was born. She became her companion and remained with Annabelle until the day she departed for America. She was a faithful companion and nursemaid for the baby. In fact, Annabelle was living as a fine lady, except for the meager cottage. Franz brought her clothes of the finest materials…brocades, silks and satins. She dressed daily as though she were being taken to the theater. When Franz arrived each day, and as the baby grew, the nurse would take Paula to the brook to play by the gurgling water. The lovers had an idyllic existence, entwined in each other's love, until Katrina ended it all."

Suddenly Janos' voice, insistent and repetitive, broke through to Annabelle. "Annabelle, we are here. We are at *Anyóka's*. Do you hear me? Let's go inside, now."

With tears in her eyes, she awoke, mumbling, "Janos, I am sorry. I was just thinking about my life. Yes, let's go inside."

CHAPTER FIVE: ALFREDO'S NEW YORK

As soon as he opened the door to Luigi's apartment, Alfredo heard her voice. He hoped that the turning of the knob had not given him away, as he stealthily pulled the door closed and left.

Lucia was everywhere he turned. He ran down the steps back into the sunshine, striding in the opposite direction to his brother-in-law's place of business. It would only be a few minutes before Luigi arrived behind him, coming to see what had happened to him.

Now what would he do? He strolled through the streets of the city, lost in thought. His mind wandered to Annabelle as it had done again and again since that day at Ellis Island.

He came upon a small triangular park, not far from Christopher Street, and looked for an empty bench. Finding a place not far from the old men playing checkers, he watched their game in the sunset and planned his strategy.

He would have to see Annabelle again.

The vendor on the street corner was hawking sausages; Alfredo could not resist. Counting out his money carefully, he decided to practice his very weak English.

"I'll have one," he said.

The vendor inquired, "Peppers and onions?"

Alfredo shook his head, "No, *grazie*."

Feeling proud of his first independent exchange, he was inspired with courage.

He pulled the crumpled paper from his pocket and stared at Annabelle's address. It was one thing to buy a sausage and another to find his way alone from Sheridan Square to Cherry Street.

He had not mastered enough of the language to freely ask directions, but he did trust that his brother-in-law Luigi would help him, even at the risk of incurring Maria's anger. He was a man's man, not to be intimidated.

Glancing at the fading sky, Alfredo decided that tomorrow at work he would seek Luigi's help. He was sure that it was safe to return home now; Lucia always had to be home before dark.

Whistling, he climbed the stairs two at a time and threw open the door with abandon. He tossed his worn jacket on the chair in the hall, and energetically entered the kitchen. No one was in the room.

He stopped at the mirror in the hall to examine his face and smooth his hair. He adjusted his collar from its turned up position and patted down the fabric of his shirt, tucking it into his pants around the dark blue suspenders.

He was so engrossed in thought that he had not heard the voices in the other room. Not only was he now facing Lucia, but also her mother and father.

With exaggerated politeness, he bowed in greeting to her parents and acknowledged her with a half-smile.

"Alfredo, we're so glad you finally arrived," bellowed Lucia's father.

"It's a pleasure to see you, too," Alfredo commented, lapsing comfortably into his familiar language.

Maria could tell from the expression on Alfredo's face that an explanation was in order.

"Alfredo, I forgot to mention to you this morning that we would be having company for dinner."

"Yes, I see that you did," he replied without any hint of annoyance in his voice. He was proud of his ability to remain calm and detached.

Maria held her breath as he continued, "Since it is always a delight to be in the company of such charming people, and because you were not here when dinner was ready, we ate without you. I hope you do not mind."

Alfredo replied, "That is not a problem. I would not have wanted you to wait until this late hour or worry that the food might be ruined."

Lucia chimed in, "I am so glad to see you, Alfredo. You never seem to be here when I stop in to visit."

Luigi interrupted, glancing at his wife with a warning look, "Alfredo has been very busy lately. I'm teaching him the business and it's important that he spends as much time as possible at the market."

"That's very enterprising," commented Signora Della Cesare.

Alfredo stared at the matronly figure dressed in black seated at the far end of the table.

Her face was overworked with excessive rouge and heavy lip color. The corners of her eyes were pinched into a smile, and the wrinkles flowed downward into the pasty color on her cheeks; her hair was fixed in the style of the day, but the choice was too young for the woman he viewed. To Alfredo, Signora Della Cesare was homely and lacked elegance, unlike his own mother who was a stylish older woman. He was struck by the resemblance Lucia had to her mother. It frightened him to realize that one day, she would be an ugly old woman, too.

Lucia's father sat back, enjoying the scene. He felt before that he had made a good match for his daughter. Now that he understood that Alfredo would be a partner to Luigi, he was even more excited. Luigi's business was the most popular market on the Lower East Side; he had the freshest fruits and vegetables at the most reasonable prices. Yes, he thought, Lucia would have a good future with Alfredo.

Lucia's father cleared his throat. "Actually, Alfredo, we came here tonight to discuss more than your business interests, although I am pleased to see that you take your future so seriously. I really want to speak with you about the agreement your father and I made for the marriage between you and Lucia. My daughter informs me that she is willing to be your bride, so I have provided handsomely for her dowry. I know you will be pleased, not only with the beautiful woman you will wed, but also with my generous provisions."

Alfredo swallowed forcedly, careful not to reveal his feelings.

"I understand your concern, Signore, but I do not feel that I am ready to discuss the wedding at this time. I have just arrived in this country and I am unable to take on such responsibilities until I can provide for my own household. At that time, we can continue this discussion."

Luigi cleared his throat. "I think that would be a wise decision. Let's give Alfredo a chance to get settled here."

Maria rose with nervous alarm. "Lucia, help me to clear this table. Then we can serve the pastries."

Although sorely disappointed, Lucia smiled bravely. The last thing she wanted would be to let Alfredo know that she was desperate for him. She had to be more coy and cunning than that.

"Yes, that's a good idea, Maria," commented Lucia. "Anyway, I am too young to marry," she continued. "After all, I am only seventeen."

Signora Della Cesare shifted in her seat, as the younger women continued to arrange the table. "Nonsense, my child," she stated. "You are a woman now. Many respectable young ladies of seventeen are already married."

Signore Della Cesare interrupted, "I think my wife is right. Tomorrow I will have the papers drawn up."

Alfredo started to feel overcome by panic. He had to delay them somehow.

"If you want to do that, fine," he continued. "After I have thoroughly examined the papers, we can talk about a possible date. But not before I am ready to set up my own household. I refuse to have my wife living under someone else's roof."

"Alfredo, my dear," cooed Lucia's mother, "We would be only too happy to have you both stay with us for the first year or so."

"I am flattered, Signora, but my pride requires me to be an independent man. Again, we can talk about this more in the future. For now, Maria, where is the Anisette?"

Wednesday was bright and sunny, just the kind of day Alfredo needed to launch his new life. And that life, he determined, would include Annabelle. Over lunch, he broached the subject with Luigi.

"You know, Luigi, how I feel about Lucia. I don't want to marry her, even if my family has decided that I must."

"It is obvious to me that you don't love her. But what will you do? Surely, your father will pressure you to follow his wishes."

"I am going to arrange to marry someone else instead. And my father will have to accept it."

"But he has made a contract with Della Cesare!"

"Without consulting me. I am an adult, fully capable of making my own contracts. And it was a verbal one, at that! If I can convince Lucia that she doesn't want to marry me, her parents will not force her to go through with the wedding."

"Alfredo, that will take a lot of convincing. That girl is in love with you."

"Young girls are fickle. She is not in love with me, only with the idea of marriage. I will take care of changing her mind, don't worry about that. Now I need your help to find the young woman I met on the boat in the crossing. This is her address. Can you tell me how to get there?"

"What are you thinking? Are you sure of what you are doing?"

"I am very sure," replied Alfredo.

"Well, it is not far from here. Come, I will draw a map for you."

With the stub of a pencil, Luigi traced the pathway from Cherry Street. "Here, go one block to Clinton and south to Delancey; make a left when you get to Delancey and go six blocks to Orchard Street and turn right." He pointed out the landmarks along the way so that Alfredo felt certain that he could find the address.

"Be sure, Alfredo, that you do not mention this to your sister, or your upcoming marriage will not be the only marriage in trouble."

"I know my sister, Luigi. You can be sure that I would not do that to you. She is too fiery. You would never hear the end of her complaining about what you have done."

"Listen, Alfredo, this will require your immediate attention, if you want to do this, do it today. It is already getting late and coming home to dinner after Maria expects you will only cause suspicion. Go now. I can watch the market for the rest of the afternoon. Wednesday is never too busy with customers."

"Thank you, Luigi, You are not just my brother-in-law, but a real friend."

Alfredo embraced him with enthusiasm and sped down the street, even forgetting to remove the apron he was wearing. He was two blocks away from the market before he realized it was tied around his waist. He ran back, throwing it over a hook by the front door.

Alfredo lifted the knocker of the house on Orchard Street and waited. He could hear movement up the stairs and soon saw a pretty head poke out the window. He recognized Rowena from the day at Ellis Island and bowed respectfully. He could hear Janos' voice in the background; he wondered if he had just come in from work and had opened the windows to let the slight breeze into the house.

As he waited at the door, Alfredo thought how some time had now passed since he and Annabelle had arrived in the New York harbor. Maybe these people would not remember him; maybe Annabelle would not remember either. She had been going through so much upheaval, he was not sure if she would recall how he had guided her through the immigration process. Maybe they would not welcome his interest in Annabelle, or perhaps she had married by now. There might have been someone waiting for her here in New York City.

His mind kept jumping from one thing to another while he awaited a response. It seemed that hours had passed by the time Janos came downstairs. The wooden door squeaked open, and Alfredo saw those piercing blue eyes sizing him up. He shifted uncomfortably.

"Well, well, you are the one from the ship," Janos said. He reached his hand out for a warm greeting and pumped Alfredo's arm up and down while he continued, "We never really thanked you for helping Annabelle that day."

Alfredo smiled nervously. He could understand most of what Janos was saying, but his English was very limited. He had practiced what he had to say with Luigi, who made him write it down, should he forget the words.

“I hope I am not intruding.” He spoke haltingly with a thick accent. He suddenly became aware of his own voice, faltering as he nervously continued.

Janos had been in New York for so long that he was able to figure out the essence of speech from the many languages he heard. Though Alfredo was coming along in his language studies, his English was not so easy to decipher. Yet Janos seemed to be managing to interpret his words.

“It is not a problem. Please come upstairs with me and meet my wife. Feel welcome in our home,” offered Janos, as he gestured to Alfredo to follow him.

Alfredo trudged up the narrow and steep stairs, following closely behind Janos. The afternoon sun had dimmed and the interior shadows made it difficult to see. They entered a small room, sparsely furnished, but clean and cared for by a woman who loved it. The floral curtains fluttered in the afternoon breeze, and the hand-embroidered pillows graced the plain and worn chairs. The one piece that caught Alfredo’s eye was the highly polished cherry rocker; it reminded him of his mother’s rocking chair, at home. A wave of nostalgia overcame him. Gracing the rocker was a colorful afghan that was surely carefully crafted by this caring woman. Everything had a woman’s touch.

Rowena was standing shyly behind her husband, as much for his protection as to indicate that she belonged to him. Her figure betrayed her approaching motherhood, yet she was as beautiful as he had remembered.

Alfredo glanced around furtively, looking for signs of Annabelle. She was obviously not there right now.

“Can we help you with something?” Janos inquired.

"I came to see Annabelle and find out how she is. I was in the neighborhood and decided to stop by. If this is an inconvenience to you, I apologize," Alfredo responded.

"No, this is not an inconvenience. Would you like to join us for the evening meal?" Janos asked.

Alfredo replied with embarrassment, "No, I had no wish to upset your day. As I said, I wanted to ask about Annabelle."

Janos continued, coming right to the point, "Surely by now you are settled in the city and are wed yourself?"

"No, I am not wed," Alfredo stammered, trying to think how to tell Janos that his family had plans for him.

"I see," Janos muttered, trying to size up the situation and wondering once again what the fascination was for Alfredo. Annabelle had not expressed any interest in him and, since he and Rowena saw her quite regularly, Janos was sure of that. His mind briefly drifted to Annabelle, who was getting better very slowly. At least she had taken an interest in her handiwork and was trying to learn the language of this country.

To Alfredo, he replied, "Annabelle is not here." Rowena gave him a warning glance. She did not want to reveal any additional information to someone they did not know, even if he did provide a kindness to Annabelle. To divert the conversation, Rowena offered Alfredo refreshments and a seat by the window.

Alfredo declined. "I must go. Can I contact Annabelle, perhaps by mail?"

Janos took over the conversation, knowing that Alfredo was having a hard time finding his words. "I will mention to Annabelle that you inquired after her. If she wishes to see you, I will contact you."

Luigi had written the address of the store, in case Alfredo needed it, so Alfredo handed it to Janos. The two men shook hands, and Alfredo made his way out of the building. He had a sinking feeling that he would never hear from Janos, or that Janos would never mention his visit to Annabelle. He left feeling totally disheartened.

What he did not know was that Rowena was anxious to get Annabelle settled for once and for all; she did not want to have her husband continue to assume responsibility for Annabelle. Even with the long distance between them, she thought Annabelle consumed too much of Janos' attention, always worrying about her welfare and wanting to make frequent trips to see her. She thought that he was spending too much money on her needs.

Janos, on the other hand, was turning over in his mind the strange behavior of this man. What prompted him to take such an interest? Naturally suspicious, he felt there was some ulterior motive he could not understand. He never accepted a situation at face value, except when it was easy to do so. He was careful about people he didn't know and even about those he befriended, even after a friendship seemed to be established.

Janos and Rowena stared silently at Alfredo from the window as he walked away. He was neatly dressed with shoes that were polished. His shirt was clean and starched, and the fedora he wore had a neatly shaped brim. He wore a suit of conservative cut, in a brown wool. Janos thought that perhaps he had wealth; he certainly seemed to be doing well here in the United States.

Alfredo knew that it was Luigi's kindness to him that allowed him to lavish himself with proper clothes. He liked to stroll past the men's clothing stores, gazing at the newest European fashions. Then he would examine the discount vendor's wares to select the most up-to-date styles he could find.

Sometimes he would seek out the tailors on the Lower East Side with the best prices and secure what he could afford. He did not want to look or act like a refugee; neither did he want to speak like one. He had breeding and wanted to re-establish himself at that level of society. He took great pains to practice the English language and to learn how to communicate with everyone with whom he came in contact. Being unmarried allowed him to be able to buy things for himself as he wished.

Yes, Alfredo had great plans for himself and, he thought, for Annabelle, if he could only find her, if he could only get to know her better.

Still he had the problem of Lucia. Try as he might, he could not shake her attention or her family's persistence. Somehow he would have to stall them all; he would not accept a contract, and he did not want to take on a wife at this time, at least not before he had the chance to make a connection with Annabelle.

Annabelle was the girl of his dreams. Sometimes in the evening when he lay in the darkness, he could picture her face before him, the nagging look in her eyes that betrayed her helplessness and the sweet smile she only fleetingly displayed. He thought that she represented everything he had hoped for in a woman.

He tried to recall the girl he had first seen with the gypsy, the one with the self-assuredness and the spunky attitude. He knew, in time, that person would surface again. Her grief would lessen and nature would take over. He wanted to be around when that happened.

He was frustrated; in spite of Janos' words, Alfredo knew his chances were slim. He was subject to the whims of this couple. He had no idea where Annabelle had gone, not even the slightest clue. Of course, he knew that he could only politely inquire, lest they start to distrust him. He had no prior claims, after all, and had no reason to be able to make any kind of demands. He would wait and see. For now he had to turn his attention to devising a tactic that would dilute Lucia's interest and make her less concerned with him.

He returned to his sister's home feeling dejected. And there again he found the persistent Lucia, claiming to be fostering her friendship with Maria. If he put her off too convincingly, she would press her father to seal the agreement. He knew that Lucia was accustomed to having her own way. He also knew that she would do whatever it took to get what she wanted. He decided to invite her for a walk in the early evening air.

Lucia tucked her arm in his and prattled noisily about her day. Although he tried to pay attention to her words, he found great difficulty in having interest in her at all. She seemed so superficial, so unreal, so self-interested.

"Alfredo, I had the most interesting time today. Maria and I visited with Signora Argenta. You know who she is. She lives on the next block and, oh yes, she has six children…do you remember? Never mind, her house has the geranium pots on each side of the front door. Say you remember. Anyway, she has promised that she will help me furnish our apartment. Alfredo, where will we live and when do you think you will be ready to set the date? I know it's not for me to question, but I am ***so*** excited."

Alfredo tried to think of other things until the voice next to him stopped droning on. Then he just nodded, hoping to avoid answering her.

"Alfredo, I asked you, when do you think you'll be ready to set the date?" The irritating pitch of her voice made him turn with a start.

"Soon, Lucia, soon."

She seemed satisfied with his response and squeezed his arm affectionately, but not for anyone else to see.

Alfredo sighed. She was troublesome, very troublesome. Perhaps he could take her home now. When they arrived at her parents, she invited him inside. Not to draw undue attention to his absence and to meet all the standards of propriety, Alfredo agreed to step inside, into the foyer. Lucia hesitated for a moment, slightly pressing herself against him in the crowded entryway.

She turned, blocking his passage, to prolong the moment.

"I had such a lovely time, Alfredo. We will have so many wonderful times together like this."

She inclined her head towards his shoulder and looked up into his eyes in an innocent fashion. Alfredo could smell the heavy scent of her perfume; it was making him feel heady in these close quarters. Her presence was suddenly enticing to him, not because it was Lucia, but because he had not been with a woman in a very long time, not since before he left home. And he realized how foolish he was acting because he had no real interest in Lucia.

He suddenly remembered how his father had taken him to that isolated section of his city, and introduced him to Anna who he said, "would take care of him." She had, painstakingly, taught him whatever he needed to know. He had become fond of her, paying her weekly visits. She was much older than he, but experienced. Alfredo enjoyed her. Lucia's perfume was reminding him of Anna, dragging him back into those times that were so personal to him. He began to feel a tingling in his loins and thought it best to get Lucia inside before he forgot his resolve.

But Lucia had a different mindset. She was determined to prolong this moment as long as she could; she sensed his vulnerability.

Just when Alfredo was feeling helpless, the door to the foyer opened from inside, and Lucia's father bellowed, "Now, my children, we have plenty of time for that. Perhaps Alfredo, I should have the contracts prepared sooner than we discussed."

Alfredo blushed with anger. Lucia had set a trap for him and had won a point. He would have to be more careful. He felt it best not to respond to her father's comments and, rather than draw further attention to himself, he tipped his hat politely to Lucia and left.

Time dragged on. He continued to wonder about Annabelle but could not think of any way to get in touch with her. He had not heard from her cousin or his wife. He realized that two months had passed since he had stopped to ask about Annabelle. His own wedding was drawing nearer, despite his efforts to forestall the event. What more could he do to avoid this event? And, though he did not want to think about it, if Annabelle was not interested in him, maybe he should consider this marriage to Lucia.

It was September 19th, the feast of San Genaro.

This was Alfredo's favorite time of the year. The fall was so invigorating. He loved to feel the cooler temperatures and to see the leaves turning colors. He enjoyed this feast day and the celebrations around it. As he walked through the streets of Little Italy, hearing the accordion music playing his native tunes, he felt his first wave of nostalgia. Up until now, he had barely given a thought to the Italy he knew so well and left behind so easily. He reminded himself that in New York they celebrated what they called Thanksgiving, and that feast was coming soon. It was good to offer thanks for all you have been given. He was grateful, too, and ready to engage in that practice. Unfortunately, he felt conflicted right now.

Suddenly, he recalled the soft rolling hills and the smell of the mountain flowers of Italy.

He could feel the air and hear the goats baying. The aroma of his mother's bread seemed to fill the recesses of his mind, so much so that he found that he had a longing to see her. So engrossed was he in thought that he was hardly aware of the crowds around him.

The food purveyors had their carts filled with appetizing and comforting food. He longed for his mother's cooking; all of those memories of home overcame his senses. He stopped for a sausage sandwich, relishing the smells and already tasting the soft Italian bread that the vendor was loading up with the sausage and pepper combination.

He heard the music in the background; it had a lilting sound, bright and cheerful. Some of the immigrants had made a circle in the roped-off streets, beginning the traditional Tarantella dance. Others were standing around, clapping hands in unison with the beat. Alfredo stopped at the outskirts of the crowd, only slightly aware of the dancing. His mind was still distracted as he imagined tasting his mother's gravy and eating her cheeses. The memory was as stirring as any experience could be, so that he was startled when he felt a tug at his sleeve. Turning slowly, he was pulled back to reality. Expecting to see Lucia, he steeled his face, suppressing the annoyance that was building up inside him.

Instead, he saw Annabelle and her cousin Rowena. Melancholia was replaced by a dizzying lightheadedness. The moment he had thought he was prepared for, that he had rehearsed time and again, was at hand. However, he was caught off guard and totally unprepared. He did not have any idea how to respond. He hoped he was not putting her off.

In his imaginings, he was sophisticated and controlled. He had thought he would bend and kiss her hand, inquiring after her health. She would smile, impressed by his appearance and manner, commenting that she was glad to see him. He would have the right words, spoken with ease and little trace of an accent. He had practiced over and over again all the conversational phrases he could muster. Luigi's mother, a natural linguist, had taken a liking to Alfredo and was coaching him in his English. His motivation, of course, had been this very moment in time. Now, he could not remember any of the phrases he had learned, even though he had practiced them over and over.

Annabelle shifted nervously. Perhaps, she thought, he did not recognize her.

He suddenly felt foolish. Yet Rowena had said that he had come to Orchard Street, searching for her. So he must recognize her.

Rowena would not let this moment pass. She was intent on cementing this relationship, so she ventured, "My husband and I have wondered what became of you. We have not heard from you in some time now."

Alfredo replied, "I am pleased to see both of you again," and, turning to Annabelle, said "especially you, Signorina. I have thought of you many times since the day we parted at Ellis Island."

"Thank you for thinking of me and inquiring after me," Annabelle blushed and stammered in her own broken English. "Also, thank you for the care you offered on that terrible journey and…through the difficult time I had." She could not mention Paula's name; it was still too painful for her.

Turning full circle and sweeping his arms in an outstretched position, Alfredo continued,

"What brings you to the festival? I did not expect to find you here. I did not believe you would be interested in this feast."

Rowena again took over. Annabelle seemed shy and reserved, not at all as he had imagined she would be. "We were home alone today – my husband is at work—and I had heard about the festival. We decided to come and see what it is all about."

"Are you sure, Signora, that it is safe for you to be walking unattended through the city at such a time? Wouldn't your husband be concerned that you have come here alone?"

Rowena knew he would not be happy about it but said hurriedly, "We spoke of it yesterday, and since Annabelle is here with me, he thought it would be fine."

Annabelle studied her shoes so that she would not have to face either Alfredo or Rowena. This was all wrong. Rowena had talked her into this adventure; Janos would be furious if he learned that they had wandered off unescorted, especially with Rowena expecting a child. But who would know them here? None of their people would be at this feast, she thought. He could not hear about them coming here to this feast from anyone that knew them. So there was nothing to worry about.

The banter continued awkwardly between Alfredo and Rowena, while Annabelle wished she could fade into the background. She was only understanding bits of the conversation. She was not assertive and found new friendships difficult at first, especially since she had lost Paula. Any self-assurance she had before had disappeared.

Alfredo studied Annabelle as he tried to answer Rowena's questions. "I am working with my brother-in-law; we have a vegetable market not far from here called, Luigi's. Today we are closed because of the *Festa*, but otherwise we would be open for business."

Rowena said, "You must show us exactly where so that we can shop at your market from time to time."

"Surely it is too far for you to walk. Come now, let me show you around, and, I would be pleased to offer you something to eat."

Annabelle was just about to decline the offer when Rowena's eyes lit up with excitement.

"Oh yes, that would be so nice."

Since her pregnancy had advanced, Rowena had begun to feel more and more lost. Janos seemed to pay less attention to her and her needs, so the thought of a gentleman's consideration was appealing to her. It was Annabelle's turn to feel sorry for Rowena, as she began to realize what was happening.

Alfredo, with one lady on each arm, took them from stall to stall showing them the delicacies available. He pointed out the handmade articles for sale. When Annabelle accidentally touched his hand, it made his heart soar, but most of the conversation was directed towards Rowena. He felt too embarrassed to look into Annabelle's eyes. He thought he might betray his own feelings. Also, he felt afraid.

It was only a matter of time until they met Lucia with her parents. Alfredo was faced with the task of explaining how he had two attractive women with him. He told of the trip to New York, how he had met both of them, and he had to also explain about Rowena's missing husband.

"Signor and Signora Della Cesare and Lucia, I would like you to meet Signora, eh Signora Rowena and her cousin Annabelle."

Lucia leaned back and in an icy voice said, "I remember you, Annabelle, from the ship. You are the woman who lost a child."

Annabelle's eyes filled with tears. Who was this cruel woman, she wondered; she could not remember seeing her before.

Rowena interrupted, "Yes, that is true, but it is in the past."

Alfredo controlled his steadily mounting anger. "I am afraid we have to be going now. I promised my friend that I would personally bring the ladies home. It was nice to see you all again."

"Alfredo, don't forget our appointment tomorrow evening," chimed Lucia sweetly. "You promised to review our marriage contracts."

She was publicly proclaiming her possession of him, brazen in the presence of her parents. Alfredo was angered to the core of his being. We will see, he thought, who will keep that appointment.

Annabelle got the message quickly and felt more ashamed than ever. She should have realized that such an attractive man would be betrothed.

As soon as the Della Cesare's had left, Annabelle cleared her throat and attempted to get her thoughts across to Alfredo. "I am sorry if we caused you any embarrassment. I should have realized that your future was well planned."

Alfredo reassured her. "Nonsense. You did not cause any problems."

He led them through the streets until the singing was behind them. Then, he secured a carriage to escort them home; he was concerned about Rowena's condition. She was now uneasy. Carriages were a rare sight, so she knew that Janos would hear about this, after all.

At the door of the building, Rowena excused herself, claiming tiredness. She quickly mounted the stairs so that she would be adequately prepared for Janos' return home. She was hoping he would not discover that they were not home all afternoon.

Downstairs, on the street, Alfredo lingered with Annabelle. "Annabelle, are you now staying here?" he inquired.

"No," she answered, deciding that it was best to lie to him. "I have just gotten word that my friend's mother died in Hungary, and I will be returning there for a time. I owed my friend a lot; he and his family took care of me after my father died, and I feel the need to return to pay my respects and see if they require any help from me. I had a little cottage of my own there; I can probably stay there again."

Alfredo's heart sank. "It's a long way to travel to pay respects."

Alfredo hesitated but decided he had no choice, so he continued awkwardly, "This is bold, I know, but time is of the essence. Can I convince you to remain here and make a life with me? I know it is sudden, but it appears that I have no time for planning and for a respectable courtship. I knew when I first saw you that I wanted to build a life with you."

Annabelle replied, blushing intensely, "I cannot expect you to make such an offer. Your family would never allow it if you have a wedding of your own in the making. Neither would Lucia's family. I can tell that from meeting her for a few minutes. You really know nothing about me."

"I know you are beautiful and sweet and wonderful," he foolishly rushed ahead.

Annabelle became more uncomfortable. "I have done a terrible thing today, Alfredo. I have intruded on your life, and now I will disappear from it completely. My apologies."

She picked up her skirts and fled up the darkened set of steps.

Alfredo called out," *Aspetta!* Wait, please wait." But she was gone. All his plans were squelched. She would not be back; that was clear to him. The pain of rejection overcame him; he ran blindly through the city, weaving his way back to the sounds of the music and loud cheering of the crowds. It was the heart of the Italians that made him feel so happy here. There was no time for distress and for failure. What will be, will be, he told himself. His fellow countrymen had a zest for living, and Alfredo prayed that it would carry over to him and embrace him tonight.

He turned the last corner, only to come upon Lucia and her parents once more.

"Alfredo, I am so glad to meet you again. Have you taken the young ladies home?" inquired Signore Della Cesare.

"Yes, Signore," answered Alfredo, feeling more and more frustrated and trapped.

"Well, we are about to return home. Lucia would like to stay a little longer. Can we count on you to escort her home later?"

"Of course, Signore," replied Alfredo, as Lucia took the arm extended to her. He was no longer angry, only defeated.

Lucia was tender and understanding with him. Though she knew nothing of what happened, she sensed a crisis had occurred, so she remained uncharacteristically quiet, disarming him even more. Perhaps, he thought, it would be a good idea, after all, to marry her. At least everyone else would be satisfied, and he would no longer be able to yearn for what could not be. Annabelle clearly did not want him anyway.

Dusk had settled in as Lucia and Alfredo watched the candlelit procession passing in front of them. The priest led the way with the altar boys close behind him, elevating the religious statues. Alfredo prayed that God would give him the guidance he needed. It seemed to him that Lucia's hand, slipped silently into his, was a sign from heaven. His resistance was weakening.

Lucia now seemed to be the one leading him to her darkened doorstep. Pulling him into the foyer, she assessed that her parents had gone to sleep and that the house was still and quiet.

"Alfredo, come in for a moment. We have to be quiet, though, so we don't wake up my parents."

"I don't think I should stay," was Alfredo's quick reply.

"No, please do. Wait, I will be back in just one minute."

She tiptoed up the stairs to the bedroom area and could hear her father steadily snoring and her mother's light breathing. She leaned over them, "Mama, I'm home. I am going to sleep now myself."

"I am so glad you are here. I can rest well now." Her mother rolled over, muttering something more that Lucia could not understand. Her father was not a problem. Once asleep, he could not be easily awakened. They would have the house to themselves.

She then checked her sister's bed and saw that she was also sleeping. The time was ripe, thought Lucia.

Downstairs, Alfredo was pacing nervously. His senses warned that this was dangerous. He should be on his way home. As soon as Lucia returned, he would bid her good night.

She came back to him, whispering, "Alfredo, take off your jacket. Let's talk a little while. We have hardly spent a moment alone together."

"Lucia, I don't think your parents would approve of us sitting in the dark while they are sleeping."

"Then let's light the candle."

The glow from the candle cast a spell on Alfredo. Lucia's face was dim and unclear. He was too tired to think clearly as exhaustion set upon him. He was thinking of the events of the day, the excitement and then the disappointments, the rejection from Annabelle that he had experienced, the see-sawing of his emotions. He felt very vulnerable and really wanted to get away, to think things through.

Lucia squeezed in next to him on the loveseat, slipping her arm through his and placing her head on his shoulder. She had inclined her body slightly, enough for him to feel the softness of her breasts, round and firm against his arm. He felt too drained to fight her advances.

“Lucia, I think I should be leaving right now. I’ll see you tomorrow as planned.”

She held onto him more tightly. “Please don’t go, Alfredo. I have so much to say to you. I have thought of nothing but you since my parents first spoke about arranging a wedding. Then, when I learned it was with you, I realized that it would be harder for me to resist you because I already loved you. I have known you all my life and, even though I am young, I will promise to make you a good wife.”

She brought her face closer to his. The scent from her hair intrigued him again, and before he knew it, he was kissing her. She wrapped her arms around his neck and edged even closer to him. Then, suddenly she was on his lap, and he was exploring her body.

He had to stop himself, he vowed. This was Lucia, not Annabelle. This was the Lucia he did not really want. But it was too late for Alfredo. The dejection he had experienced fed the longing. She gave her body freely so he continued to follow the wave of desire until he satiated himself with the sweetness of the experience. He lifted her skirts and pressed the line of her leg into the warm damp region of fulfillment. Before he knew it, they were one. Alfredo and Lucia were so involved with each other that they never heard the squeak of the stairs and the soft footsteps that retreated hastily.

Spent and fatigued, he kissed her again, resigning himself to his inevitable future.

CHAPTER SIX: THE WEDDING

Lucia was radiant. She thought that even Alfredo would have to admit that she made a beautiful bride. As she gazed into the mirror her mind wandered over the past few weeks. She knew she had Alfredo in the palm of her hand. It did not matter that she had tricked him into marrying her. She finally had what she wanted; she achieved what she was striving for. And, she thought, that sorry excuse for a girl, Annabelle, would never be able to have him now.

Just for an instant Lucia's brow wrinkled. She knew what was expected of her.

Suppose she couldn't get pregnant right away? She dismissed that thought immediately. All the women in her family were good child-bearers. She would make it her business to have a child right away; maybe she would even conceive on her wedding night. Anyway, she would keep him in bed long enough to guarantee a pregnancy. She knew he was a family man, and because he now thought she was carrying his child, he agreed to marry her.

Lucia reflected on how easy it had been. Alfredo was discouraged. Annabelle's rejection of him had sent him into her arms. He was ripe for the attention of another woman and she had guaranteed that she was that woman. She hovered around him at every free moment, arranged those family dinners he had been so reluctant to attend, and had been patient and understanding through all of his moods.

Alfredo knew that he had been susceptible to Lucia's charms because he had learned that Annabelle was returning to Hungary, and that there was no chance for him to be with her. He felt that she had made that clear. Until that time he had been able to keep fighting Lucia's attention. That night of rejection had changed things so that he no longer resisted her.

He resolved himself at that point to what he now considered the inevitable—a loveless marriage. He hoped that, in time, he would grow to at least feel comfortable with Lucia, even though he knew he could never really love her. They just did not speak the same language.

Lucia, on the other hand, was reveling in the taste of victory. The sweetness of her success was overwhelming. Though she knew she would face Alfredo's anger if and when he discovered that she really was not pregnant, she thought the chance was worth taking. No one, not even her own mother, knew her secret. She always told her mother everything, but not this time!

She thought if she waited a decent interval, Alfredo would become accustomed to her so that he would be more open to her news. A nagging fear at the back of her mind made her wonder if he really would show up at the church today. But then again, he had the dignity of his family to protect.

She studied her image in the mirror. She hardly recognized herself. Her mother had rapidly made a gown that would rival any other; with embroidery and pearls interspersed in its folds, the gown represented a level of society that few others could imitate. Its perfection would be appreciated by all. Her veil with its delicately embroidered dogwood blossoms swept the floor; her face was made to look elegant; her hair was perfect. She felt confident that Alfredo could only be impressed when she walked down that aisle.

She thought about the wedding arrangements. Her father had hired an accordion player; the food would be provided by the best Italian shop in New York City, and her mother had personally prepared all of the select pastries that Lucia loved so well. Even the hall was festive. Tiny hand-fashioned blossoms were on each table as a centerpiece.

Her reverie was interrupted by her mother's voice. "Lucia, my baby, so beautiful!" she exclaimed proudly.

Her sister ventured, "You will be – how do they say it? – the 'talk of the town'."

Lucia smiled, "Mama, thank you for everything; it is so perfect."

"Lucia, I wish I was getting married," wailed Anna Maria, her sister.

"You will have your turn too, when you reach the right age and Mama and Papa find the right match for you."

"But will I be able to trap him the way you trapped Alfredo?"

Lucia spun in anger. "What do you mean – trapped? He asked me to marry him."

"Only because of what you did. He really kept trying to postpone the wedding, so I don't think he wanted to marry you at all," continued Anna Maria.

"Now, now children," Lucia's mother interrupted. "This is not the time for disagreements. Come. Alfredo will be waiting."

Anna Maria shouted out," I'll bet Lucia *hopes* that Alfredo will be waiting. Maybe he will change his mind and run."

"What makes you so evil?" Lucia screamed. "Get out of here. I hate you."

"Now that is enough," Lucia's mother sternly replied. She grabbed Anna Maria by the arm and pushed her out the door.

Jealousy had consumed the younger sister. Lucia always got what she wanted, no matter how much hurt it brought to others. Just this one time, Anna Maria wanted Lucia to feel the sting of pain she usually caused her.

She popped her head back in the doorway and yelled, "Don't worry, Lucia. If you treat me nicely, I will never tell Alfredo what you have done to him."

With that, Anna Maria was gone. Lucia paced back and forth nervously. How did Anna Maria find out about everything? It was her secret and only hers. She was always nosing around in corners where she did not belong, eavesdropping. Maybe she had been hiding behind the French doors the night Alfredo brought me home from the *Festa*, she wondered. Nonsense, she was sleeping. I checked on her myself. Maybe she was listening when I told him of the pregnancy. Lucia's color heightened until she was beet red. But even if she did, she would not know that I am not expecting a child.

She rushed to the other side of her room and started rummaging through her dresser drawers. That had to be it, she concluded. Anna Maria found my diary and was reading it. But I keep it locked. I'll bet she forced the lock. That had to be how she found out.

She picked up the diary, turning it around again and again to see if it was tampered with. She could not see any evidence of damage. Somehow, Anna Maria had discovered the truth, or maybe she only guessed. That had to be it, she was just guessing.

Never mind. The wedding would take place, nevertheless.

Determined to save the day for herself, Lucia tapped on her sister's door. "It's Lucia. Let me in."

She pushed the door open only to see Anna Maria's expression of victory. She had to control her temper. "Anna, I don't want this day to be spoiled by a disagreement between us."

"There is no disagreement. I just want you to know that I am aware of all your tricks, even if no one else is wise enough to discover what you have really done."

"Whatever are you talking about? What kind of tricks?"

"There is no sense in discussing this at all. You know what I mean. I keep my eyes and ears open. Maybe Mama and Papa are fooled, but I am not."

"You think you know everything, don't you? I suppose you were reading my private journal as well?" Lucia continued.

"Lucia, how crude do you think I am? Your actions are transparent. If you don't stop bothering me, I will speak to Alfredo myself, and the truth will be out."

"Don't be ridiculous. Do you think he would believe a mere child?" Lucia turned on her heel, letting the door slam behind her. Anna Maria was laughing in the background.

The Church was crowded with Signore Della Cesare's associates and friends. Alfredo stood in the sacristy, peering through the partially opened door to see if the few friends he had invited had arrived. He was proud when he spotted Maria and Luigi, handsomely dressed in the garments he had provided for them for the occasion. He smiled as he recalled Maria's enthusiasm over the purchase of a new frock; it was his way of demonstrating his gratefulness to them.

He could hear the organist softly practicing the songs that Lucia had chosen. Yes, this whole wedding is planned just as Lucia wanted it. She has finally won, he thought. He had no choice, but he had to admit that it was his own foolishness and weakness that had him standing in this church today. He could blame no one else, and he never would abandon his responsibilities.

He vowed to himself that he would always remember the beautiful face of Annabelle, especially when things became too difficult to bear and Lucia was too overbearing …whenever he needed to recall that life can be blessed with exceptional people.

He shifted his weight as he heard the bridal march beginning. Luigi came around behind him, prepared to witness his union and support Alfredo whenever he needed it. Only Maria sat in the front pew. Alfredo realized how sparse his guests were. Only twenty people were invited, most of them friends of Luigi and Maria. The bride's side of the church was filled to overflowing. He knew the scales were tipped against him.

"Are you ready, Alfredo? The priest is motioning for us to come now."

"Eh, yes, I am ready."

He waited at the side aisle in the front of the church, looking down at his newly shined shoes. Suddenly, the gasp from the guests made him look up to see Lucia in all her splendor, clothed in the best that her father could afford. He had to admit that she looked beautiful and graceful.

He walked to the center aisle, watching Lucia make her way towards him, her eyes downcast in a shy, retiring attitude. How out of character, he thought. There was nothing shy about Lucia, especially when she had her mind set on something.

Never mind. They would raise a family, and he would grab what little happiness might flash through his life. He would make the best of it. He was committed.

It was easy to see that Lucia's father adored her. With tears in his eyes, he lifted her veil and kissed her, handing her life over to Alfredo in one rushed movement. She seemed to hardly notice her father, so intent was she on looking around at the guests and smiling at everyone. This was the day she had dreamed of, and it clearly was exceeding her expectations.

Alfredo could hear the soft crying from the front row; he did not have to look to understand that Lucia's mother was giving a memorable performance. Signore Della Cesare slid in next to her, handing her his handkerchief and consoling her. Alfredo watched detachedly, feeling as though he was witnessing a tableau.

The ceremony was quickly concluded, and he barely realized he was reciting lifelong vows and that he was entrapping himself in a life he did not want. Lucia was calm and steady, determined and in command.

There was the rush down the aisle with showers of rice and pats on the back. Hurrying through the vestibule, Alfredo never saw the figure hiding in the shadows of the confessionals. The young woman stood solemnly, her face partially covered, tears streaming down her cheeks. Though she hardly knew him, Annabelle felt overcome, felt she was grieving for what might have been. She waited until the guests had vacated the church before venturing into the sunshine, careful to keep her head down and to push between the people crowded around the bride and groom.

Annabelle walked the streets of the city until the darkness obscured her way. With alarm she realized that she had wandered very far from Cherry Street; Janos would be wild with anxiety and Rowena would not know how to handle him. It was Rowena who learned of the date of the wedding ceremony from Alfredo's brother-in-law, when she went to purchase the fine produce they sold. But she never told Annabelle, fearful to add more pain to her life. Annabelle found out when she overheard Rowena talking to Janos about it.

Annabelle started to take stock of her life. What had begun as a short visit with Janos and Rowena was turning into a very long stay. She was becoming more and more uncomfortable as time passed, because she could sense Rowena's displeasure with her presence. Annabelle had planned to stay at her grandmother's house all this time, but when Rowena started to suffer complications in her pregnancy, Annabelle offered to help with the heavy housework and to be there in case of difficulty. After all, she was obligated to repay them for their kindness. Surprisingly, the two women had started to become better friends. Annabelle was glad for this temporary diversion; it had put any thought of returning to Hungary completely out of her mind. Now she had finally resolved herself to being without Franz.

When she finally made that decision, and after she offered to stay with Janos and Rowena, she decided to try to foster a friendship with Alfredo and set out to find the market. In reality, she had begun to hope that there could be more than a friendship between them. When she finally reached the market, she found it closed for the day; the proprietor in the next store told her about the wedding that was taking place. So she decided to see if she could get a look at the couple. Now she realized that she had been holding onto the fragments of the hope for his attention just like, as a child, she used to cling to her worn dolls.

She picked up her pace heading toward what she thought was the main street that would lead her home. She suddenly became aware of heavy footsteps behind her, gaining in momentum. Her heart was pounding rapidly, and she began to run. She heard the footsteps running faster and getting closer and closer behind her. Her arm was jerked backwards, causing her to lurch forward as she let out a scream. Spinning around to face her attacker, she encountered the angry face of Janos.

"Annabelle, where have you been? You have made us sick with worry."

"I was walking, trying to make decisions about my life. I didn't realize how late it had become."

"No decent woman walks through these streets unescorted. Do you have any idea what could have happened to you?"

"I really did not give that any thought," she replied. "I was trying to figure out what I should do now. You and Rowena will soon have your baby; there is no place for me in your daily lives."

"And you plan to do that by strolling through the streets of New York? I bet you have been with that Italian, haven't you?"

"No, I have not. For your information, he is married now, so there is nothing for you to fear from him."

"I will not continue to listen to this prattle. You are under my protection now. We will return home right away and talk about this some more tomorrow."

"There will be no more discussion, Janos, because I will be leaving as soon as possible."

"Where are you going? Where do you think you can go?"

"I will go back to Grandmother's for the time being. Then I will be on my own."

"Women do not live on their own. You are not thinking clearly. Where is your common sense?"

Annabelle reddened as her anger flared. "I will find a way, rent a room and find a job."

Raising his voice, he angrily continued, "Doing what? Cleaning floors?"

"Maybe, yes."

Janos fell into silence. The darkness swallowed up the two figures threading their way through the city. Janos pulled open the front door, hearing muffled sounds from the apartment above. He took the steps two at a time with Annabelle close behind him. She knew that Rowena's time had come.

"Run for the midwife, Janos. I will take care of her."

Annabelle deftly took charge. She had helped her mother deliver many of the babies on her father's estate; it was second nature to her. To Rowena she whispered, "Take deep breaths and don't worry. Everything will be fine."

Annabelle had always admired Rowena's flawless complexion and flowing blonde locks and had felt intimidated by her appearance. But Rowena was not so beautiful at this moment, thought Annabelle, as she struggled with the pain of childbirth. She suddenly seemed so much more human.

"I am going to prepare the hot water. I will not leave you. Don't be fearful," assured Annabelle.

Rowena cried, "No, please don't leave me. I am so afraid. I cannot be alone."

"Rowena, you will be absolutely fine. Don't be such a child."

Annabelle turned to leave her, and then decided to light some additional candles.

"There you are, Rowena. With more light, you will feel more secure."

Rowena's face was laced with pain and the tears were freely running down her cheeks. "I will not be all right. I am afraid I may die."

Impatience burst forth from Annabelle. "You will not die. You will deliver this child as all women have their children, and you will be proud and happy to do it again."

Rowena continued whimpering as Annabelle busied herself with the preparations, gathering clean towels and setting water to boil. A silent prayer crossed her lips, "Please God, help us safely through this night, and let me know how to do all the right things."

CHAPTER SEVEN: AFTER THE WEDDING

Alfredo was discovering his new wife, and she was full of surprises. He had expected some degree of restraint from her in spite of their previous experiences, just because she was a new bride, and might be tender as a result of pregnancy. He was unprepared for the events that unfolded.

Lucia had dressed herself in the sheerest of garments. She was provocative and showed no hesitation as she approached him lustily. She unveiled her cream colored breasts, the nipples standing up proudly. And she attempted to remove his clothing.

Alfredo was much more inhibited. The fact that she was not at all shy and retiring set him further back in his advances. He had expected that she might be embarrassed, especially about her pregnancy, but she showed no signs of this. Rather she acted like a whore, even disrobing in front of him. He felt cold and trapped. He envisioned a woman who would display some sense of modesty, hesitant at first, one who would allow him to take the lead.

But Lucia, on the other hand, thought that all men were the same, only interested in the woman's body. So this was fine with her. She was only interested in being married, being his wife and having a place in the social strata. It had been easy enough to seduce him before; it should be easier now.

She became frustrated by his lack of response. She forced herself to try to compensate for both of them, but he increasingly became more unresponsive. He turned his back to her in the darkness, images of Annabelle assaulting his mind, making him wonder how it would have been with her. Consummation was more than just another chore to shoulder.

Lucia slept fitfully, hoping that tonight she might have become pregnant.

Alfredo and Lucia settled into a routine. He would dress early before she awoke and leave for work. That made one less hour that he would be forced to listen to her talk aimlessly about the most nonsensical topics.

Lucia was lazy. She slept late and lay in bed until eleven o'clock each day, having convinced her mother that she needed extra care. So her mother arrived early in the day, prepared her breakfast for her and undertook the task of keeping house.

Two months passed after the wedding and Lucia was finally pregnant. She had not yet figured out how she would explain the time difference in her delivery to Alfredo. Anyway, what did men know about having children? She would just explain that she was late in delivering the baby.

Alfredo attempted to act the role of proud husband. His father-in-law was impressed with his virility. To be expecting a grandchild so soon! What a blessing, thought Lucia's parents. Surely, that meant that Alfredo really cherished Lucia. But Alfredo was overwhelmed with the magnitude of responsibility. He tried to work late at the market most nights to minimize the time he had with Lucia. He explained to her that he had to make as much money as possible with this new member of their family on the way.

Truthfully, the relationship between the couple was strained. It became difficult for Alfredo to take those steps towards home.

As days progressed, Lucia was also glad for the limited time she had with him. This was less than an ideal arrangement. She felt she was not getting enough attention from Alfredo, so she looked to her mother to cater to her needs.

Pampered by her mother, she would dress up lavishly so she could visit the shops, ordering more than they could really afford, and sending the bills to him at the market. Her female friends marveled at Alfredo's generosity. They saw him lavishing her with luxuries.

Alfredo forced himself to couple with her, allowing his mind to fantasize that he was fondling Annabelle, and filling her with his love. He imagined what it would be like to have someone he loved who was tender and caring, and who really loved him in return. The only comfort the marriage brought to Alfredo was the fulfillment of these physical needs and the thought that he would soon have a child to dote on.

The thought of this baby coming blinded him to everything else. What did it matter if Lucia was overspending? Women in pregnancy had to be coddled. When the baby was born, he felt that she would be consumed with motherhood, and become the loving mother and the gentle helpmate he had always yearned for.

When Dr. Santoro confined her because of her pregnancy, both were happy to avoid intimacy, she because she was faking her ardor and Alfredo because he no longer had to force himself with images of another woman.

Today, Alfredo sped towards home. He decided to leave a little earlier than usual, because he had made up his mind to make this arrangement work.

The air was heavy with the threat of rain. Even as he rushed forward, he heard the thunder becoming stronger. A streak of lightning flashed in front of him, taking him off guard. He pulled his coat more tightly around himself. As he reached the doorstep, a torrential rain started to fall. This was the first time he was really glad to be arriving at home. Things would definitely get better for them. He made up his mind that he would do whatever would be needed to make this marriage work.

Taking two steps at a time, he whistled cheerfully. Bursting through the door, he was startled to see Anna Maria.

"Anna Maria, I didn't expect to see you."

She responded nervously, "I was just leaving. Mama sent some dinner for you both."

"That's not necessary. Tell your Mama that Lucia is a good cook. I have not had meals as good as these since I left my mother's home."

Lucia stepped up behind Alfredo. Seeing her there, Anna Maria blurted out, "Lucia has not made one meal for you yet. Mama sends dinner every night. And on Sunday, you eat with us anyway."

Alfredo whirled around in anger, facing his wife.

"Is this true, Lucia?"

"Of course not, Alfredo. Are you going to believe me or a little girl?" She flashed Anna Maria a threatening look. But Anna Maria warmed to her topic. "Be careful of her, Alfredo. She is crafty; she has tricked you before."

Lucia screamed, "Get out of here, you evil child. Go home." To Alfredo she said, "She is always telling stories. Mama has had a lot of trouble with her because of her storytelling. Why, she was even called to school because of this behavior."

Now Anna Maria started to cry. "That's not true, Alfredo. She is the one who is lying. She even tricked you into marrying her by telling you she was pregnant when she wasn't. There, I have said it. I had wanted to tell you this before, but I was afraid of her."

Anna Maria gathered up her skirts and fled through the door. Alfredo called out, “Wait, Anna Maria. Wait until the rain passes. It is storming too hard to allow you to leave.” But Anna Maria did not return.

His tone was remarkably even, in spite of the anger he felt building within him.

Lucia was whimpering at the window, her back to Alfredo.

He addressed her, “I will return shortly, and then we will discuss this. In the meantime, set the table for dinner. I am taking your sister home.”

He found Anna Maria huddled in the doorway, watching the wall of rain.

“I am sorry, Alfredo. I didn’t wish to spoil anything for you. I should have told you before now. I knew what Lucia had done because I read her diary.”

“Do not be upset, Anna Maria. What is done is done. You must learn not to get involved in other people’s problems. There will be no further discussion about this.”

Anna Maria sobbed, “Mama will kill me when she finds out what I have done.”

When Alfredo returned, Lucia was shaking with fear. Now that she was really pregnant, maybe he would abandon her. She would be the laughingstock of the community and bring shame to her parents. All because of that miserable idiot of a sister! Lucia said aloud, “She has always been jealous of me, and this is her way to ruin my life”.

She forced herself to appear calm. If she acted as though the child were telling tales out of school, she was sure that Alfredo would believe her.

Then she remembered the diary. Anna Maria must have read the diary. The evening fire was already set, so she realized how she could solve the problem.

She ran to the bedroom to retrieve her diary so she could throw it into the flames before he returned. She was panicked, nervously searching through the linens for the hidden book. It was her own foolishness. She should have kept her secrets to herself, but she needed someone to confide in and, without that, she used the diary.

She was just tearing out the last page and throwing it into the fire when she noticed Alfredo quietly standing behind her.

"So, it is true. I was hoping that Anna Maria was having a childish tantrum, but I now realize she was telling the truth." He turned away in disgust.

"Alfredo, please listen to me. Let me explain! I loved you so much that I could not bear the thought of you not marrying me. I knew you only would marry if I had a way to force you to do so. So I lied to you. But I am expecting our child now. Dr. Santoro told me today that it will be in September."

"Lucia, listen carefully. I will support you and my child because I have taken vows. But nothing more. You will now do as I say, as far as the child is concerned. But I no longer care what you do. You can do what you wish. But every day, you will awaken early and become what a wife should be. You will prepare my breakfast, keep our house clean without your mother's help, and make all of our meals yourself. If there is one word of this disgraceful situation to anyone, I will leave you. Now you can eat alone. I am going to sleep in the other room. You will no longer be bothered by me."

Lucia stared into the fire, watching the castles she had built quickly disintegrate. She started to plot. Somehow she would win him back. When he saw the child swelling within her body, he would feel differently, and when he held the baby, everything would be fine again.

Or so she thought….

CHAPTER EIGHT: NEW BEGINNINGS

Annabelle had been living with the Krugs, a family that hired her upon Janos' recommendation. After a week, she already knew that it was not going to work out for her.

She had previously looked daily for work but was scrutinized by every potential employer. They turned her down when they discovered she had no family and no husband. Without Janos' intercession, she never would have gotten this job. But they really did not like her and were both curt and impatient with her.

How would she ever make it alone in the world? Perhaps she *should* return to Grandmother's house. Yes, that was what she would do. New York had only brought her bad luck. All of her happiest memories were in Bayonne, so she packed her bag by candlelight, intent on leaving the next morning. She would explain it all at breakfast.

Closing her eyes, her mind traveled back to Franz once more. He was the only one that had given her the kind of unconditional love she wanted. Yet she admitted to herself that even there he was using her. He had led her to believe that things could be worked out for them. And then he followed his mother's orders anyway. So was it really unconditional love?

It was time to start over and put the past behind her.

The next morning, the sun shone brilliantly through the front windows of the house. It was an omen, she told herself, an omen that her future would be bright after all.

She lifted the last remnants of her belongings from the dressing table, pausing only a moment to visualize the face of her sweet child. For Paula's sake, she had to succeed.

She left before the household came to life, deciding to place a note and the few coins she owed on the hallway table. Softly clicking the lock behind her, she walked with lightheartedness towards Janos' house. Once more, she would have to ask for his help, but she vowed that this would be the last time. She wanted to make sure that they knew where she would be. She felt a newfound freedom by coming to this decision, because it was something she wanted.

She knew the baby would be awake, so Rowena would also be up and about, tending to the child. In one way she hated to go there now. Seeing the baby only brought sadness to her, making her recall Paula as an infant. The pain in her chest intensified until she was blinking away tears.

She turned her thoughts to the holidays in an effort not to dwell on the loss of her child.

Christmas was only two weeks away. The thought of celebrating it with Grandmother was so exciting. She always prepared the traditional delicacies, making the house smell like a bakery. Oh yes, and how festive it looked. They would gather boughs from the pine trees outside, dragging them into the house and draping them over the handrails, red ribbons adorning them. The odors were intoxicating, and the whole experience would make her feel like a child again, protected just for a little while. She had no doubt that Grandmother would welcome her.

She climbed the stairs quietly, being careful not to disturb the other tenants in the building. Pausing momentarily to listen, she heard Rowena's voice cooing to her baby, so she knocked lightly.

"Who is it?" came the voice from within, slightly fearful in tone.

"It is Annabelle, Rowena. Please open the door for me." Rowena rushed to release the lock, calling out as the door opened, "What is wrong? Is there more trouble?"

"No, of course not. No trouble at all. Why are you always thinking of the worst thing that could happen? You even seem more nervous now that the baby is here."

"Oh, I just want everything to be perfect for Janos," she replied. "I cannot have anything happen that will cause an upset."

"You worry too much about pleasing Janos. You should be trying to find some happiness for yourself."

Rowena went on. "I am happy when he is happy. You will understand that when you find a man to love who loves you in return."

Annabelle's face betrayed her annoyance.

"I am sorry, Annabelle. I didn't mean that the way it sounded. I meant…."

"Never mind. I know what you meant," Annabelle interjected. "Let's not waste time on this silliness. Do you have any coffee? I am so hungry."

"No, I am sorry that I don't. I wanted to get some, but money was short. I can give you a cup of tea, instead."

"Yes, I would love that, and anything you can give me for breakfast would be appreciated. I want to go to Grandmother's and have to figure out how to get there."

"I thought you didn't want to go there, that you wanted to be independent?"

"I thought so, too," Annabelle responded. "But I guess I am not yet ready to be independent, so going to Grandmother's will give me the chance to think more about what I have to do."

"Do you want to stay with us?" Rowena asked, because she knew Janos would expect that of her.

"No, I cannot intrude on your life any longer. I think I can find my way with Grandmother's guidance. She will help me work it out."

Rowena quickly responded, "Don't say that you feel you are intruding. Janos will be angry with me. He will say that I made you feel uncomfortable."

"Don't worry, Rowena, this is just between the two of us."

"What is between the two of you?" asked Janos. "Also, Annabelle, what are you doing here, so early in the morning?"

"I came to tell you that I am going to Grandmother's. I am saying my goodbyes."

"Well, at least I am relieved about that. She will be good for you. How do you plan to get there?"

"Janos, don't be so overprotective. You would think I am a woman of the streets, the way you carry on."

"Don't be silly, Annabelle. I just mean that Grandmother will put you on the right path."

"Yes, at least we all agree on that point."

"Since it is Saturday, I will get a carriage and drive you. I am not working today."

"No, Janos. Just tell me how to get there. I want you to spend your time with your family."

Turning to Rowena, he ventured, "Do you think we can take the baby also? Grandmother has not seen him yet."

"I don't think so," replied Rowena. "The weather is too changeable lately, and I don't want to risk ending up in bad weather with the baby; he is too little. Let me stay at home. You take Annabelle."

“Yes, I guess you are right, Rowena. I will take Annabelle and get back as soon as possible. I should make it back here by early afternoon.”

She answered him, “I have so much to do that by the time you get back, I will be finished and maybe we can take the baby for a stroll, if the weather holds.”

“I guess that’s settled,” Annabelle commented wryly. “Both of you seem to forget that I am a grown woman, capable of caring for myself.”

“If you ask me, you haven’t done a very good job of that at all,” Janos responded shortly.

The trip to Grandmother’s was silent, Annabelle bristling under Janos’ criticisms. On one hand she understood his concerns; on the other she resented his overprotective attitude and the protection he seemed to think that he owed her.

By the time they finally reached Grandmother’s, the tension was so high between them that Janos elected not to stay, even for something to drink. Janos could not wait to leave; understandably, he wanted to get back to his wife and child.

Grandmother came out to the carriage, attempting to soothe his ruffled feelings, and inquiring about Rowena and the baby. She tried to convince him to eat with them, giving him a chance to rest from the long and tedious ride. But, he would have no part of it. He wanted to get home.

Annabelle conjectured that he might finally have an opportunity to concentrate on his wife and child, instead of constantly fretting about her activities. Maybe worrying about me and my problems will no longer burden him, she thought.

Before he pulled away, Annabelle jumped up, attempting to put her arm around his neck, realizing that peace should be made between them.

He had already done so much for her, and she knew he did not think that she was appreciative.

"Janos, thank you for all your trouble in taking care of me. Please forgive me for not doing what you think I should do. I love you and Rowena and the baby very much. You will always be close to my heart."

Janos didn't respond to her words; his body stiffened under her touch, but Annabelle knew this was his way of protecting himself, and expressing that he was right about everything. When he tipped his hat as he made the turn, Annabelle knew that all was forgiven. His strength was a plus and a minus, depending on how he chose to use it.

She then turned to *Anyóka*. No words were needed. She went into her arms, nestling in the protective warmth that emanated.

"Annabelle, I know the time for you is coming. I am so happy that you came back to me. I was fearful that you would wait too long. I need you here to help me with my work. I have so many people coming daily that it is difficult for me to handle them all."

"What can *I* do for you?" she inquired.

"You can set the times of the appointments and talk to those people who are waiting to see me. I cannot do both things, and the demands are becoming overwhelming. In addition, you can help me with the house and the garden. By the way, I have company for dinner tomorrow night. A young man whose mother was from my village is going to do some repair work for me, and I have invited him to have dinner with me. We will have some time to prepare, and you can help me."

"Don't tell me the matchmaking is already starting."

"Annabelle, don't be ridiculous. How did I know you were coming today? It never hurts to meet new people, especially an eligible young man."

Annabelle knew what she had in mind; Grandmother turned her back and suppressed a satisfying grin.

She was glad her grandmother had directed her to rest before the company arrived. She laid in bed, staring at the ceiling. The diminishing afternoon light flickered across the cracks in the walls, conjuring up visions of things that might have been. She tossed and turned restlessly, finally deciding that she would plan the next day for herself. But that proved to be a fruitless exercise as well. No matter what she tried to concentrate on, her thoughts kept returning to Alfredo, seeing him enraptured, as he hurried down the aisle, his bride on his arm.

Somehow, she thought she owed him something for the long trip from across the Ocean, and for the attention he gave her in her time of need. No one else was there to help her and he came forward. He didn't even really know her.

She did want to thank him for his protectiveness and was angry at herself that she did not encourage his attention. She decided she would write a note of congratulations and send it to him at the market. In this way she would satisfy her conscience without angering his wife. She hoped it would not seem too aggressive or overbearing to Alfredo.

She stretched her body the length of the bed and sighed. She had not been this peaceful in a long time, feeling safe and secure at Grandmother's. She slowly coached herself out of bed and went to sit at the writing table. She lit the kerosene lamp and searched around the room until she found some paper and a pen. She could always count on Grandmother to provide everything she needed. It was going to be difficult to motivate herself, if she decided to leave and move on her own. She would have to make her own life, but she knew it would take time.

She really needed time to heal. She had not allowed that to happen and was glad that now she would be in a safe and protective place.

She scribbled hesitatingly in Hungarian…first, the message she really wanted to send:

> *Dear Alfredo,*
>
> *I am destroyed by your marriage. I was so foolish not to allow you to become my suitor. I should have considered your offer of marriage very seriously, and now find myself thinking of you all of the time. After some time going over the situation, I have come to the conclusion that it would be a good idea to get to know you better. Your reaching out to me at our last meeting was more than I could bear; I was not ready to think about starting a life, so I lied to you about returning to Hungary. I really had no intention of going and wanted to stay here and work things through, before I encouraged you. When I finally got the courage to try to connect with you, I found that it was your wedding day….*

She shamefully scratched out the message, quickly tearing up the paper, even frightening herself at how forward she sounded. Start again, she directed herself. Writing in her native tongue made it easier to pull her thoughts together. She would ask for help to translate the note into English.

Dear Alfredo,

I learned of your recent marriage. I really wanted to let you know that I wish you the best. My plans changed and I never actually left America. Please realize how grateful I am to you for the help you gave me aboard ship. I will remember your kindness for the rest of my life. I never would have survived that journey without your help. I only hope that God will repay you with the very happiest of lives.

Annabelle read and reread the letter until she was happy with the contents. Then she decided to copy it over so it would be more presentable to show her grandmother, who could help her get it ready to send. She wished she felt able to confide in *Anyóka* so that she would tell her if these were the right and proper things to do. Yet she felt shy about asking her opinion.

Based on how she felt, Annabelle was glad that she was doing what she thought would be considered polite behavior. Tired from the task of writing out her feelings, Annabelle threw the discarded copy into the fireplace and folded the other, knowing she would wait for the right time to ask for help.

She hoped that tomorrow she could arrange to have it sent, in case she changed her mind about the message. At the very least, she would be able to say that she had behaved with dignity.

The next morning, Grandmother had a sumptuous breakfast waiting with sausages and eggs, biscuits fresh from the oven, fresh butter and homemade jams. Annabelle had not eaten with such gusto since before she left home. Within her was a peacefulness that she had not experienced since she arrived in America. She could recall living at home before her father died and feeling this way at that time.

Her mind wandered to her father. She thought of him so seldom, yet he probably had the most influence on her personality, next to Grandmother. His proper appearance and dignified carriage clearly demonstrated his nobility. He had a certain way of letting the world know that he demanded respect, and respect is what he got from all, except for her mother. It saddened Annabelle to recognize that her mother did not love him. The fact that she did not love her father was a mystery to Annabelle. She could not reconcile how anyone could fail to love him; he was such a generous and giving man.

Grandmother interrupted her thoughts, "Annabelle, my child, what are you thinking about? I have been speaking to you for the last few minutes and you haven't heard a word I have said to you."

"I'm sorry, *Anyóka*. I was remembering my father."

"Yes, a good man but not appreciated by your mother, even if it sounds like I am criticizing my own daughter."

Annabelle interjected, "Why did they ever marry?"

Grandmother thought carefully before responding to Annabelle. "In the first place, your father was a charming man, but, more than that, your mother saw that he had land and plenty of wealth. Your grandfather arranged the match between them, making your mother as pleased as she could possibly be. I had only seen her this happy when she got a new gown that no one else could match. She was the envy of the countryside."

"Do you think they loved each other?"

"Love? A funny word; it means many different things to different people. To answer you, I think your father was devoted to her and was pleased to have an attractive wife who had the ability to entertain his business contacts with graciousness. But ***love***? That depends on what you think love is. It can have many definitions."

"I don't know what love is, other than feeling safe and content and able to be myself with someone who does not criticize me. I had that with Franz."

"Ah, yes, Franz. Yet he was not deserving of you. He took your affections but was not man enough to stand up to his mother. Instead, he compromised you and your child. He proved himself to be unworthy of you."

Annabelle paced back and forth, wringing her hands nervously. "I'm afraid I will never find the right man for me."

"You will, my child. Just give it time. Speaking of men, Dorothy's nephew Johann is coming for dinner tonight. He is about your age and just completing his studies at the University. I think you will like him."

"*Anyóka,* I am not certain that I can even act interested in anyone at this point in time. Not even for you."

"Annabelle, he is interested in establishing a medical practice and is setting up an office in his home. My friend, Dorothy, tells me that he inherited the house from his uncle. I think he has a lot to offer."

"Why then is he going to do repair work for you, if he is going to practice medicine? I suppose he is seeking a suitable wife to keep his home and impress his potential patients."

"I imagine that's true. But that is not why I invited him. Remember, he was invited before you arrived here, and he is going to fix one of my windows because he knows how and because he needs money at this time."

Angrily, Annabelle snapped, "*Anyóka*, I cannot believe you are pushing someone on me. I expect this from Janos, but not from you. Of all people in the world, you are the only one who can feel my pain and understand what I have been through. I am not interested in being auctioned off to the highest bidder." Annabelle's eyes filled with tears as her anger built.

"Annabelle, aren't you getting carried away by your feelings? No one, least of all me, is trying to marry you off. In fact, Johann may be coming with a woman who I suspect might marry him, and there may be no interest at all in you."

Annabelle arose from her chair and kneeled in front of her grandmother, penitent. Putting her head on her grandmother's lap, she muttered," I am so sorry, *Anyóka*. I should have trusted you; you are the only one who has never betrayed me."

Margaret caressed her hair, feeling the warmth of her tears seeping through her thin cotton dress. "Cry, my child. You have an ocean of tears to release your grief."

Annabelle spent the better part of the afternoon peeling apples for strudel. The aroma from the kitchen was tantalizing; it made her mouth water and improved her mood. Grandmother knew how to create magic in the kitchen, she thought. Maybe I can learn how to do the same thing.

She told her grandmother that she wanted to help prepare the dinner. She then started the chore of shelling the peas and cleaning the potatoes. The pork was in the oven long before the dinner hour, so Annabelle basked in the tantalizing scent of the roast while she prepared the vegetables. Sweet cabbage was simmering. She then began to stoke the fire and ready the table for the evening meal. All of these tasks distracted Annabelle from dwelling on her own situation and, for a time, she forgot her problems.

"Annabelle, time for you to get ready for dinner," her grandmother piped up.

Alarmed, she jumped up, "Do I have time to freshen up and change my clothes? The sun is so low in the sky."

"You have plenty of time. I have heated water so that you can bathe if you so desire."

"That would be delightful. I will wear my orchid dress. That's appropriate since I am still in mourning."

"It flatters you, Annabelle. Here, add this white lace collar to brighten your complexion. You have been looking so drawn. And be sure to put a blush on your cheeks."

"*Anyóka,* you think of everything," Annabelle said as she kissed her on the cheek. "But what about you? When will you be able to get ready? Do you have enough time?

"Shortly, my child. Don't worry about me. Go now, before it gets any later."

Back in her room, Annabelle began humming a song, a little folk tune that her grandmother used to sing to her at bedtime. She gazed in the looking glass, pinching her cheeks to restore some color to her face. Maybe she would be able to enjoy the evening after all, if the conversation was good and the food was acceptable. If *Anyóka* had been doing all of the cooking, there would be no doubt about how good the food could be. Yet with her help, who could guess the outcome?

She placed the combs in her hair and spun around once more to judge her appearance. I *will* have a good time, she resolved. No matter what anyone does or says. Tonight, will be the beginning of a new life for me.

She heard voices in the hallway and hurried down the stairs. Margaret was still greeting the guests as she descended, the swishing of her taffeta dress announcing her arrival. She stopped suddenly. There were two young men awaiting her greeting. The first she knew had to be

Johann, because he looked just like his grandmother and Annabelle had met her. But the second? Who was the second? He looked so familiar, but she was unable to recall where she had seen him before.

She completed her descent cautiously, trying to gather herself together. She was not much for surprises, and she was put off by the arrogant stance of the mysterious gentleman. All eyes were fixed on her, but she had to resist the strong inclination to turn and run. Instead, she tilted her nose higher in the air and pulled back her shoulders in expectation.

Grandmother's voice rang out, "Annabelle, Johann has surprised us with his friend." She continued to Johann, "This is my granddaughter, Annabelle, who has come to stay with me."

Johann interrupted, "Annabelle, I am pleased to meet you. This is my closest friend, Miklos Katika."

Annabelle curtsied and said politely, "I am pleased to meet both of you." She extended her hand while one and then the other pressed their lips to it. Miklos was staring at her in a way that made her feel undressed; she was anxious to avoid him. She knew she had met him before, but where? She felt so confused.

He commented, "Remember, Annabelle, that I met you at Franz's home. We had dinner together, though I admit it was a very long time ago."

Stunned, she did not answer. A wave of despair was building within her and she tried to resume her composure. She made no reply.

Ignoring Miklos, she turned to Johann. "My grandmother mentioned that your fiancé would be with you."

"She had intended to come with me tonight, but has taken ill. So, I took the liberty of bringing Miklos along with me. I didn't think that Margaret would object."

Margaret replied, “It is fine. We always have enough food to feed one more person, and I already expected to have two in your party.”

Sensing the strained atmosphere, *Anyóka* hurried everyone into the dining area. “Dinner is just about ready. Take a seat, gentlemen. Annabelle and I will start serving. Unfortunately, my husband is not here this evening. He would have liked to have met you, Miklos.”

“Where would you like us to sit?” Johann inquired.

“If you both sit on the left side of the table, Annabelle and I will face you.”

They watched as the women brought in a luscious salad topped with cucumbers and tomatoes.

Margaret settled in her chair and continued, “Let us join hands and recite our prayers of thanksgiving together.” She chanted a short Hungarian phrase and ended in English, “May God bless our days and bring us peace. We thank Him for his good graces and the food we are about to share. And may Rudolf’s mission be completed with safety and happiness.”

Johann broke the silence. “I want to know more about Rudolf and his trip.”

Grandmother answered politely, “He was called to his sister’s because of some family problems. We look forward to his return next week.”

Annabelle offered, happy to change the subject. “Johann, tell us when you will be getting married.”

“Not soon enough,” he quickly replied. “I had hoped it would be in May, but she wants to plan the wedding in September.”

“He is really smitten,” Miklos said. To Annabelle, he directed, “Can you tell us more about you, since you have been here in the United States.”

Annabelle studied Miklos' face. Why was she feeling such apprehension? She ventured,

"How do you know Johann and how did you know that I was here?"

Johann and I went to university together. When I arrived in the United States, I contacted him to let him know I had arrived."

Annabelle interrupted, "And how and why did you find me?"

"Franz let me know where you were staying. He asked that I check on you, and when Johann mentioned his invitation to dinner, I realized this was the very same place that you were living."

Startled at his answer, Annabelle stared at the table before replying, "It seems strange to me that such a coincidence could occur."

"Life is full of surprises" was Miklos' reply. He continued to inquire, "I imagine now that you are with your grandmother, you will be seeking a husband."

"You are quite forward," she retorted. "But you are mistaken."

"Well then, I should think you would have many suitors," he continued.

"I do not think that is something I wish to discuss with you, Miklos."

Margaret decided to rescue Annabelle. "Come, my child, let us bring in the rest of the meal. Then we can sit and talk without interruption."

Annabelle breathed a sigh of relief. What was it about Miklos that she so instantly disliked? She was beginning to remember that she felt the same way when Franz had brought him to meet her.

She expressed her anger to *Anyóka* as they were gathering the dishes they were planning to present to the guests. "He is *so* rude. What is wrong with him?"

Grandmother responded cautiously, "It seems that he has not learned how to approach an attractive young woman. He certainly has shown that he does not know what is appropriate to ask."

They carried the steaming platters to the dining room. Pork baked to a golden brown and topped with apples in a delicate blending of flavors, scalloped potatoes, creamed peas, piping hot biscuits and fresh butter graced the table. The young men moaned in anticipation of the food.

"Gentlemen, it seems you have not eaten in weeks."

Miklos answered, "I have not had food this good in a very long time, so appealing and so well prepared."

"We are glad to provide you with a good meal," responded Grandmother.

While everyone ate, the conversation flowed smoothly, and Annabelle began to relax.

"Gentlemen, I am happy that you seem to be enjoying the meal," Grandmother commented, as they continued to unabashedly heap food on their plates.

"I agree with Miklos; I have not eaten food this delectable in weeks," Johann replied.

"But I know your grandmother well, Johann, and she is a wonderful cook."

"Yes, that's true," said Johann. "But her meals, though hearty, cannot compare with this. They are much simpler in nature."

"Be assured that we do not feast like this every day. This is an occasion. I have looked forward to this time with you, Johann, and am anxious to have you look at the problem I have encountered in the back hallway. With Rudolf away I am concerned about waiting until he returns. The water is coming through the ceiling. But never mind, all this can wait until after dinner."

"Aunt Margaret," Johann responded," I will be happy to help you. It has been much too long since I have seen you and I have gotten too caught up in my own life. I am sorry for that."

Now that the attention was focused on Johann, Annabelle breathed a sigh of relief. But, the color came quickly to her cheeks when Miklos suddenly addressed her again.

"We had been discussing whether or not you would be considering marriage at all."

Unsure of how to handle him, Annabelle answered shortly, "Not at this time. But you are making me feel very uncomfortable."

He ignored her response and continued. "I am sorry that I am making you upset, but I would hope that you would consider me a suitor."

She turned to him suddenly, "And you, are you married? And how do you think that Franz would feel about that?"

It was his turn to color, "No, I am not married, but I think that Franz would approve of my interest. After all, we were the best of friends, and he would want the best for you, under the circumstances, especially after losing the child."

"Wait, how do you know about what happened to Paula?" Annabelle interjected.

"I was on the ship when your child got lost."

"And you who claim to be so interested in me, never tried to help me?"

"I did not want to interfere. There were plenty of people surrounding you, especially that one young man who took interest in you."

He hesitated to see her reaction, but then he blundered forward. "I have not been able to find a woman with the grace and beauty that you display. I know it seems forward, but I would very much like to see you again. I know what happened with Franz having to marry another, and I think that I could make things much easier for you."

She embarrassed herself. "I am not prepared to discuss this now. Perhaps in the future. We will see."

Miklos turned to her grandmother, "If it is agreeable to you, I would like to come tomorrow and take Annabelle for a ride in the countryside."

Margaret looked at Annabelle. "I think that is Annabelle's decision, not mine, but I do not object if she does not."

Annabelle just shrugged her shoulders, responding, "I am not ready to see you again."

"Well, then I will consider that an acceptance and will be here at noon tomorrow."

"You may come, if you like, but I am not interested in seeing you."

Johann struggled with his discomfort and tried to change the subject. The rest of the dinner dragged on while Annabelle offered several excuses to postpone this meeting. Yet, Miklos persisted and Annabelle tired of the argument. So she resigned herself to the appointment, though she dreaded it, and vowed it would be only once and done with.

When the dessert arrived, Johann could not compliment enough the delicious seven-layer torte filled with jelly and topped with chocolate. Miklos commented favorably on the crisp apple strudel that Annabelle had prepared.

When the door closed after them, Annabelle breathed a heavy sigh. "*Anyóka*, I don't know what to do. I do not want to insult Johann, but I really do not like Miklos. I find him too aggressive. He is looking for a wife, and I don't want to be that person. I got the impression that he has been considering me for that role; I know it sounds self-centered, but I am not ready for a new relationship, especially not with him. I haven't recovered from losing Franz and then Paula, or even from having my hopes dashed about Alfredo. And I do not like the fact that he was on the ship with me and did not make himself known to me."

"Time heals all wounds, my child. Wait, you will see. This distraction could be healthy for you. Someone who makes you feel attractive will boost your morale. If he is not right for you, you will know it soon enough. You do not have to seriously consider him at this time, or at any time in the future."

The next morning was misty, the fog hugging the earth and obstructing the view of the road at the end of the drive. Annabelle said a prayer of thanksgiving, certain that she would not have to deal with Miklos. He would never find his way in this weather. Yet, as the sun appeared in the sky at midday, the fog drew back, revealing a bright, warm afternoon. Not long afterwards, the sound of carriage wheels announced the arrival of Miklos.

Annabelle, dressed in a subdued, dark brown frock that hid her figure well, was hoping to find ways to discourage Miklos. She had pulled her hair back from her face in a severe bun that she thought made her look stern. Determined to be disagreeable, she hoped to make this the first and last meeting, Annabelle appeared in the doorway when Miklos knocked on the door.

"How stunning you look today," he commented with a flourish.

Annabelle felt the hairs on the back of her neck tightening. Don't be irrational, she told herself. You have to play the game. You have nothing to fear from this man.

Miklos continued with a smile. "Take your parasol. The sun is hotter than you might think."

"I have my bonnet, thank you," she replied, fastening the ribbons of the brown straw hat under her chin. She tucked in the stray wisps of hair which wanted to escape into curls and hoped she looked severe enough.

He continued, "I was unable to sleep last night, after meeting you. I kept envisioning your face again and again. I have decided that we will be spending quite a lot of time together."

Annabelle snapped back, "Well, I have not decided that we will be spending any time together. I think I have something to say about that."

"Of course, you do. My apologies if I seem too forward. But fate has put you in my path. That, I cannot ignore."

"It has nothing to do with fate. It is insignificant. Friendships must have a more solid foundation than a twist of fate, anyway."

"My dear, Annabelle, I was thinking of much more than friendship."

"Sir, if you have gotten the impression that I am anxious to marry or even interested in considering such a development, please let me correct you. I am most satisfied with things as they are."

"What future would you have as an unmarried woman? You will have no purpose in life."

"I don't think my purpose in life has anything to do with a man. And I have my own plans in my mind for me. And these, I will not discuss with you. Perhaps you should go home right now."

"Ah, so I have offended you. I am sorry. I shall have to arrange more time for you to get to know me."

"I hardly know you, and I am happy to have you leave now."

Miklos interjected, "Well then I will have to give you more time to get to know me."

After that, Miklos became more docile and, with the change in his attitude, the afternoon turned out to be surprisingly enjoyable. Annabelle actually found herself basking in his attention; it had been so long since she was treated with such indulgence.

They traveled the river road until they came to the Inn at the Four Corners. There they stopped for refreshment and a walk in the gardens. Miklos was proving to be more interesting than she had first judged, relating the story of his childhood and his current rise to good fortune.

"So, that is how I came to be living with my own grandmother. Isn't it strange that we are both living with a grandparent?"

Disregarding his comment, Annabelle asked, "How does that explain the vast acreage you say that you now own?"

"My mother had only one brother who had no children. When he passed away two years ago, he left me his properties. I have been working to fix the house and so I temporarily moved in with my grandmother. This is why I came to live here."

"What about your uncle's wife?" Annabelle continued.

"Unlike me, he was a confirmed bachelor," Miklos smiled.

They paused under the shade of the horse chestnut tree which took them out of the bright sunshine. Miklos took Annabelle's hand into his own. "Last night when I saw you coming down the stairs, something magical happened to me. I felt happier than I have in a very long time. But I will attempt to control my enthusiasm for you. Make no mistake, however, I think we were meant to be together."

Annabelle turned slowly away from him, pulling back her hand. "I have too many painful memories in my past, and I still must deal with them. I have not recovered from them and don't know if I will ever be able to do so. I think you should search elsewhere for the fulfillment of your dreams. You are hoping for a wife unlike me. I will not fulfill the dreams you have."

He grasped her shoulders and turned her back towards him. "Would you like to talk about these things that trouble you so much?"

"Not now, and maybe not ever. Please take me home now. I really need to help my grandmother with many of her chores. I promised her I would not be too late in returning."

She was hurrying to dress when the letter arrived. Days had passed, and Miklos had promised that they would attend the local theater presentation. Annabelle, in spite of her misgivings, had actually begun to look forward to such an outing. She had not been out in public at any kind of event since she was with Franz. She admitted that she was beginning to enjoy Miklos' company more, now that he had stopped pressing her. Tonight, she had a new gown of glistening, mauve satin, and although more than a year had passed, she felt guilty for wearing such a color. Grandmother had assured her that it was appropriate.

She stood in front of the looking glass, gazing at her own image. The letter sat unopened at the edge of the dressing table. Now that she was feeling happier and more content, some of the old frustrations started to manifest themselves.

She looked at the address and realized that Alfredo had sent the letter. What could be in it? It was probably a courteous note of appreciation for my considerations, she thought. I'll open it later, in case.... A little voice in her head was nagging her. "Open it now, Annabelle. You have been hoping for a contact from him. Open it now."

She turned it over and over again, laughing at his handwriting, so childish for a man so in control of himself. She tore the letter open without regard to the seal, then hesitated to unfold the neatly pressed paper. This is foolishness, she thought.

She became pale as she read on.

....and I realize I made a terrible mistake by marrying Lucia. She has deceived me so that I can no longer have any trust in her. Life has become unbearable for me. But we have a child on the way now. I would really like to see you again, though I have nothing to offer you in my situation. Yet, the sight of you would be a comfort. Please let me know if you would consider meeting me. I hope this finds you well.

Not another arrangement as she had had with Franz! What was he suggesting? No, she was not buying that again. She crumpled the letter and tossed it in the corner. The tears fell softly as the anger raged inside of her, choking her so she could not breathe.

Aloud, she vowed, "Tonight will be different. I will make every effort to open myself to all possibilities, and to try to see if Miklos might be a suitable husband for me. It is time to think about you, Annabelle."

The reflection in the mirror nodded in agreement.

CHAPTER NINE: TROUBLE IN PARADISE

Signore Della Cesare sat across from Alfredo.

"I hope you did not mind meeting me here at the *taverna*. I did not want my wife or Lucia to know about our little talk."

Alfredo looked back with eyes of steel. "What is it you want to talk about?"

"I…mmm….have been noticing that my daughter has not been herself lately."

Alfredo snapped, "Did Lucia ask you to speak with me?"

"She has not mentioned anything to me, but it would take a fool not to notice that the child is unhappy."

"Lucia creates her own unhappiness," Alfredo retorted.

"I know you will now be telling me that I have spoiled her. That is true, but now she is expecting your child. This should be the happiest time of her life!"

"Are you suggesting that it is my fault that she is unhappy?" asked Alfredo.

"I am questioning why two people who have been married less than a year cannot bear to be in each other's company."

Alfredo answered thoughtfully, "Sometimes it is discovered that the two may not be well suited to each other."

"All new marriages are difficult," said Lucia's father. "You, my son, you must learn to overcome those small differences. It is the lifetime that counts, not what happens at the moment."

"Signore, I have respect for you, and I don't wish to insult your daughter, but Lucia is a self-centered woman with no concern for anyone else's feelings, other than her own. I have stopped trying to change this. Until now, I have allowed her to have her way, but I will no longer cater to her, and I find it impossible to love her. I am now resigned to what I have to look forward to."

"Are you asking to arrange for an end to this marriage?"

"After the child is born, I think that might be the best thing for both of us and for the baby. But I want to make sure that she has all she needs in preparation for this child and is properly cared for. The child is mine. I will always take care of it."

With sadness overtaking him, Lucia's father continued. "In the meantime, Alfredo, reconsider. Youth is careless, and you are the man. You can make it work if you set your mind to it. You can be firm with her; she has a good heart and will come around to your ways."

"I will try to do what I can. But I cannot promise more than that."

"I will have her mother speak to her. She has a way with Lucia, and I know she can make her listen to reason."

Lucia revolved in front of the full-length mirror, surveying her swollen body. How she hated her appearance and this child within it, causing her so much grief! She was so absorbed in studying herself that she failed to notice Alfredo standing in the doorway.

"Admiring yourself?" he asked sarcastically.

She turned around in alarm. "No, I am not. You know how much I hate being pregnant and don't want to be so misshapen."

"I thought a child was what you wanted?" he continued. "You certainly made enough attempts to ensure that you would conceive."

For just a moment, a flicker of shame fleeted across her face. "Alfredo, I have apologized about that so many times. How many more apologies do I have to make? How can I make it up to you?" Tears flowed freely from her eyes, and she groped for something to use to wipe them away.

He surprised her by responding tenderly. He gently fingered the raven curls escaping to frame her face. "I had almost hoped that we could have a real opportunity for happiness."

"We can, Alfredo," she replied, tentatively putting her arms around him. Laying her head on his shoulder, she whispered, "Please, can we start all over again?"

He could feel her tears seeping through the starched white shirt he wore. It softened him because it seemed to him that she was sincere. "I was discussing you with your father today. He seems to think that within you is a really loving person. Is that so?"

She stiffened in response to his comments, but ventured, "Alfredo. I *love* you. You know that," she said accusingly.

"I think I know the answer to whether or not you love me. What concerns me is whether or not you do or can love our child."

"Alfredo, if I did not love you, why would I be carrying your child? I could have told you that I had miscarried the first time, when you thought I was pregnant and I was not."

"Deception seems to be your natural inclination, Lucia. Now answer my question."

Lucia's face reddened, and her heightened color and streaming tears made her look puffy and unattractive. "What was the question?"

she responded in a voice that seemed to climb an octave every moment that passed.

"Will you love our child and care for it properly?" he repeated.

She turned away so he could not see her face, afraid of betraying her true feelings. "That is a silly question. All mothers love their children."

He grabbed her shoulders and turned her towards him, "You and I both know that is not true. Just being a mother does not guarantee love. I guess you have answered the question for me, after all."

Frustrated with him and the pressure he was putting upon her, she screamed, "Alfredo, you are trying to trick me!"

She grabbed him and tried to pull him to her, desperation overtaking her completely. She began to beg him, crumbling up his neatly pressed clothing. He pulled roughly away from her, and she responded by covering her face with her hands and sobbing uncontrollably.

His face was set in determination, and his voice was stone cold without emotion.

"I am telling you something, and I want you to listen carefully to me. Here are the rules I am setting down."

Fear overcame Lucia, as she realized that her life was suddenly changing in a way that she never expected.

He continued, "You will care for my child just as a 'model mother' should do, I will expect you to assume the responsibility for this child and not depend upon your mother to take care of the baby. I want to see you caring lovingly for our child and preparing our meals yourself, making a home for us as I had experienced in my childhood. If you do this, I will stay with you. If you decide you cannot or will not do this, then our marriage will end. That will bring disgrace upon you and your family."

"Please Alfredo, I have known you all your life and you have never been harsh like this. What has happened?"

He sat on the side of the bed, his shoulders drooping, a beaten man. The effect of this whole dispute was evident to anyone looking at him. He had aged and hardened. His face was set in unsmiling lines, and his forehead sported a permanent frown.

Turning to face his wife, he breathed deeply and began, "When I knew you at home in Italy, you were just a child and spoiled by your parents, used to having things your way and subject to fits of temper when everything did not go smoothly for you. I had wanted a woman who could meet my expectations for happiness. That is why I was not anxious to marry. However, you made sure that I did not have a choice. Now, when I look at you, I realize that you are still that child in a woman's body. You will have new responsibilities, so things *must* change. As much as I threaten you, I will *not* abandon you at this time. But if things do not significantly change, you will force my hand. There will be no future for us. It is your decision, Lucia."

Lucia's heart was beating uncontrollably. She would have another chance, after all, a chance to make him see things her way.

"I promise you that I will try to do as you ask. But I must have help from my mother because I don't know how to manage alone. With her help, I will try to learn." She studied his face to see how he was receiving her comments.

He eyed her carefully, "She can help you to get started and teach you what to do. But she will not help you every day. You will learn how to cook our meals yourself, as I thought you had been doing during the last few months."

Lucia smiled to herself for her cleverness, for she had her mother bring the day's meal in the morning while Alfredo was at work, and take the food that Alfredo provided for the next day's meal home with her, so that they were eating what he knew was available to them. She had also been smart enough to arrange for weekend meals at her parents' home, or with Luigi and Maria. She had succeeded in fooling him many times.

Pleased with herself and the way the conversation had gone, she approached him, putting her arms around his neck. "I am so sorry all of this has happened. Things will be different, you will see. I will make you love me."

She pressed her lips against his, but he was like iron, unresponsive to her advances.

Refusing to accept defeat, she pleaded, "Alfredo, I am so lonely for you. Please let's make it up between us. Make love to me."

She nestled into his neck, her breath coming in quick jerks, as her tears warmed his skin. Reluctantly, Alfredo put his arms around her. Starved for attention, he allowed himself to be drawn to her, knowing that things would have to work out, after all.

In the back of his mind, he pictured Annabelle and remembered the hastily written letter he had sent. Ashamed of his impetuous gesture, he vowed to hold back, waiting to see how things were going. Surely, Lucia would manage to become more loving, more tender, more concerned, and she would keep the promises she made.

He felt spent and dissatisfied. He had hoped that he could rekindle feelings for Lucia, slight as they were. But she was too vacuous, too insensitive. She accepted his overtures and encouraged his interest; then she lay still expecting him to service her, to excite her, to give of himself, while she gave nothing. No, Lucia was not the woman he needed. He turned on his side away from her, vowing that after the baby was born, he would make a trip to see Annabelle before it was too late. He would figure out how to end this loveless marriage. He had to grab onto his star, to make it to the rainbow.

Annabelle again stared at the paper before her. Common sense. Yes, use common sense, she thought.

After retrieving it from the trash, she read Alfredo's note, over and over again, trying to decide what to do next. If she were wise, she would be casual, not putting too much importance on his words. After all, he was a man committed; he even admitted that himself. Yet, if she could see him even one more time, maybe it would be easier to decide what was right for her, and what to do about Miklos. Even if there was no future for her with Alfredo, she needed to decide if she could live happily with Miklos. But she did not want Alfredo to perceive her as a "loose" woman.

Miklos. Another puzzle. Something about him was so intriguing. Maybe it was the way he attended to her. No one, not even Franz, had ever made such a fuss about her and given her so many gifts. Yes, he never came to see her without some small thoughtful gift, a bouquet of flowers, a book of poetry… but was he sincere? Or just trying to manipulate her? She was so confused.

Annabelle, do not deceive yourself, she thought. After all, it's not the gifts that count. There is the deception. I must not mix material things and the happiness these things bring with the basic love and caring that is core to a relationship. Alfredo has no pretenses; he is what he says and offers nothing but himself. And he has already shown that he would take care of me in a crisis, even when he did not know me.

Yet, I know he is married now, and even if I had hope for a lasting relationship with him, I know it cannot come to be. It is impossible.

I am trying to use Alfredo to measure Miklos against him. I am wrong and I know it, but I cannot figure out any other way to decide what I should do.

She rose and strolled to the window, looking out at the peaceful surroundings. The leaves had just begun to fall, and the air was becoming crisp and refreshing, that coolness that makes one feel clean and whole. She studied the colors and the intensity of the reds and greens. She was always amazed at the varying shades of green. Every tree had its own appearance, some dark green, some light, some more yellow than green, some now a combination of gold, orange and red, and some still in the process of changing. This is the way it is with all of us, she thought. We are all different, and we all choose our paths. Some of us are like the tall oak, sturdy and straight and dependable; some are like the old tree in the back of the lawn, twisted, distorted and misshapen with no real direction. I wonder, she thought, what kind of person that old tree represents. I must be careful not to allow that to happen to me; I am already on that path. I must not allow myself to become so tangled with the challenges of life so that I end up like a broken and mangled tree.

That decides it, Annabelle proclaimed. She took pen to paper and wrote…

Alfredo,

I have just received your letter and am overjoyed for you at the news of your expected child. Sometimes, even the best of marriages offer challenges and suffer problems. Nevertheless, these things can all be worked out. It is difficult for your wife at this time while she is waiting for the child. Pregnancy is not easy. So you must be patient as well.

Alfredo, I am eternally grateful to you for your continued interest in me. I will never forget how you helped me in my time of need, through the greatest loss I have endured in my life. I am not taking that lightly. I will try to return the friendship and, as a friend, will listen to the frustrations you are undergoing. But I will not interfere in your marriage or the future of your child.

I hope that you will find that the birth of this child will bring peace and joy to your new family and allow you to experience the contentment that you deserve to have.

As for me, I am going forward with my life and have finally met a man that is providing me some of the peace I have needed for such a long time. Sometimes in life, things do not work out as you have hoped; perhaps they are not meant to be. All the same, I wish you 'love'.

Annabelle

That sounds correct now, she thought. It is not encouraging him; it is supportive, but it does not cut him off completely. If he realizes that he was too impetuous, he can now bow out gracefully, and it makes me more conscious of what I have.

Feeling light-hearted again, Annabelle primped in front of the looking glass. It was too nice a day to remain inside, she decided, and grabbed her shawl. The action brought a sudden ache in her chest as she remembered how she had wrapped Paula in this very shawl. She let her mind wander. If only Paula were here now; she would love to pick up the pretty leaves and stuff them in my bag. Even as a toddler, she was always collecting leaves or rocks or flowers. Stop this, she told herself. I have to go on and put these memories out of my mind. I cannot deal with them right now. It hurts too much.

Running down the steps, her eyes brimming with tears, she shouted to her grandmother who was in the kitchen, baking apple pies, "*Anyóka*, I am going for a walk. I will be back soon."

"Annabelle," came the reply, "please pick some more apples for me. Here, take the basket. I don't have enough for the strudel."

"All right, I will. I'll bring them back with me." She grabbed the well-worn basket by its handles and swung open the back door. She heard the carriage before she saw it. Unmistakably, it had to be Miklos. He was committed to surprise visits and she would certainly not want to see him now. She was much too confused, and surely he would detect her mood and demand an explanation. She hurried off behind the trees at the rear of the porch before he could take advantage of her indecisiveness. She really did not want to offer any explanations about why she was so emotionally spent.

Running quietly, she disappeared into the grove of maples and collapsed onto a bed of leaves. A nice, solitary place to think, she considered. She hoped that her grandmother would discourage Miklos and not invite him to await her return.

She listened to the whinny of the horses. The air, so biting and crisp, made it possible for her to hear everything, as though she were standing at the back door of the kitchen. Yes, there.

The carriage is leaving. Good. He's gone. She relaxed and breathed a sigh of relief. No need to hide any longer, though her emotions had not quieted.

She started back into the clearing, so that she could cross the lawn and stroll along the banks of the stream at the south end of the property. Deep breaths of fresh air, Annabelle, she thought.

It was a day to remember. Twenty years from now, I will be able to pick this time out of my memory and relive every moment, as though it were happening again. She stooped to pick up an acorn. How could I have explained this to Paula, she wondered. From this tiny casing comes the grandest of trees. She found herself talking aloud.

Swinging right, onto the Jones' property, she stood by the split rail fence. There were only remnants of corn, dried and strewn bits of husks where the wagon had stopped to pick up the bundles. She realized that all of that crop was in the silo already, so that winter was not far behind. Thinking about it gave her a chill. Another year is passing and I am still where I was when I arrived here.

Turning slowly, she gasped to discover a human form behind her. Her voice shook. "You startled me!"

"I am sorry," was the reply. "You were too beautiful to disturb, and I was lost in watching you."

"Why...why are you here?" she stammered, staring at Alfredo.

"Didn't you receive my letter? In it, I explained…"

"Yes, I received it and had just penned an answer to you. I have it here in my hand."

"Forgive me, Annabelle, I should have sent a message in advance, but I was sure that you would not agree to see me."

She stared at Alfredo. He had changed in ways that she could not exactly pinpoint. The gleam in his eyes was gone; the sense of solidity and stability was not there. His clothes were less than perfect, and his hair needed attention. This was not the man she remembered.

Awkwardly, she offered, "How is your wife, Lucia?"

"She is doing well in her pregnancy. But I have been a foolish man. There is little hope for me, because I have allowed you to slip through my fingers."

This would be a new role for her, to be the consoler instead of the consoled. She extended her hand. "Come, let's walk. It's too pretty a day to stand still, and I want to hear about your life and your family. Tell me all about Lucia."

"There is little to tell, I am afraid. I married in haste and gave in to family pressures. Everyone had decided what was best for me. I knew it was not right, yet I still did it. After seeing you the last time, I felt there was no opportunity for me, and I was angry at the thought that I would never have you in my life. So I relented, and allowed myself to become involved with Lucia. Our families had arranged our marriage, though I never really wanted it. I thought you were returning to Europe, and I would never be able to see you again; because of that, I agreed to marry Lucia."

He stopped and turned to her. "When I met you on the ship, I was sure that I would never marry Lucia. I knew you and I were meant to be together, and now look at what I have done."

"Alfredo, you are a romantic. Sometimes things just don't happen the way we envision them. It happened to me also."

"You mean with me?" he asked, as the excitement built within him.

"No, I was referring to my life before I met you." Then gently, "Please do not be hurt or judge me too harshly. At the time when I met you on the ship, so many disappointments had come my way that I was unable to cope well. I only had Paula and then when she was taken from me, I could only think of the loss of my child. The pain is still as acute as the day it happened more than a year ago."

"It was foolish of me to presume," he continued. "Anyway, I became involved with Lucia, and she told me that she was expecting my child, so I married her. What else could I do?"

They walked in silence, neither one commenting.

Annabelle swallowed, pushing the lump back into her throat. "Alfredo, I feel I am somewhat responsible for this, since you told me that my going away was your deciding factor. You see, I lied about returning to Hungary, and I never should have done that to you. I had just met Lucia with you, and she made it clear to me that you were going to be married. I didn't want to interfere in any way with your plans and expectations. Nevertheless, now you have a family to consider, so there is nothing to be done except for you to remain with them. In time you will find happiness, perhaps through your child."

"I am understanding that you are saying that you do not see any chance for us at all."

"That is correct, Alfredo. You are married, committed to a family and I, well I am thinking of getting married myself."

"Marriage for you? Now? I am embarrassed. I had assumed that somehow there might be some chance for us in the future. I am ashamed of myself."

"Never mind," Annabelle responded. "If you were free, it would be different for us. If we had met at another time and place, then perhaps…who knows what might have happened. But not now. Now you have an obligation, and I respect that."

Alfredo silently stared into the clouds scattered in the bright, blue sky. He tried to gather himself together before he answered her. "I understand what you are saying, and I do not take my responsibilities lightly. Perhaps you think I am only trying to gratify my own needs and not take you into consideration at all. You need to know that is not the case, but I will respect your decision, though I will never stop thinking about you. Perhaps you are right. I was just too presumptuous."

He bowed ceremoniously and kissed her hand. "To your future happiness. I will never forget you."

Tipping his hat, he turned and walked determinedly across the clearing. Annabelle stared after him, fighting a desire to call out after him, and wondering if she had made the right decision to send him away so abruptly. Yet she knew that with a child on the way, there would be no other choice.

Darkness had crept over the meadow by the time she returned to the house. It was too late for the basketful of apples, anyway, even though she apologized dutifully to her grandmother. The table had already been cleared from dinner, but Margaret had kept her food warm near the fire. Annabelle couldn't eat anything; rather, she listlessly climbed the stairs to her bedroom.

Perhaps tomorrow she could decide what to do. It seemed she was always putting off making decisions. Whether they were the right decisions when she finally decided, was another question. She just felt more confused than ever.

CHAPTER TEN: THE ENGAGEMENT

Winter had set in firmly. From her window, Annabelle could only see the drifts of snow piled high along the edge of her grandparents' property. Even the Jones' fence was no longer visible. She had a sense of security and solitude, looking out onto the rolling lawns and knowing that she was warm and comfortable inside. Pulling her shawl more closely around her shoulders, she threw another log on the fire.

Piled high in a large copper kettle in the corner of the room, the split wood spoke of hours of labor, felling trees, cutting them into large sections and splitting them into manageable logs. She had learned from Franz that there is an art to building a fire. How the wood is stacked in the fireplace allows for a better fire, and the harder woods would guarantee a longer burning time. Yet to start the fire, it was important to have some soft-wood kindling and some pinecones. She peered out the window to survey the woodshed and tried to estimate if they had enough firewood to last through this storm. Rudolf, her grandfather, had worked really hard to store what he thought was enough wood for the winter.

From the kitchen came *Anyóka's* melodious voice as she related the activities of the day to Rudolf. She was so much happier now that Rudolf had returned from his long and hazardous trip to visit his brother. The distance was so far, and to make it especially challenging, traveling alone was difficult at his age. Margaret was glad he was back safely.

Annabelle heard Rudolf chuckle at Margaret's comments and could just imagine the exchange of expressions between them. Maybe being married for a long time gave you that sense of satisfaction from knowing and understanding each other.

No one had come calling in a week, so impassable were the roads. She had even begun to miss seeing Miklos whose authoritative mannerisms had become more natural and more acceptable to her. At first, she had railed against his dominance; now she had decided that it was just a symbol of someone who would protect her from harm. Let him tell me what to do and where to go, she thought. Let him take care of me. It is so much easier than having to worry about things myself. Yes, I guess I am happy having Miklos provide for me. She pivoted in front of the looking glass, allowing herself to wonder what it was that Miklos found attractive. Was it her long flowing hair or her trim figure? Her face was not too bad, she admitted, although she had a tendency to paleness. Yes, she decided, I am happy with the attention he shows to me, even if I am not really sure about him as a prospective husband.

Two weeks ago, he had brought her a puppy, just a ball of light brown fur. He called it an early Christmas gift. Curled up by the fireplace, the puppy was barely visible, so well did it blend in with the honey-colored hues of the golden hearth-rug. She had called her "Mez" because of this golden color, the Hungarian word for honey. She thought how Mez seemed to camouflage herself in the room, coming forward for affection just when Annabelle needed something to demonstrate that something or someone cared about her.

She had never had a puppy before; the pup was so small and helpless as she lay curled up. She sank to the floor to sit next to Mez and began to pat her belly. The puppy stretched out full length in total contentment.

It felt wonderful to have something to care for once again, and she was grateful to Miklos for thinking of it.

"Mez, Mez," she whispered. The puppy let out a squeak of joy and climbed onto her lap. Annabelle picked her up, bringing the puppy to her face for a soft kiss on the top of the head. Stroking the delicate fur, she drifted off, remembering other times and places. She allowed herself to indulge in these reminiscences; she decided that her grandmother was right and that she deserved a little bit of happiness. Enough bad things had happened to her, and she was determined to turn things around. And she accepted that this puppy was a symbol of the comforts that Miklos could offer her.

Her grandmother called out from the bottom of the stairs. "Annabelle, we have a guest. Please come down."

Like a schoolgirl, she skipped down the stairs two at a time, wondering who was paying a visit. She thought perhaps Mrs. Jones had come to borrow some eggs.

In the kitchen, with the sun sparkling on his wet hair, was Miklos.

"How did you get here?" she exclaimed. "I thought all the roads were blocked."

"By sled," he answered. "Would you like to go for a ride?"

"That would be so much fun," Annabelle laughed heartily. "I have to get my wrap."

"My dear, you will need much more than a mere wrap. You will have to bundle up nice and warm. The wind is rather fierce, though the sun is shining brightly." He continued, "Make sure you have a scarf to cover your face as well."

Margaret smiled as she watched Annabelle, responding in such a lighthearted manner. It had been a long time since she had seen that smile. “Be sure not to return late. I will have supper ready. Not any fuss. Just plain food.”

Miklos bowed in appreciation. “Even your plain food is more delectable than anything else I have ever eaten.”

He helped Annabelle with her long coat. She fastened the collar under her chin and wrapped herself in the red woolen scarf that Grandmother had made for her. Hidden behind his back, Miklos suddenly produced a fur muff. “I thought this would help to warm your hands.”

Annabelle squealed in surprise, “It’s so beautiful. How thoughtful of you!”

Mez hopped up and down at Annabelle’s feet, begging to be picked up. She had already learned the signs that meant she wanted to go outside, and that she wanted to go with Annabelle.

Annabelle stooped down to gently pat her head, “Not today Mez. We would lose you in a snow drift, and you are still much too young to go outside in such cold weather.”

Miklos’ brow furrowed as he listened to Annabelle. “Anyone would think you were talking to a child. Take her along if you like. You can hold her on your lap and wrap her in a blanket.”

“No Miklos, not today.”

“Fine then,” he said, “Let’s be on our way.”

Annabelle struggled with her skirts while crossing the snowbanks in the front of the house. Miklos lifted her up, trudging through the sparkling snow and placing her carefully in the sled. Then he pulled the heavy seal-lined woolen blanket across her lap.

The countryside was breathtaking. Annabelle was elated to be out of the house; she had been so confined for the last week or so. Such a magical feeling overcame her as she basked in her good fortune. She reveled in the purity of the meadows, untouched by humans, she admired the soft, rolling mounds of white, as far as the eye could see. Once in a while, some movement could be seen, as a cottontail skirted across the undisturbed landscape. She felt joy enveloping her chest and she gave a gleeful exclamation.

Miklos stared at her from the corner of his eye. He would have her, he determined, no matter what it cost him. He marveled as the color built up in her cheeks, as much from excitement as from the cold, crisp air. He began humming a tune, an old Hungarian folk song that his mother used to sing to him. To his amazement, Annabelle joined in, her voice clear and pure. They stopped along the roadside to watch a group of children skating on Wilder's Pond. Boys and girls had joined hands in a whimsical ballet on ice. Annabelle wished she could skate, but she had never learned how. She imagined herself gliding across the perfect ice in effortless motion.

She thought Miklos had read her mind as he said, "Some afternoon, we shall have to plan to come here and skate with the others."

Embarrassed, she responded, "Oh no, I couldn't. In the first place I don't know how to skate and I am much too old to learn now."

"Nonsense," he corrected, "I will teach you. You can learn to do anything you really want to do."

They alighted from the sled and followed the worn path towards the pond. The snow was packed solid, and the walking was easier than Annabelle had thought it would be. So many others had passed before them and packed down the snow.

Spontaneously, Annabelle turned to Miklos, "You have made me happier today than I have been in a very long time. Thank you."

He was taken back by her response and put his arm around her shoulder as they made their way to the edge of the pond to watch the skaters. She continued, “I have a lot I must tell you before we continue to see each other.”

“Let time take care of everything, Annabelle. I am in no hurry. Whatever you have to say can wait.”

“You don’t understand, Miklos. I have to tell you about my past unless you want to be hurt.”

“There is nothing about your past I want to know, as long as I can have you with me. Anyway, Franz already told me anything I need to know.”

He turned towards her, lifting her chin ever so slightly upwards and gently pressed his lips to hers. “I am afraid I am falling in love with you,” he confessed.

She leaned her head on his shoulder, confiding, “I am afraid of that too, Miklos.”

“Come now.” He changed the tone of his voice to a brisk banter, “Things are getting much too serious here. Perhaps we should try to get back before the sun goes down. We have come some distance.”

As dusk crept in, the mystical quality of the day seemed to increase for Annabelle. The shadows cast their magic on the landscape, providing a mysterious feeling. She basked in the change in the atmosphere, and Miklos stopped to light the lantern on the front of the sled. Riding back through the countryside, she recalled the other snow-filled evenings she had shared with Franz and allowed herself the luxury of contentment. She enjoyed watching the horses make their way carefully, lifting their heads, their manes blowing in the wind.

By the time they returned home, Margaret had dinner prepared. Rudolf was full of chatter about the day’s woodcarvings. He had displayed a few of his finished works on the shelf in the dining room, so that he could explain to Miklos the process he followed with his wood chisels and fine handiwork. The rich color of the woods displayed and the fine finishes set off by the gleam of candlelight made these works of art even more appealing. Rudolf lifted the walnut "ibis" bird from its resting place, demonstrating the delicacy of its dogwood beak. Miklos listened politely as Rudolf explained every fine detail. Filled with a little too much brandy, he was talkative enough for everyone. It was fine with Annabelle, who was basking in the warmth of the homey atmosphere. She was mystified at how a man could envision a form in the wood that he chose to carve. She had watched his carving for many hours and knew how painstaking it actually was. Getting the wood to respond to the cuts he was making; gently teasing the shape from the form; carefully sanding the wood to smooth it down for the delicate finish he wanted to achieve. Annabelle really appreciated the artistic skills he embodied. As many times as she stared at a piece of raw wood, she could never envision any kind of shape within it. It was magical to experience the outcome.

Miklos also seemed content and surveyed Annabelle with an air of possession. After dinner he joined her as she settled by the fire, Mez at her feet. Grandmother served coffee in the drawing room along with her coveted pastries. Miklos indulged himself and Annabelle wondered how she had ever doubted that he could be a part of her family. Everything was moving along just as Miklos had planned. He was proud that he could fit himself into the atmosphere and that he was being accepted by her family.

When the snow started to fall again, Margaret suggested that Miklos stay over in the extra room suitable for guests. Not wanting to take advantage of her hospitality, he refused. The sled was equipped with lanterns, and the moonlight was strong, in spite of the flurries coming down. So he felt he would have no problem traveling, in spite of the weather.

Taking his leave, he bowed graciously to Grandmother, shook Rudolf's hand energetically and paused momentarily to gaze endearingly at Annabelle, pressing his lips to her hand.

Then, just before exiting, he turned to Rudolf and Margaret. "The next time I visit, I will have a serious matter to discuss with you. In the meantime, thank you for a wonderful dinner and evening."

Annabelle stood at the front window for some time, gazing at the falling snow. She held Mez close to her heart, and watched the faint outline of the sled fade into the distance, as Miklos made his way home. Yes, maybe things would work out after all.

The next day was Saturday. The sun was shining brightly, the air fresh and clean as it always is after a new fallen snow. It was invigorating as was the memory of the night before. Annabelle felt that, finally, life was working perfectly for her. Tonight she expected Miklos for dinner again, and this time she was preparing the meal as she had promised. She wanted to impress him with her capabilities in the kitchen since she had learned so many different dishes under her grandmother's tutelage.

She hardly thought about Alfredo now in any hopeful way; she would not allow herself to consider what might have been. But every time the loss of Paula came to mind, so did Alfredo.

His tenderness and dedication to her that horrific night would always be a part of her most special memories, the ones that brought tears to her eyes.

She forced herself to think about the child that would soon be born, Alfredo's child, and his commitment to the baby and his new family. She could not help thinking how the child might look just like him as an adult with his quick smile and furrowed brow. Never mind, she chided herself, my life will be with Miklos. Hopefully, I will be happy, and I will not have to worry anymore.

She decided that she was pleased with Miklos' attention, and when the nagging question of love came into her mind, she pushed it aside, considering rather how wonderful life would be as the wife of a well-to-do landowner. She would be treated as a lady, respected for her position in the community. Her father would have been proud of her, saying that she was following in her mother's footsteps, as the belle of the ball.

She chopped the carrots, potatoes and cabbage into small pieces, adding them to the simmering beef broth. Peppers and celery were next to go into the pot. What a surprise for Miklos! He had once mentioned his love for *marhahus leves,* beef soup. She would serve it with homemade liver dumplings.

Margaret popped her head into the kitchen. "That smells delicious! Do you need some help?"

"Not really, *Anyóka*, unless you want to taste it and tell me what it needs."

Her grandmother ventured over to the cauldron, lifted the lid and dipped in the ladle. "Add some peppercorns and a little more parsley," she suggested, "You're right. I forgot the peppercorns. They should have been added in the beginning, before the vegetables."

"Don't worry, Annabelle. It always comes out right, even when added later in the preparation. I have done it myself many times."

"I am so nervous and want everything to be perfect," Annabelle murmured. "This is my first try at making dinner for a guest, and a special one at that."

"Can I help you with the desserts? What is the main course?"

"Esterhazy steak. Do we have capers and white wine?"

"Yes, both. This ***must*** be a special occasion. Are you preparing for something you might think will happen?" she asked playfully.

“I had not really thought about that. A dish commemorating the nobility! I guess it does look like I expect something special to happen. At least that is what Miklos keeps telling me.”

She moved over to wash the cauliflower and break the florets into small pieces while Grandmother started to sift the flour for the Linzer Torte.

“*Anyóka,* I really do have plenty of time. You are always the one cooking. Please go inside and relax. I can finish here.”

“Good, because I expect Rudolf’s cousin Klari to be here soon. She wants to see me about a problem she has. She has not been feeling well for some time.”

Annabelle’s face revealed her concern. “Do you have any idea about what is wrong?”

“I am afraid I do know, and that is precisely the problem for me. I have to tell her what I think and try to give her some help as well.”

“I’m sorry,” Annabelle continued. “Here I am being selfish and babbling about my life, when you have so many serious things to deal with.”

“Annabelle, my dear. When you are young, you should enjoy being young. The difficulties of the world have already plagued you enough. Take this time for happiness; it is sometimes too short-lived.”

Margaret turned on her heel and went into the sitting room to meditate before Klari arrived.

She really needed to clear her mind.

Annabelle stared after her, puzzled by the mysteriousness that her grandmother projected.

So many times, she knew the answers, Annabelle thought. Yet never did she take away a person’s right to make his or her own decision, not even when she knew what would be best for all. Annabelle wondered if that was what she should do. With the power to foresee, should she warn someone, stop them from disaster? She pondered whether or not her grandmother would stop her, if a marriage to Miklos was not the right thing for her. On the other hand, she remembered how *Anyóka* always said that each person has their own journey in life, and has the right to choose the path they wish to take.

As another nagging doubt crept into her mind, Annabelle dismissed it as foolishness, forcing herself to concentrate on the preparations in the kitchen.

Soon Klari was coming up the walkway. She painfully manipulated her cane. It was difficult for her to walk, and each step was laborious. Annabelle heard her grandmother as she met Klari at the front door.

"I am so glad to see you, Klari." Margaret hugged her soundly.

Klari smiled half-heartedly. "Margaret, I am glad to be here, too, but I don't know if I will ever see the springtime."

"Let's take you into the parlor and let you rest for a while. I have made a special brew for you to drink; it will make you feel much better."

She settled Klari on the sofa and slipped away. Klari closed her eyes and sighed deeply, grateful for the warmth of the fireplace and the coziness of the room. By the time Margaret returned, Klari was asleep.

Margaret took the brew, setting it on the table and opening the container she had brought from her storeroom. The herbal mix it held was potent. Klari stirred as the fragrance wafted towards her face. Margaret smoothed her brow and rubbed some of the mixture on her temples. It seemed to relax her so that her breathing became more even. She sat by Klari's side for a very long time, pressing her hands on the top of Klari's head. She finally coaxed Klari to drink some of the brew. Then she left the room, rejoining Annabelle in the kitchen.

"Do you mind if Klari stayed for dinner? I know this is your dinner party, but the trip back will be too much for her to make tonight."

"Of course. There's more than enough food for all and I, for one, would be delighted to see her. I have not enjoyed her company in such a long time; she is so entertaining. As soon as I learned that she was coming, I expected her to stay the night."

"Well, we'll see how entertaining she is when she awakens. Perhaps not as much as you might expect."

Changing the subject, she lightened the tone of her voice. "Let's use the best china and set out the sterling silver candlesticks and add the linen tablecloth and matching napkins."

"Yes, of course, *Anyóka*," Annabelle replied. When her grandmother scurried out of the room, Annabelle began to check the menu. Her hands were shaking as she went through the list she had made. Mushroom-stuffed eggs, beef soup and dumplings, steak, cauliflower, salad, and, best of all, coffee.

Coffee was saved for occasions, special occasions at that. Annabelle smiled to herself. She had done a good job and she could hardly wait to serve the meal. She remembered the spiritual saying, "Pride goeth before a fall." She knew she should check her enthusiasm and get back to the fine details.

She ticked things off in her mind. She told herself: one cut glass goblet goes in front of each rose-patterned china plate. Light the candles and make sure each setting has the proper number of forks, knives and spoons. Then she stepped back to admire the table setting. She realized she had forgotten salt and pepper, so she rushed to find the set that matched the china. When she returned, she again took stock of the table setting.

The glimmer of candlelight was accentuated by the cut of the crystal. Dancing images of the glass were projected on the walls. She wondered what Miklos would think when he arrived. Would he think she had made a fine enough presentation, enough for the wife of an influential man? Was she just imagining things that might happen?

Rudolf busied himself stoking the fire; soon the room was ablaze with warmth from the sweet smelling wood. Klari still slept.

Rudolf doubtfully considered Klari. "Margaret," he called. "Are you certain Klari is all right?"

"She's fine", came the calm response as she busied herself with some final touches. "Wake her, if you are worried," she instructed.

She watched carefully as Rudolf woke her, shaking her ever so gently. Klari opened her eyes, not seeming to know where she was. She hesitated, taking in the room and its occupants. He wiped her brow, as if to sweep away the cobwebs.

"How long have I been asleep?" she whispered.

"Since midday," replied Rudolf, reaching out to touch her hand.

Klari swung her legs around in one youthful movement. Rudolf stared in disbelief. Last week, when he visited Klari at home, she needed help to get out of her chair. He turned to his wife, an inquisitive look on his face. But, he said nothing; instead he chose to watch in astonishment.

Klari didn't seem to recognize that anything had happened. She stood, stretched her arms above her head and let out a deep sigh. "That was the best rest I have had in a very long time." Margaret watched silently, but Annabelle could see the satisfaction in her eyes.

Annabelle, who had not seen Klari in years, seemed confused. "Klari, you look fine to me. *Anyóka* mentioned that you have not been feeling well."

"I suppose that's true," she replied. "But right now, I feel wonderful."

Rudolf turned to Grandmother, "Margaret?"

She disregarded the question and Rudolf's probing looks. "Let's sit by the fire and warm ourselves. Soon Miklos will be here."

Annabelle felt chills running up and down her spine as she watched Klari move around without any effort at all. Rudolf tugged on Grandmother's sleeve. "Come with me into the kitchen so you can show me what has to be moved to the table."

Grandmother nodded, understanding the silent questions that she was receiving.

"Margaret, what have you done to her?" Rudolf insisted. She couldn't get herself from the chair to the table last week."

"I have done nothing, Rudolf. Perhaps, that rest was just what she needed, in the company of those who love her." She kissed him gently on the cheek, turned on her heel, moving towards Klari in the other room.

Rudolf scratched his head. He could not figure out Margaret. In fact, he had never been able to do so.

Upon his arrival, Miklos dominated everything and everyone. Instead of Annabelle, he became the center of attention at the dinner table. It seemed that he even overshadowed the amazing meal that Annabelle had prepared, charming Klari and entertaining her with his stories of his accomplishments.

Klari, who was always skeptical about new acquaintances, fell under Miklos' spell. Annabelle began to think how proud she would be as the fiancée of such a captivating man.

Suddenly, Miklos reached across the table, taking Annabelle's hand in his own. He turned towards Margaret. "I would like your permission to marry Annabelle," he said. Annabelle blushed with excitement. Everything was just too perfect.

She arose from her seat and walked around the table to Miklos. The shimmering rustle of her rose taffeta gown added to the romantic setting. It seemed that the flickering candles even accentuated the color of her cheeks. "Miklos," she said, "you have not yet asked *me*." Miklos bowed to kiss her hand. "Do you have any doubts, my dear?"

Rudolf had his doubts; he did not like Miklos and harbored his suspicions; no man was this smooth in his actions. It was not normal behavior. He preferred the more restrained gentleman, not the flashy suitor he saw before him. He held his tongue, not wanting to upset either Margaret or Annabelle and, of course, Klari, their special company for the evening.

Brandy followed in the parlor; combined with the aroma of after-dinner cigars, the atmosphere was charged with coziness. If Annabelle were to paint a picture of an ideal setting, she could not have cast a more accurate scene.

After the dishes were cleared and the gentlemen had completed their private discussions, Margaret, Klari and Rudolf excused themselves to allow the couple a few moments of privacy.

Alone with Annabelle, Miklos again took charge. Withdrawing a small jeweler's case from his vest pocket, he released the clasp, presenting to her a startling diamond in an ornate filigree setting of polished gold. Annabelle let a cry of surprise escape her, as she beheld the brilliance of the stone. The light caught the diamond cuts, causing the firelight to create a cascade of star-like images on the walls of the study. Her hands were shaking as he gently placed the ring on her finger.

Taking Annabelle in his arms, he pressed his body close to hers. She remained passive, fearful of the reaction of her heart beating strenuously against the delicate bodice of her gown. She was breathless, overcome by the moment.

Miklos turned her face to his, tenderly caressing her cheek as he bent to softly capture her lips. His kiss became passionate, lingering there. Annabelle fought her own tendencies to respond, reminding herself to remain proper. Was it Miklos or the magic of the night? She questioned her own need to wonder about him and to decide if she was truly in love with him.

Yet, it was perfect, so right in every way. How could she object?

Miklos wrapped his arms more tightly around her. She attempted to hold herself back, but he was in control of her. Tentatively, he stroked her breast. The effect was electrifying and frightened Annabelle. He was moving much too quickly, and clearly, she was not ready for this. Determinedly, she disengaged herself from his embrace.

"Miklos, the hour is late, and too much has happened already, and much too quickly at that."

"But, Annabelle, we are betrothed."

She turned away from him. She had never before felt this kind of resistance inside herself, not with Franz, not even with her imaginings of what it might be like with Alfredo. "I know," she whispered. She placed her hand softly on his face, "But I am not ready for this yet. You must allow me time."

He abruptly let her go, clearly angry. She began to feel guilty; he had been so kind, and she had insulted him.

"Please Miklos, too much too quickly."

He took his cloak from the peg in the hallway, striking a formal tone. "We will have a party to announce our engagement and the wedding will follow within the next few months. Discuss with your grandmother when it will be convenient for her. I will make all the arrangements, and tomorrow I will return to inform you of the details."

Annabelle was startled, taken back; he had suddenly become another person. From a considerate, kind suitor to a demanding, but restrained man. Suddenly, she felt like he was almost a stranger. She was shocked; tears made their way down her cheeks, but he took no notice of them. He quickly put his coat on and left.

Later, in the privacy of her room, she considered what had happened, going over it again and again. She thought he would be understanding, but she knew she had spurned him. She decided to accept his sudden departure with grace, giving him the benefit of the doubt. She reasoned that he would calm down, think about what had happened, and realize he had moved too quickly.

She climbed into her bed, pulling the quilt around her; suddenly she was so cold. Could sex be that important to him? What about the friendship they had shared? Or had she imagined it? It seemed that their relationship had completely changed, turned upside down.

She turned on her side, fingering the precious diamond. She would have to adjust to his ways. Men had different needs. In time, she would learn how to please him, but she was determined that he would have to wait for that physical closeness until after the ceremony. She knew that intimacy would only confuse her more deeply, and she was already deeply confused.

CHAPTER ELEVEN: CHRISTINA

Alfredo met each new day with apprehension. As Lucia grew bigger with child and more discontented, she became smaller in her behavior and less generous. It was as if the child blossoming inside of her was robbing her of life. She was withdrawn into herself, excluding everyone around her, even her own mother.

Alfredo rested in bed listening to her uneven breathing. After his last meeting with Annabelle, he had decided that he had to resume his role as husband and concentrate on becoming a father. He admitted to himself that he was obligated to do so. It was the right thing to do, and what he had vowed to do.

Unfortunately, other than mechanically satisfying his own urges, he felt nothing, no warmth within him, no outpouring of love, not even a hint of love. And Lucia did not reciprocate at all. He expected nothing of her and got nothing from her. So, at times like these, in his loneliness, his thoughts returned to Annabelle.

He got lost in thought as the minutes passed by. He tried to examine his own mind, to determine why he was attracted to Annabelle. He finally decided that it was her femininity. He witnessed that side of her on the ship, how she expressed her feelings for her child. Annabelle was flexible emotionally; she could bend with emotion. Lucia was hard and unyielding. The only emotion she displayed was anger, when she was trying to get agreement for something that she wanted. He recognized that he was trapped in a loveless marriage, but would make the best of things, even if he had to resort to his own imaginings.

Since the sixth month of her pregnancy, things had become more difficult for Lucia. She was unhappy with her appearance; she did not like being pregnant and could not even make herself look forward to the birth of her child. Every day she was becoming more dissatisfied with herself, with him, with their home, with everything around her.

Today, when Alfredo returned from work, he found her in the corner of the room, sitting listlessly on the small upholstered chair he had bought her as a wedding gift. Her eyes were reddened from crying; Alfredo felt sorry for her.

Lucia despised the reality of pregnancy. She did not want to see herself and had forced Alfredo to remove the looking glass from their bedroom. She hated the sight of her misshapen body, and she did not seem to be able to connect with the child growing within her.

He was not sure how to respond to her; he did not know how to handle these moods. He turned towards her now, lying on his side and draping his arm around her. Perhaps, if he was more gentle with her, but even in her sleep she pushed him away, annoyed at his touch. He turned away; maybe the birth of this child would make all the difference in their relationship. She would see the beautiful being they had created together.

He slid from beneath the quilts, trying not to disturb her sleeping figure, as much for his own presence of mind, as for her benefit. Despite his efforts, a blast of cold air hit her back; she growled in her sleep. She grabbed the quilt, pulling it tightly around herself. He felt her forehead; she seemed feverish. He would stop at her mother's and have her come to stay with Lucia today. She would know what to do to soothe her, to make her feel better. After all, her time was getting near. And he was certainly at a loss about what should be done. He had little understanding of birth and delivery.

He prepared his own breakfast as he had taken to doing the last month or so. It saved him from having an argument with her. Lucia would never get up when he did, nor did she seem to care if he stayed or left. But, then, too, he did not have to spend awkward minutes trying to think of something to talk about with her. They had nothing in common, no interests that were the same, except for the expected baby. He had to admit that he had a limited inquisitiveness about her; there did not seem to be any depth to her. He tried to remember if he always thought she was this way. He recalled how, as children, she had prattled on about what was happening to her. She never asked anyone else anything about themselves, none of the boys and none of the girls. He kept telling himself that pregnancy did not really agree with her.

Tonight he would bring home book-work from the business. It would keep him busy and allow him to avoid any conversation with Lucia. Sometimes he devoted his spare time to studying English, another excuse for avoiding Lucia. How would he ever be able to manage the rest of his life if everything remained like this? He pushed the negative thought out of his mind, concentrating on tying his necktie. As he looked in the hallway mirror, he studied his own face. Were those age lines forming or just worry lines? In either case, he admitted that he was starting to look sickly and older. He was just too young for this. He had to find a way out, some way to settle things for once and for all. He had to be the dominating figure, to make the rules, or Lucia would devour him.

Maybe after the birth of his child….

He closed the door softly behind him. Tonight, he decided, he would try one more time, one more attempt at a truce between them.

He looked at his pocket watch; it was early, but the Della Cesares would be awake. He would ask the Signora for her help and advice. She was the only one who seemed able to control Lucia, to get her to understand and to cooperate.

He crossed the street and gingerly lifted his hand to knock. They were always awake before 6:00 A.M., so they would not mind, especially if it was for Lucia. Why was he so hesitant? Yes, it was a matter of pride. Here he was having to beg for help, admitting that he could not control his own wife. What would they think of him now? They already were disappointed in him; the Signora, visibly, did not like him. He steeled himself for the reaction he was expecting.

Signore Della Cesare cracked the door open. When he spotted Alfredo, he became alarmed. "Alfredo, what is the matter? Is it Lucia? Mama, Mama, come quickly," he called to his wife.

"No, Signore. Everything is fine, at least I think it is. I wanted to have the Signora go over to Lucia early this morning. She is restless in her sleep and slightly warm to the touch, maybe feverish. I thought she would know what to do."

Signora Della Cesare was untying her apron. "I'll go right now."

"Yes, thank you. And please, if you can wait one more moment…Lucia and I…well, ummm, we are not getting along quite as well as I had hoped. Could you, that is if you can find the way to do it, can you speak to her and tell her that I am determined to make this marriage work? It is needed, especially now with the baby on the way! However, I need her to try, too."

It was probably the longest speech that Alfredo had made in his entire life. He watched Lucia's mother's expression as it changed from concern to annoyance.

“Why are you speaking to me? You should be talking to your wife about such matters!”

He shuffled nervously from one foot to another. “I have tried and tried to speak with Lucia; she does not listen to me; she does not answer me.”

“Mama, you know how headstrong she can be,” Signore interjected. Turning back to Alfredo he continued, “My wife will talk to Lucia and convince her to be a proper wife and partner.”

Alfredo bowed his head. “Thank you, Signore, Signora.” He tipped his hat in respectful acknowledgement of their authority. He could see in the background the small figure of Anna Maria listening, while peering around the doorway. Was he just imagining a grin on her face?

The day progressed uneventfully. Alfredo thought there were more customers than usual, or perhaps it was that he was more tired than usual, or more distracted with worry about Lucia. He had dark circles under his eyes, lending him a gaunt appearance. Several of his customers asked if he had lost weight. He would study his own image more closely.

Perhaps he should return home at lunchtime today and try to settle things with Lucia. But, by the time the noontime hour arrived, Alfredo was even more disheartened. He knew he could not handle a disagreement and then come back and work the rest of the day with a positive frame of mind. He had to be cheerful and friendly to his customers; better to save the meeting for later that evening. Maybe Signora Della Cesare will have calmed Lucia down and changed her attitude towards him. In the back of his mind, he doubted that he could be so fortunate. He had been struggling with this for so long now; it almost felt hopeless to him.

Alfredo buried himself in thoughts of the market, taking more than his share of the customers, driving himself harder with each hour that passed by. Was he trying to punish himself for being unable to control his life?

Luigi commented, "Alfredo, what is wrong with you today? More trouble with Lucia? You do not look well; this marriage is bad for you, Alfredo. Please, let's talk about it. Come home with me tonight. We can ask Maria. She always knows what to do."

"No Luigi. No one can help me. I must find my own way in this, even though Maria, my sister, may have advice for me. I know how wonderful she is, but I cannot discuss this today; it is too difficult for me, maybe tomorrow."

It was late afternoon, and suddenly, it seemed as though the whole neighborhood had decided to shop with them at the same time. Well, Alfredo thought, at least it keeps me busy and allows me less time for thinking. When they had closed the doors and were taking care of the end-of-day tasks, Alfredo worked slower and slower as if he could delay the inevitable conversation he would need to have with Lucia when he returned home.

Suddenly they heard a frantic knocking at the door; looking out they saw Anna Maria, breathless and pale as she shouted, "Alfredo, you must come now. Quickly. It is Lucia. She is having a hard time."

"Are you telling me that she is having the baby? Is she all right?"

"I don't know. I was told to come and get you right away. They did not let me see her."

Alfredo tore off his apron and started to pull on his jacket. With fear creeping into his throat, he turned to Luigi, "I am going now."

Luigi waved his hand. "Go…go."

What if he lost this child? Or what if … no, he would not allow himself to think of that. It was too much to bear, and not a solution to his problems. He sped down the street with Anna Maria close on his heels.

He had forgotten his jacket, but the chilly day did not seem to affect him at all. The passersby were pulling their wraps more closely around them. Alfredo didn't even notice the glances as he ran past.

Dr. Santoro's carriage was already there. Fear climbed from his chest into his throat as he took the steps two at a time, unmindful of his wild appearance. He had forgotten about Anna Maria completely.

The room was quiet when he entered. Everyone must be in the bedroom, he thought. As he approached the doorway, he could hear his mother-in-law weeping. He hesitated, his hand on the knob. Whispering a prayer for strength, he stepped into the room.

The midwife was in the corner attending to the baby. It was squirming and crying, screaming its dissatisfaction at having to make the journey into this cold environment.

No one had noticed him. He felt like he was watching a play, all the characters moving in exaggerated fashion.

Dr. Santoro was bending over Lucia, administering medication. Signore Della Cesare was comforting his wife who was twisting her handkerchief into a knot. Lucia was still and pale, barely responding to the Doctor.

Perhaps this is the way it is, he thought. The birth must have been difficult, but waited a moment to gather his thoughts before speaking.

"Dr. Santoro, Anna Maria came to get me."

The Doctor, in turning, betrayed a concerned expression, so serious that Alfredo's heart skipped a beat.

"What is wrong, Doctor?"

"Lucia has had a very hard time. I doubt that she will survive this And the baby is early and needs attention."

Stricken, the color drained from his face. In spite of his desperate fear, a glimmer of hopefulness snuck into the back corners of his mind. God forgive me, he thought.

Instead, he responded, "But she is so young. How can that be possible?"

"Age has little to do with it. The baby was almost strangled by the birth cord. You are lucky to have this little girl. Lucia, on the other hand, has lost a lot of blood and is very weak. I fear infection is setting in as well. I have given her something for it. I advise you to spend every moment you can with her. She may not last until the morning."

Alfredo paled. How would he ever manage with an infant? He was by himself? Who would care for the baby while he was working? So many questions, so many problems.

Signora Della Cesare turned towards Alfredo, hatred evident on her face. "My daughter told me today how you have mistreated her, how you forced her to work so hard to care for you and the home, how you would not allow me to help her out. This is all your fault. If you had not done those things, she would be just fine right now."

Alfredo opened his mouth to reply, but because his mother-in-law was screaming at him, he thought better of it.

She continued relentlessly, "If my child dies because of you, I will see that you pay for it."

Signore Della Cesare motioned to Alfredo to be silent. When he faced his son-in-law, his eyes were filled with tears. "She was my baby. I will not allow you to step inside my house again. I hold you responsible for this."

Alfredo was speechless. There was no way for him to defend himself. He watched, stunned, as his in-laws retreated into the sitting room.

Dr. Santoro came forward, "Alfredo, you must forgive them; they are overwhelmed with grief. Perhaps she will pull through. Sit with her. I will talk to her parents for you."

The Doctor took his bag, starting towards the door. Alfredo asked him, "What happens if we need you? Why would you leave us now?"

"I have done whatever I could do for her. There is nothing more I can do to help her now. I will check in on her in the morning. I know what happened between the two of you. Lucia told me. I am sorry for you. She was not the easiest woman in the world, but you are young and you have a healthy child."

"Thank you for your concerns, Doctor. Can the midwife remain to care for the baby, at least through this night?"

"Yes, for now. And I will arrange for a wet nurse."

Alfredo shook his head in agreement and shook the doctor's hand. "Thank you once again. I will see you tomorrow morning."

"Yes, Alfredo. Send for me if there is any kind of drastic change. Give her this medicine every two hours through the night. We will see how she is in the morning."

Alfredo sat at the side of the bed, taking Lucia's hand and studying her face for signs of life. She was too quiet, much too quiet. He bowed his head in prayer, for Lucia, for himself, and for the new baby. He tried to quell the feelings of guilt he was having about the possibility of being out from under Lucia's clutches. Instead, he prayed and asked God for forgiveness and for strength to do the right thing for his family.

The Doctor entered the sitting room and sent Lucia's parents home. "You both need some sleep. Come back first thing in the morning." To Anna Maria who was cowering in the corner, he said, "Go with your parents, child. You too can come back after you have had a few hours of sleep. There is nothing more any of us can do now. It is in God's hands; only He decides her fate."

Alfredo stared after him, listening to the exchange of words in the next room. He decided to stay where he was, with his wife. Sitting close to her, he called her name softly. Her eyes fluttered open in recognition of his voice. "Lucia, we have a beautiful little girl. You had an exhausting experience, but the doctor says you will be fine."

She seemed to want to say something, so Alfredo moved closer to her. He could barely hear her words, she was whispering so softly. "Alfredo, I will not see the light of day. I am sorry for the pain I have caused you."

"And I you," he said. "But I don't want you to concern yourself with this now. Tomorrow when you are stronger, we will talk. Together we will figure out how to go forward and make a family. We cannot continue like this, living without love. Sleep now and think of a name for our child."

"Christina," she whispered.

"Christina is a good name," Alfredo whispered back to her.

Lucia sighed and closed her eyes.

Alfredo sat by Lucia's side all night long. Periodically, he would awaken and check to see if she had returned to consciousness. When Dr. Santoro returned Alfredo was still sleeping, his head resting on Lucia's mattress.

"Alfredo, wake up. It's all over," said Dr. Santoro.

"You mean the suffering is over and she will recover? Thank God."

"No, I mean she has died."

Alfredo felt the tears brimming, but he was unable to speak, so overcome was he with the situation. The weight of the news had grabbed his heart, suppressing his breath. His next thought was, what would he do about his child?

Dr. Santoro could sense his helplessness. "I have asked the wet nurse to make herself available to you. She agrees to remain with the baby until you can make other arrangements, after the funeral."

"How can I manage? What will I do? I have no idea." Alfredo offered. His confusion was apparent; the worry lines in his forehead had deepened, and the darkness under his eyes had spread and intensified.

Dr. Santoro continued, "Perhaps the grandparents can be convinced to take the child. That would alleviate the burden for you."

Alfredo emotionally replied, "No, I will not allow it."

Dr. Santoro continued, "Alfredo, you are not thinking clearly right now. You are a young man with a whole life ahead of you. You will find another wife, one more suitable for you, and you will have a chance at a happy marriage."

Alfredo quickly jumped in, "This is not something I want to discuss or to even think about right now."

Dr. Santoro patted him on the shoulder in an effort to offer some kind of feeble comfort to the grieving man. "For right now, I suggest you consult with Lucia's parents. There are arrangements that must be made right away. I know that they would want and need to be included; they probably have preferences for taking care of their child."

They did indeed make the decisions for Lucia's burial. Alfredo allowed them to take over and relinquished control to them. He remained in the background, not even offering to share his opinions, or to explain his feelings.

The local parish priest, Father Sabatti, came to see Alfredo. He was sympathetic to the young man but was really an agent of Lucia's parents.

He wanted Alfredo to allow him to work directly with the parents to handle the services in a way that pleased them. Alfredo happily agreed; this was not something he felt he was ready to handle himself.

He lurked in the background, hiding in the shadows while the priest performed the necessary last rites. He allowed the body to be held in the Della Cesare's home where friends of the family and of Alfredo were received. Most of the next few days were a blur to Alfredo.

He found himself standing by the graveside, watching the oak coffin being lowered into the ground. He was oblivious of the people around him, nodding to those who offered their condolences. Surprisingly, throughout the whole monstrous affair, Lucia's parents did not say one word to him, not even about Christina or what was to become of her. He had no idea of how, or even if these grandparents would ever be part of his daughter's life. If they were not, that would be all right with him. All of his support came from his sister Maria and her husband Luigi.

Alfredo slowly began to feel somewhat better; the baby was flourishing under the loving care that Maria offered. The kindness of Maria and Luigi could not be measured. They allowed both Alfredo and his child to move in with them so that the small apartment became even more crowded; Maria and Luigi no longer had any privacy. They were willing to wait as long as it would take for Alfredo to find a solution to his problem.

As time went by, Alfredo came to realize that the baby was closer to Maria than to him. It was only natural; she was the one who was with her all day long and Christina responded to the sound of her voice, and to the tenderness that she offered.

He did not know how to respond or how to be a father. It was somewhat of a relief to him to hand the reins to his sister. But he also knew he was just postponing the inevitable decision that he would have to make, sooner or later. Maria, in taking the responsibility from him, had given him an excuse to do nothing. He basked in the vast emptiness inside himself. But Luigi was not going to let this continue. He decided that he had to force Alfredo to make a plan for the future.

He did not mind having the baby, or even having Alfredo with them. He worried that his friend would never be the same, and so decided to push him a little. He applied gentle pressure, trying to get Alfredo more interested in life. He suggested some social activities, but Alfredo promptly refused.

Alfredo was mystified. Although he had never really loved Lucia in the real sense of the word, or what he imagined marital love was all about, he was lost without her. He had lost not just his wife, but his home, his sense of family, his reason for being. His life had little purpose, except for the moments he shared with Christina, when he returned from work. He was amazed at the vast emptiness within him. It seemed that life had little purpose now. Because Maria had relieved him of all the responsibility for Christina, he had an excuse to do nothing, and could not seem to reach within himself to find a pathway to survival.

Until today, Luigi had been careful to venture tactfully into a discussion of the situation. However, now he decided to take a stronger stand with his brother-in-law.

"Alfredo, you cannot continue in this state of mind. I know you still have your apartment, and I know you have not been back there since Lucia died. Now it is time to resume living your life. You have everything you need for the baby at your home."

"But Luigi," he protested, feeling the color rising in his cheeks, "How can you expect me to work and care for a child at the same time?"

Luigi stared in amazement. "Alfredo, of course you cannot. But there are other ways. You could take Christina home at night and bring her back in the morning. And, also there is that other woman, the one you met on the ship, the one who came to the Festa. You seemed to like her. Maybe there is some hope there. She is not married. Maybe she would consider you. I know you were taken with her, and I think she felt comfortable with you, too."

Alfredo walked away, trying to control his anger. "Luigi, what is wrong with you? How can you expect me to go begging to someone, to ask her to consider me out of pity, instead of out of love? I could never." His voice rose as his anger increased. "I will never."

"Alfredo, don't be angry with me. Reconsider. I think she might be happy to be with you, too. You said she has no one. And, you told me that she lost her own child as well."

Alfredo spun back around, facing Luigi and looking at him directly. "If you are telling me that you and Maria no longer want to help me, then I will try to make other arrangements for the baby and for myself. I am sure I can find someone who would be willing to care for Christina."

Now Luigi started to get angry, "Don't be silly, Alfredo. That is not what I was trying to say. Of course we will help you; we are family; we are always here for you, no matter what happens. But because we love you and want you to be happy is exactly why I am talking about this with you. You need a life of your own. You need someone to love and to love you. You cannot continue like this indefinitely."

"Luigi, finding a wife is not like shopping for produce in our market. Women are not out there, waiting to be picked." Alfredo turned on his heel and left the building.

Alfredo walked into the cool night air. The darkness was just starting to settle on the city. He walked through the streets, among other people, watching them carefully. He studied the faces; he watched to see if the men and women had affection for each other.

As the breeze picked up, he pulled his jacket tighter around himself. He knew that leaving the apartment as he had done, he had left Luigi staring at a blank wall. At this point, he did not care.

His anger and frustration, his self-pity and unhappiness carried him forward through the night to the pub at the other end of the town. There he sat, downing one glass of wine after another, until he wove his way back home. Rain was heavily falling on him, but he was unaware. When he arrived at Luigi's, his brother-in-law put him to bed. Now, both of them slept uneasily.

Lucia and Annabelle filled his dreams. He felt as though Lucia was telling him to go to Annabelle, to reach out to her for the sake of their child. She seemed to want him to ask Annabelle if she would marry him. Lucia was telling him that she wanted a stable home for Christina, and that she was sorry for the pain she had caused him.

In the morning he had made up his mind.

CHAPTER TWELVE: MIKLOS

After the night of the engagement announcement, Annabelle found herself having mixed feelings about Miklos. The balance of their relationship had changed. Although she could not tell exactly what had happened, she knew that now Miklos felt that he had power that he could exercise over her, power she had not experienced before. His demeanor had changed; what he expected of her had changed. It was clear that he thought that she now owed him something because he had given her a ring, because he wanted her to become his wife. He acted as though she should be grateful for this. Even with Franz, who could never entirely commit himself to her, she felt more appreciated, felt more equal to him, even felt like a couple. With Miklos she now knew that he had convinced himself that she was his possession, his very own to use as he pleased. She did not know if this was to continue like this, but she knew that she could not survive in a marriage built on that kind of relationship. She felt she had enough sadness in her life and was not anxious to get caught up in another difficult situation.

Since the misunderstanding between them, he had not again mentioned it, but he still was courteous, yet distant. She felt a coldness spilling out around her, a coldness that he was happy to impose on her. He still sent her small gifts of appreciation; a book of poetry, a bouquet of flowers, a little perfume, yet he did so without enthusiasm. She was now very uncertain about him. She decided that she had to speak to him directly about what had happened to cause this change between them.

Shortly after he came to take her for an afternoon stroll, she decided to approach him about the situation. He seemed determined to give her all the outward signs of attention. Today, he seemed to be in particularly good humor, so Annabelle felt comfortable with broaching the subject.

"Miklos," she ventured tentatively, "I am not exactly sure about what has happened between us. It is just a week since you gave me the ring, but I feel you have withdrawn from me, that we are not as close as we were. I wanted to talk about our misunderstanding."

Miklos looked at her with no emotion showing, "I don't know what you are talking about Annabelle. What misunderstanding? Have I not been treating you with care?"

Annabelle did not want to push him too hard, so she tried again, carefully.

"I was referring to what happened when you made those romantic advances to me, and I was unwilling to respond."

"Annabelle, now you are making a lot out of nothing."

"To me it is something important. Don't you remember what you said and how you acted with me?"

His voice became stern. "I remember that we are engaged and that you should be prepared to do exactly as I say. That is exactly what you *should* remember."

"Please, Miklos," she proceeded, thinking that she would be able to smooth things over, thinking that it was only his masculine pride that was hurt.

She reached up, wrapping her arms around his neck. She felt his body stiffen as he pulled her arms from around him. He made it clear that her discussion would not be honored.

He continued, ignoring everything else that was said, he repeated, "Annabelle, the engagement party will be in a fortnight. I spoke to you of this. I will make all the arrangements. I will create the guest list; I will provide the music and the food. I will even bring my servants to the party so that you and your grandmother can enjoy the celebration. All you have to do is to ensure that your grandparents can cooperate with the date. It will be held here, at your home, of course."

"Don't you want to know my thoughts about the engagement party? It is very close to the end of the year and my grandmother feels like we would be dealing with weather problems. You said what is convenient for my grandmother. Don't you want to hear about that?" she asked.

Not even considering the courtesy of a reply, he took her hand; she looked at him in amazement, as he refused to answer her. "I will think about it," he finally said.

"Now let's go for that walk." She felt a cold hand grip her heart as she realized that there was not a chance that he was going to acknowledge her concerns. It was clear that he did not care what her thoughts were.

He not so gently placed his arm through hers and led her to the door. "Where is your wrap?" he demanded.

She turned away in frustration, so that he would not see the tears brimming in her eyes. She lifted a gloved hand and wiped away a tear that escaped down her cheek. She instinctively knew that he would not care about that at all.

She thought, how can I ever relate to this man who ignores what I am saying, who refuses to listen to me, who organizes everything to his satisfaction without consulting me? I can now see that he has to have the final say in everything. Seeing that now, she thought. What am I to do?

Returning an hour later, she immediately sought out her grandmother. Margaret was in the kitchen, in the process of baking bread.

Without looking up from what she was doing, Margaret offered, "And how are the young lovers getting on today?"

"That's what I wanted to talk to you about, *Anyóka*. I am not certain myself," Annabelle ventured.

Margaret stopped kneading the dough, wiped her hands on her apron and looked directly into her granddaughter's eyes. "Clearly something has happened," she said. "What is the problem? How can I help?" She drew up a chair at the table, Annabelle settling in across from her.

"I am now uncertain about Miklos. Suddenly, he seems so different."

"In what way? Tell me," Grandmother continued, "What makes you feel this way?" She studied Annabelle's face, while waiting for an answer.

Annabelle shifted uneasily in her seat. "It's hard to know where to begin, and I don't want to go into details. I feel uncomfortable talking about it, but the final thing is that I don't think I really love Miklos…not at all."

"What brought that on?" Grandmother asked.

"He seems to have so much to prove; he wants to have everything his way, he has not even asked me what I want or how I feel about the arrangements for this party. He is suddenly acting like he owns me. And I told him that we should have more time elapse for the engagement party, as you asked, but he does not seem to care."

Grandmother tried to tread lightly. "Are you looking for romance, an unreal romance, like you had with Franz?"

It was hard to answer honestly, and Annabelle felt embarrassed. "I actually thought about that myself, I really did. But I don't think I really am looking for that."

"What are you looking for, child?" Grandmother inquired.

Annabelle stopped to think. "I am looking for someone who will treat me with kindness, who respects me as a woman, who cares what I say and feel…."

"Maybe you are just nervous. Maybe you are being too hard on yourself and on him?"

Grandmother cautiously watched Annabelle's face as she considered this question.

"It's difficult to find the right words, but there is something about Miklos that scares me, some underlying trait. Something about how he is now treating me. He now makes me feel like a possession of his, like one of his pets."

"In the beginning, when you started to be interested in him, did you feel that way?"

"No, I didn't. But something happened, something I don't want to talk about. This thing that happened, changed things between us. Now I feel like an awkward child."

"Is it something you can fix? Did you talk about it with him?" Grandmother continued.

"I tried to talk to him. But he would not listen to me. He just told me I would have to learn how to do what he tells me." Annabelle put her face into her hands, letting the tears come, her body wracking with her sobs. "*Anyóka,* I am so confused. Never in my life have I felt like I had so little value, even when things were falling apart with Franz. I was not afraid of Franz. However, I am afraid of Miklos."

Grandmother went to Annabelle and put her arms around her. "You need to sleep on this. You have had a very difficult year. You need to be certain you are looking at things realistically. Come now. Dry your eyes. Things will work out fine in the end. You still have time to change your mind, if that is what you decide is necessary."

Annabelle wailed, "I don't know. I just don't know."

Miklos, too, was thinking about the day. In his mind, he was going over the exchange he just had with Annabelle. He did not like it, not one bit. She was going to be a problem; he could see that. He was going to have to become even more adamant about what he wanted her to do, and how she should behave, as his prospective wife, and after, as his wife.

At his next visit, Annabelle tried once more to smooth things over with Miklos.

She pleaded, "Please, Miklos."

She reached up and placed her arms around his neck but felt his body stiffen. He again unwrapped her arms from around him.

"Annabelle, as I keep telling you, the engagement party I spoke of should be held in a fortnight. I said I will make all the arrangements for the guest list, the food and the music. I told you that I will be bringing my own servants with me so you and your grandmother can also enjoy the party. But if you need more time for the party, we will do it after the winter. Now, let's go for a walk."

To himself, Miklos thought, "I will do whatever it takes to have my way in the end."

When she returned to the house, she again spoke to her grandmother. "I don't know. I just don't know. He will not talk with me about the problem I am having. This is the second time he has just ignored me and ordered me to go for a walk with him. But he did consent to allow more time to pass before the engagement party takes place. Please, *Anyóka*, can't you tell me what to do about marrying him?"

"I am afraid, child, that this is one decision you will have to make for yourself. However, the time between now and the party gives you a chance to re-evaluate your feelings for him. Let's see what happens."

It was early on the night of May 20th, and Annabelle was dressing for the engagement party. Grandmother had decided to nap so she could be at her best that evening. She never really liked to have so many guests in her house at once, but Miklos was so insistent, making her feel that she had to agree to do just as he wished. She began to see some of what Annabelle was talking about.

The servants were in her kitchen; the aromas of the delicate preparations filled the house with temptation. In spite of her increasing nervousness, Annabelle even had to admit to herself that it was putting her in a festive mood.

There was a knock on the side door. Annabelle was upstairs but could hear Miklos' butler open the door and wondered what additional detail was being addressed. She thought everything was taken care of. It certainly seemed like Miklos thought of everything – the best food, the most beautiful floral pieces, and the most polite and most efficient servants. She went back to reminiscing and her face powder.

Then there was a tentative knock on her bedroom door.

"Miss," the timid maid ventured, "there is a gentleman to see you."

"Is it Miklos- Mr. Katika, that is? I am not yet ready."

"No, Miss, I have not heard his name before."

"Well then, it is one of the guests who has arrived too early?"

"No, Miss. His name is not on the list. And he says it is most important that he speaks with you."

"All right then. I will be down shortly. Ask him to wait in the parlor."

Annabelle felt irritated. Not so much because a guest had arrived early, but because she was sure Miklos had something to do with this, too. Somehow, he had arranged something else that he neglected to tell her about. Things had really not changed much between them. She thought that it was just another example of how he wanted to remind her that he is the one in charge. She went bounding down the stairs and impatiently and abruptly entered the parlor.

"Can I help you? Is there something I have forgotten about tonight's festivities?"

The visitor was standing with his back to her, warming his hands by the fire. As he turned to face her, Annabelle paled.

"Alfredo, what are you doing here?"

"Have I come at an inconvenient time?"

"I am afraid so. Tonight is my engagement celebration."

His face also lost color. "Perhaps then, I should leave immediately."

"No, I cannot ask you to do that. You have traveled a great distance and must have something important to discuss. It is chilly out too.. Warm yourself, first, while I get you some brandy."

"No, thank you. I do not want to inconvenience you further."

"Then you must join us. There is plenty of food, and I am happy to have you remain for the party."

"I cannot stay."

"Then, please tell me why you have come so far to see me. Let's sit down. How impolite of me not to offer before."

She found herself rambling, not so much out of confusion, as out of a desire to keep him there. Her heart had skipped a beat. Was it the shock of suddenly seeing him, or something else that made her feel this way?

Was it something she had been searching for in Miklos and could not find? It had been so long since she had seen Alfredo. He looked really tired; he did not seem like himself. His eyes were sad and his face was somewhat ashen.

He took a seat where she pointed and she settled in the chair opposite him so she could see him more clearly. He was so handsome, she thought, even though he did not appear to be well. The firelight reflected her flushed complexion, as she caught her mind wandering. Alfredo could sense her embarrassment.

"I am so sorry. I am causing you discomfort. I will not stay."

"But you must tell me what brings you here. How are your wife and your child?"

"In truth, Annabelle, I have really come about them."

"I don't understand," she whispered.

He looked directly into her eyes. "My wife has died, and the child…"

"Oh no, not the child, too!" she cried.

He knew she was reliving what had happened on the ship when she lost Paula.

"No, Annabelle, the child is fine, though she was born early. My wife died in childbirth."

"I am so sorry. Thank God, the baby is all right."

"My sister is caring for Christina, the baby."

"I am so glad for you that you have a sister who can help you."

"Yes, that is true. But my baby needs a real mother. One who will love her and care for her as her own. That is why I came. I wanted to ask you to be that woman, that mother that Christina needs."

Annabelle gasped, "Me? Why me?"

"Because you are an ideal woman. One who, I could see, loved your child more than life itself. And because, I have been in love with you since I first set eyes on you."

Annabelle's tears streamed down her cheeks.

"But, I realize now that it is too much to hope for. You are planning for your own wedding. It seems that we are always too late for each other, like ships passing in the night. I am so sorry."

Annabelle replied softly, "Yes, it seems so, doesn't it."

Suddenly, behind Annabelle came a sharp command, "And what do you think you are doing here? Kindly leave now!"

"Miklos," Annabelle responded, "this man is my guest."

"This man does not belong at our engagement party, Annabelle. I know all about him, and I do not want him here."

"And how do you know anything about him?"

"Because I heard your whole conversation."

Alfredo interjected, "Never mind, Annabelle, I will leave."

"No you will not leave. You must stay. I insist."

"My dear Annabelle," Miklos interrupted, "He will do as I say, just like you will do as I say."

"This is my home and my party, too. I will not have him leave." She felt her face reddening. Why was she arguing? He was making her angry and stubborn; months of agitation and frustration were coming to the surface.

"I am in charge here," he said, grabbing her arm roughly.

Alfredo now stepped forward. "The lady insists that you stop."

"This is none of your concern. I insist that you attend to your own affairs."

Alfredo continued, “And I am attending to my affairs. Annabelle is my affair.”

“Annabelle will be my wife. You have nothing to say about her at all.”

Annabelle shouted, “You are both wrong. I will do what I please, not what I am being told to do. Now, you let me go, Miklos, or we will be canceling this party.”

“How dare you threaten me?” he pulled her towards him, grabbing her roughly by the shoulders. “You are much too headstrong,” he continued, shaking her back and forth. “You will do exactly what I say.”

“Sir,” said Alfredo, “you will not continue mishandling her. And if you do continue, I will have to stop you. Let her go now.”

“Is that so?” Miklos angrily responded.

“Yes, that is exactly so.”

“I would like to see you try.” Miklos threatened.

Alfredo, now totally out of control, took a swing at Miklos, knocking him across the room. Miklos, rubbing his chin, pulled himself up from the floor, blood seeping from the side of his mouth. “You will pay for this,” he growled in a deadly tone.

Annabelle’s screams brought Margaret running. “What is going on here?”

“I do not know,” Annabelle cried. “I do not want to see either of them. I hate violence.”

She took Miklos’ ring off her finger and threw it at him. “This wedding is canceled, and you can have your servants tell the guests as they start to arrive. Send them all home. I am finished with you, Miklos.” She grabbed her skirts and headed for the stairs.

“Annabelle,” called Alfredo.

She turned around on the staircase. “This is all your fault. If you had not come here… Oh, forget about it.”

Miklos said nothing. He turned and grabbed his coat. To grandmother he stated, “I will leave the butler to explain things to the guests. And to tell them how your granddaughter has taken advantage of their good graces. I will make sure that she is sorry. She will regret this day and her actions.”

Alfredo piped in, “I would not make any threats if I were you, Milos. I saw you hiding on the ship, and I worried, at that time, about you and your intentions.”

Margaret, looking at Miklos said, “I guess that settles things. Perhaps you would like to tell me exactly what has happened.”

“I will do no such thing. You can talk to Annabelle, if you want to know anything about this.”

Alfredo stepped aside, quietly waiting for Miklos to leave. When he was gone, he offered, “Miklos was pushing Annabelle around and physically hurting her. I tried to stop him, but she just got angry at both of us. It was not my intention to cause any problems for Annabelle. I wanted her to consider marriage with me. My wife passed away in childbirth, and I have a baby girl who needs a mother.”

Margaret understood immediately what Alfredo’s plight was all about. “Perhaps we just need to allow some time for you to adjust and things to quiet down. Please keep in touch with me and have a safe journey home.”

As he turned and walked away, Margaret felt deep empathy for him in his plight. She hoped that things would work out, not only for Alfredo, but for Annabelle as well. In the back of her mind, a worry had been brewing about Miklos and his intentions in the future. She did not like threats, and Miklos was quick to threaten Annabelle. Maybe it was just his level of anger? Or, she feared, his true personality.

CHAPTER THIRTEEN: WHAT NEXT?

Annabelle could not seem to recover from this last outburst. Day after day, she hid in her room, ashamed of her behavior, but glad that Miklos was out of her life. She was unable to explain what had exactly caused her anger, but she knew deep down that she could never be with him. She recognized that under that fine outward appearance of gentility, he was really cruel. It all became shockingly clear to her. Further, she realized that if Alfredo had never come to her, she might be looking at marriage to Miklos. She felt lucky that she had escaped his clutches, and she was embarrassed and saddened by her reaction to Alfredo. All he tried to do was to protect her. Now, she had also lost that chance with him. She thought that she probably would never have anyone in her life to care for her and love her.

Alfredo was also discouraged. He had handled everything poorly. It was difficult to restrain himself when he observed a man who had no qualms about hurting a woman. How could Annabelle have allowed herself to be charmed by him? Maybe Miklos had not shown that side of himself before. Maybe he should try to talk to Annabelle once again? Also, he would genuinely apologize for acting as he had, though, if truth be told, he was not one bit sorry. Miklos was nothing but trouble.

Margaret was also consumed with worry. She did not like the way that Annabelle was acting. She had completely internalized everything, pulling into herself and shutting everyone else out. She knew, as her grandmother, that she had an obligation to help her and also recognized that Annabelle's decision not to marry Miklos was the right one for her. She admitted to herself that she had been concerned about that upcoming marriage, but her philosophy was not to interfere and to allow everyone to make their own way in life. She would always be there to pick up the pieces. She decided that this very morning she was ending this silence and would tackle undertaking a conversation with Annabelle.

She was preparing breakfast; the cinnamon rolls she decided to bake were filling the house with a welcoming aroma. So much so, that Margaret herself was finding it hard to resist breaking one apart and delving into it, for her own comfort. Suddenly, behind her crept Rudolf, wrapping his arms around her and whispering in her ear, "What kind of goodies did you bake this morning? I now feel like I am starving for that sweet biscuit or roll I smell in the oven."

Margaret turned, smiled and hugged her husband. How lucky she was to find a man, at her age, that was willing to put up with her and the kind of work she did. It made her realize that she had been totally ignoring all the signs and symbols flooding her consciousness about Annabelle. This child needed stability and love; too much rejection had already come her way. She had a very good feeling about Alfredo and his efforts to help Annabelle. Maybe she would offer her opinion about him. She would meditate about it and see what she could foresee. Would Annabelle listen to her? She did not want to be responsible if something went wrong in the end, but what a lonely existence for such a young woman, without anyone special in her life.

As she turned back to cooking, she heard Annabelle's footsteps. Thank God, she thought. She has finally decided to come out of that room.

Annabelle shyly greeted Margaret and Rudolf. She said softly, "I wanted to have breakfast with you both. The baking smells brought me here a little faster. I really want to talk to you both about Alfredo."

Maria had her hands full with Christina. The baby did not want to quiet down; she seemed to understand that her life was turned upside down and that her mother was no longer in the picture. Alfredo would come home from work, pick her up and rock her in Maria's favorite rocking chair until she fell asleep. But once he put her down in her bed, she was up again and crying. He felt he knew nothing about babies. What was he going to do about this poor, innocent child who had come into his life? Her grandparents had no interest in her and he knew that his sister would not be able to take on this responsibility forever. He had hoped that Annabelle would consider his offer. Not only because he found himself so attracted to her, but, thinking back, because he had witnessed how she handled her own daughter on the ship's crossing. He had watched Paula as she played on the ship and noted that she was a happy child, carefree until the violent ending that she had endured. Yet what was most important to him was the way that Annabelle treated her child, how she paid attention to her needs and how she loved her and hugged her, rocking her to sleep at night. Was he imagining what he wanted to see, or did it happen as he recalled?

Alfredo promised himself he would wait a few days and then try again to talk to Annabelle. Maybe, by then, she would not be upset anymore?

Maria interrupted his thoughts. "Alfredo," she cried, holding Christina in one arm, "I cannot take much more of this crying. What are we going to do? Maybe we need to have the doctor see the baby."

Alfredo sighed deeply. "You are probably right, Maria. I will get in touch with him. He will probably have some good advice for us. In the meantime, I will take Christina from you."

Alfredo wrapped his arms around his daughter, cradling her head and rocking her back and forth. When he started to pace the floor, she began to quiet down. Back and forth he walked, until her eyes closed and she settled into sleep. Then he put her in her small bed, willing her to remain sleeping. Miraculously, she did, at least for a while.

When Christina had quieted, Maria approached her brother once again. "Alfredo, we need a better plan. Do you think that Lucia's Mom will help us out?"

"I can ask her," he replied, "though somehow I doubt it. Right now she is overwhelmed with hate for me."

"Maybe so, but not for her grandchild," Maria insisted.

"We will see," Alfredo answered, barely above a whisper.

The next morning Alfredo set out for his in-laws' home. He knew they always were up early but was surprised by the fact that they did not answer the door. He continued to bang harder and call out their names. Nevertheless, there was only silence on the other side. He adjusted his coat, pulled the collar up tighter around his neck to block the cool breeze, and proceeded to head towards the produce stand. In his mind, he went over and over again the few options he felt that he had, and he kept coming back to Annabelle. He felt like she was his only hope, but how could he convince her that taking care of his baby would help her?

That morning, Annabelle ventured into the kitchen where Rudolf and Margaret were having breakfast. Annabelle said, "I know I have been acting strangely, but I just do not know what to do. I realize that I have expressed this thought before."

Rudolf replied, "What are you saying, Annabelle?" Margaret was quiet, assessing her granddaughter's approach. She said nothing.

"What I mean is that since the night of the planned engagement party, I have been sequestered in my room, unable to breathe and unable to think clearly. I have now decided what I want to do."

Margaret ventured forth, "Please, child, tell us your thoughts."

"First of all, I am happy that Miklos is gone. I was trying to fool myself into thinking I would be happy with him because he could provide for me. But I know deep within me that he was only interested in what our relationship would do for him; he really didn't care that much about me."

"I guess I can see how you came to that conclusion, based on his behavior the other evening," Rudolf said.

"What you both do not know is that he started to physically push me around and I was unable to really defend myself."

Rudolf angered quickly, "What did he do to you? I will take care of him."

Annabelle said, "I do not want you to do anything; I am glad he is out of the picture. But I recognize the reason Alfredo jumped to defend me. It was because Miklos was so out of control. Instead of being grateful to Alfredo, I attacked him verbally. I am sorry about that, and know that I have to right the wrong I did."

Margaret interjected, "It may be too late for that, Annabelle. You made it pretty clear to Alfredo that you are not interested in him at all."

"I know that is what he thinks, but I *am* interested in him. I have been thinking about what he said. I lost my child, and he lost his wife, but he has a baby who needs a mother. Even if nothing substantial comes of our relationship, we do get along very well, and I am yearning for a child. I know I cannot replace Paula, but I would be happy helping another little girl to find some happiness in her life."

She turned towards Rudolf, "Would you agree to take me to Alfredo's business so I can apologize and see if there is anything that is able to be fixed between us?"

Rudolf did not answer, but turned to Margaret, hoping to find the answer in her eyes.

When she said nothing, he replied, "All right, Annabelle. I can make that trip tomorrow, if that works for you. Do you know how to find him?"

"Yes, I do. Rowena and I were at a festival, and he told us where the produce market was. I think I can find it."

"Margaret," Rudolf asked his wife, "Do you have any objection if we take this trip?"

"No, I don't. In fact, I think it could be a positive thing for both Annabelle and Alfredo. I feel that it would be a good thing"

"All right, it's all settled. Be up early tomorrow and we will start out before the sun is up."

"Thank you, Grandfather, "Annabelle said, hugging him tightly. "*Anyóka*, I promise to tread carefully and hold my temper. No thoughtless comments and no foolishness either." She picked up her skirts and headed for the stairs.

Once in her room, the tears started to flow. She began praying, "God, please help me get through this challenge, protect us from harm on this journey, and guide me so I do the right thing."

She laid down and closed her eyes. Minutes later she was sound asleep, even though it was morning. Sleeping was an escape mechanism for her.

CHAPTER FOURTEEN: A SURPRISE FOR ALL

Alfredo decided to try one more time to reach out to Lucia's parents. Once more he stopped at their home on his way to work, but, again there was no answer at the door. Turning to the right, he started walking away when he noticed the curtains at the window moving. He went directly to that spot and tapped on the window. Lucia's sister peered out at him. He motioned for her to come outside and was surprised when she shook her head in agreement.

When she joined him in the street, Alfredo asked her what was going on with her parents. Anna Maria explained that they wanted no part of Alfredo, or the baby, and had vowed to do nothing to help him care for his child. She was tearful, begging his forgiveness.

"Alfredo," she whispered, "I do not feel the way they feel, but I am forbidden to help you and to see the baby. I am so sorry." Worrying about being detected by her parents, she turned and ran to the door, quietly slipping through without any noise. Alfredo was stunned, realizing that he would likely have to abandon reaching out to them. He was unwilling to try again to talk to Lucia's parents, until he gave this whole situation more thought. He was despondent.

Alfredo dragged himself to the store, full of emotions he could not handle. He wondered what could be the next step that he could take, but as many times as he turned things over in his mind, he could not come up with a satisfactory solution. He vowed to talk about it with Luigi and

Maria when they were all together tonight, after Christina fell asleep. Surely, his sister would offer some advice. She always seemed to instinctively know just what to do.

Suddenly, the customers started filling the store and he was engrossed in fulfilling orders. He actually felt a little better since he had a plan and knew that his sister and her husband would have some valuable advice for him. After four of the busiest hours he had ever had at the store, he decided to try to get a cup of coffee. He let Luigi know that he would return shortly. He had just disappeared around the corner when Annabelle and Rudolf arrived at the market.

Luigi was so involved with his customers that Annabelle felt guilty about imposing on him to ask about Alfredo. She busied herself with checking out the produce and nervously looking up periodically, to see if Alfredo would suddenly appear. Maybe he was making a delivery. She hoped he would return soon.

Rudolf stayed to the side, watching Annabelle to see how she would handle this situation. He decided that it was her challenge to overcome. Finally, Luigi looked around to see who else needed help. He questioned himself about whether that was Annabelle standing in the back staring at the apples.

"Can I help you, Miss?" Annabelle turned, startled to hear Luigi's voice. "Yes, thank you. I was wondering if Alfredo is here," she stammered. Luigi frowned, as he struggled to place this young woman. He questioned, "Are you Annabelle? I remember seeing you at Ellis Island."

Annabelle slowly shook her head yes. "I am sorry that I did not recognize you at first," Luigi offered. "Alfredo will be returning in a few moments. Would you like to sit down to wait for him?"

"Yes, thank you," Annabelle replied. She nodded to Rudolf, who stepped forward to introduce himself.

He extended his hand. "I am Rudolf, Annabelle's grandfather."

Luigi greeted him and rushed to get an additional folding chair for Rudolf. After about ten minutes had passed, Alfredo came back in, greeting Luigi, "I am sorry to take so long to return. There was a line and…"

Luigi stopped him mid-sentence. "Alfredo, you have a visitor." He pointed to Annabelle and her grandfather sitting in the back of the shop. Alfredo's complexion paled as he stared at them. He slowly walked towards Annabelle, his face portraying his anxiety.

"Annabelle, I am surprised to see you. I thought you would not want to see me again."

"Yes, Alfredo. I know I gave you that impression. But I came here to apologize to you, and to ask you if we might talk a little more about the future. I know you are working now, but I did not know any other way to get in touch with you."

"I am glad you came, Annabelle. *Uno momento, per favore* – one moment, please. I want to speak to Luigi first."

Alfredo turned away and approached Luigi with caution, since he was very involved with customers. While waiting patiently until Luigi had concluded a sale, Alfredo went over in his mind what he would say to Annabelle. He was not certain that she would want to consider a life with him. Yet she was here, of her own accord.

Luigi turned to Alfredo, "What is going on, Alfredo?"

"I am not sure, but Annabelle wants to talk to me about the future. So, do you think you can manage the rest of the afternoon without my help?"

"This is the busiest part of the day, as people are coming home from work, and stopping by to pick up last-minute supper ingredients. But, yes, in view of the fact that this is so important, I will make myself manage without your help. Go and God go with you."

Alfredo whispered, "*Grazie*" and rushed back to where Annabelle and Rudolf were waiting.

"Let us go somewhere that will allow us to talk. There is a café on the corner where I usually get my coffee. They have a few tables inside; I think we can sit there and talk."

Rudolf interrupted, "Can you deliver Annabelle to her cousin Janos's house? I think you know where that is. If you can do that, I will go there and wait for her. I think this is a very important and private conversation between the two of you, and I do not want to impose."

"Of course, I will ensure that she gets back to you safely. I remember where he lives," Alfredo replied, "as long as that is acceptable to Annabelle."

She shook her head yes and kissed Rudolf on the cheek. "Thank you, Grandfather."

Alfredo reached for his jacket and offered Annabelle his arm. Together they walked the short distance to the corner café where Alfredo purchased a coffee and pastry for each of them. Leading her to a table in the corner of the room, he turned to her with hope in his eyes. "What is this really about?" he asked her.

"I suppose this is unorthodox, and I would understand if you have no interest in me at all now, after what happened at my grandmother's house. But I have been giving a lot of thought about what you said. I know we have little understanding of each other and, yet, the situation you are in requires some immediate help from a woman. I also know that you may already have found someone that you are fond of and that you can see as part of your future. So, if this is totally futile, I will understand."

Alfredo was confused. "Are you saying that you would consider being with me and taking care of my daughter? That you would become my wife, in this set of circumstances, even though you may not have any feelings for me?"

Annabelle felt herself blushing. "I know I am being very forward, but I also know that in life you sometimes have only one chance at happiness. I know how you treated me on the ship, and how you tried to defend me at my grandmother's house. I also do not think you are one to be unreasonable or to not care about the feelings of another person, even a woman. Am I correct?"

Alfredo was stunned at her frankness. "I don't know exactly what to say to you. I have been interested in you from the first moment I set eyes on you, and I think we could really work together to make a good life. Yet I really don't know why I feel so strongly about this. It is what the Americans call 'a hunch,' just a feeling without substance."

"I know what you mean, and there is so much you need to know about me before you take such a chance," Annabelle continued. "You know I had a daughter, but I was not married. I was in love with the baby's father who promised me a marriage, but his mother objected. She had the power and refused to agree. So I am not without guilt." She cast her eyes down, waiting for Alfredo's reply.

"Frankly," he said, "I am more concerned about how you would treat my daughter than I am about your past, or even what you would offer me. I think in time we could learn to love each other, and I already know that you were a loving mother to your child. Can you be one to my child? It is a tall order."

Annabelle thought for a moment about how to answer Alfredo. "I have given this much thought, Alfredo. I think I can accept and nurture a baby. I miss my child so much. There is not a moment of the day that I do not think of her and yearn for her. I know this is a different child and I realize I would have to learn her ways, just as you would have to learn mine. But I am not quick to anger, and I think I am understanding and patient. I am willing to give it a try, if you are."

Alfredo smiled, "I had hoped in the beginning that you might feel this way, but I confess that since I have been at my sister's and seen her with the baby, I have some big expectations from a wife. I will not expect intimacy from you, but I honestly would hope, in time, that love could develop. I would expect deliberate care and comfort for my baby and for my home. I would want you, not only to take care of Christina, but I would also want you to create a warm and safe place for her to grow up with cleanliness and good meals daily. I would hope that this is something you too would want, and not something you would consider being forced to do. My wife never wanted to be a homemaker or mother, though at first she said that she wanted the baby. As time went on, I realized that her feelings had changed. I don't think she even wanted the baby in the end. I think that the reality did not match her dreams."

"How sad," Annabelle said, tears brimming in her eyes and beginning to stream down her cheeks.

Alfredo continued. "I have a nice apartment that I have not been in since Lucia died. But it is spacious and bright and close to where Luigi and Maria live. Family is very important to me.

The Della Cesare's, Lucia's parents, are also not far away, but they said that they have no desire to have anything more to do with me or with Christina. They, frankly, said that they are not interested in the baby and will never help me out with her. They blame me for Lucia's death. They say that I pushed her too hard to be the kind of wife and mother that I expected her to be. I realize that this is a lot for you to take in, Annabelle, and you may want to consider all sides of the issues. I do not want to trick you or to lie to you, or to make it sound easier than it will be. I want you to really think about it before you consent to become involved with me. It is the fair thing to do."

Annabelle sat quietly, listening to what Alfredo had to say. Even with both of their poor English language skills, Annabelle was certain she understood what he was telling her. In the end she replied, "I respect what you are saying. Can we both think about this for a few days? Then can we get back together and tell each other what concerns we have?"

"I think that is a very good idea," Alfredo commented. "Now, let's get you to Janos' house."

They had a quiet walk through the streets, Alfredo pointing out the way and some of the landmarks that would help her, should she decide to be with him. Annabelle listened to him, intently concerned with what her future might be like. She liked the hustle and bustle of the area and the community of spirit she could feel as she watched the residents interacting with each other. It was late afternoon, and men were returning home from work. Children were playing outside and people were sitting on their stoops, talking about their day and their common interests. She liked the prospect of having women friends and of being part of such an interactive community.

By the time they reached Janos' house, she began to feel a peacefulness and a hopeful outlook. Alfredo and Annabelle agreed to reconnect in a couple of days. She said that she would try to remain at Janos' for the time being, until things were settled between them. Though she had not asked either Janos or Rowena if she could stay with them, she was sure the intense family dedication they all possessed would result in her being able to stay there until an agreement was forged.

CHAPTER FIFTEEN: A LOT TO THINK ABOUT

The next morning, Annabelle awoke to the sun shining sharply through the window. At first, she could not remember where she was. Her dreams had been of Paula, and she was confused about why she could possibly feel even a glimmer of happiness.

And then she recalled the visit with Alfredo. He wanted her to really think about what she said she would do. She had to respect that about him. Unlike Miklos who was ready to dictate exactly what she was to do and think, she knew that Alfredo was concerned about her feelings. After all, he defended her, didn't he? And he revealed all of the circumstances of his life, providing her with the choice to become part of it.

How could being with him be a mistake? And, after all, what did she have to lose, anyway. Until now, it seemed like she had made one mistake after another. Even *Anyóka* could not disagree with that, and Annabelle thought that her grandmother favored Alfredo, although Margaret had not exactly said so.

That had to mean something. Surely, if *Anyóka* foresaw a disaster, she would have warned her. Grandmother's life was all about helping other people. Annabelle was the one person in the family that her grandmother had helped the most. So then, she had to wonder why she had not warned her about Miklos. This just added to her confusion.

She lazily slipped out of bed and proceeded to get ready for the day. It was going to be a good one because Annabelle knew that her decision to be with Alfredo was solid. She was not about to change her mind, and nothing he had told her yesterday made her want to say "no". She hoped, given time to think about it, that he would not want to change his mind either. Of course, she knew he had more to risk because he had to think about the welfare of his little girl.

Suddenly she thought of his daughter.

She had not seen Christina. Could she really undertake the care and loving concern for a child that was not hers? Would she see Christina only as an extension of Paula, or would she be able to recognize the beauty of her existence? So much to consider. No wonder it was a critical decision, not just for her, but also for Alfredo.

She reminded herself that Alfredo had come to see her at her grandmother's house and did not have any concern about pleading for her loyalty. Then it had been at a time when he had seemed very desperate.

Now that he had the help of his sister, he could be more cautious. He could afford to take the time to think, not to make a hasty decision. Besides, she reminded herself, he was a handsome man who could probably find lots of women willing to marry him.

Why did she want to marry him anyway? Was it to fill the void that Paula had left? Was there really an attraction to him, or just that she did not fear him, or was it because she really did not have any other alternatives?

Could she be his wife in all aspects of that obligation? Could she love someone without holding back? Could she accept love from someone and could she learn to trust? Franz had let her down; he had not fulfilled his promises and had collapsed under the power of his mother. What would happen after marriage vows were taken? As soon as Miklos had given her a ring, he had changed completely. Would Alfredo change, too?

She was giving herself a headache. She would ask Rudolf his thoughts, from a man's point of view. Now, after being so sure of things, she was beginning to feel afraid. Why did she have so much trouble making decisions?

Alfredo, on this morning, was experiencing much of the same concerns. He knew that what he decided would be critical, not only for his happiness, but also for his daughter's. In the end, if he had to do so, he would sacrifice himself, surely, just as he had been prepared to do with Lucia. But he was unable to sacrifice his child. She was innocent. She had not asked to be born. He had to make sure that her life would be a happy one, as much as he could ensure that she would be happy and safe and protected.

He thought again of Annabelle. He had seen her grief over the loss of her child. He had seen Lucia's disinterest in her pregnancy and the prospect of having a child. What a contrast between the two women.

Yet can one woman love another woman's child? He felt the physical and psychological attraction for Annabelle that had been missing with Lucia. He hoped that those feelings would not pale and disappear, and he prayed that, if she agreed to marry him, she would also find, over time, that same attraction to him. It would be a sad and lonely life for both of them if love was not part of it.

Why was he having such a hard time with this? He would talk to Luigi, a man of decisiveness. He would know what Alfredo should do.

Or, on the other hand, would Luigi be considering the situation from Maria's standpoint? After all, she did not need to be a mother to a child that was not hers. Maybe Alfredo was not looking at this in the right way at all. Maybe he should not put Luigi in the position of giving an opinion that might be used to make such an overwhelming decision.

He had no one to talk to about this. He had only himself to rely upon. He decided to make a visit to the church. He would see if the priest was available, and maybe the priest could be more objective. After all, the priest did not really know any of them, and so he might be able to more logically work out the pluses and minuses. Yes, that is what he would do today. Then, tomorrow he would reach out again to Annabelle, and together they would decide. He would lay out some terms of agreement, ones that would neither overburden either of them, but ones that would provide them with room to grow and to become more accustomed to each other.

Annabelle entered the kitchen quietly. It smelled so good. Rowena was really excellent at making a home for Janos. If she prepared meals like this every day for him, he was one lucky man. Could she, Annabelle, make a home as welcoming for Alfredo and Christina? She was questioning herself again.

Rudolf sat silently at the table stirring his coffee. He had not heard Annabelle come into the room. When she greeted him, he looked up, concern on his face. Oh no, she thought. He does not think this is a good idea, after all.

As soon as Rudolf realized that Annabelle was joining him, his face broke into a smile.

"So good to see you looking rested, Annabelle. You have not looked this rested since your break-up with Miklos."

"I guess that is true," she said. "Where is Rowena?"

"She is taking care of the baby. She said to start breakfast without her. She had made some biscuits and had put out cheese and sausage for us to eat. Are you hungry?"

"A little," Annabelle replied. "But I have been thinking about all the things that could go wrong, if I marry Alfredo."

"I thought this was what you had decided you wanted to do," Rudolf answered.

"Yes, I was certain, until Alfredo said that I really had to think things through. Yesterday, I was absolutely sure. This morning I am a little unsure."

"What is making you so uncertain?" he asked, continuing to absently stir his coffee.

"So many things, Grandfather. First of all, am I good enough? Am I a really good person? My life until now has *not* shown me to be a good person, and, yet, you and Grandmother have not faulted me."

"Annabelle, stop thinking like that. You had a mother and stepfather that drove you from the home. They did not care about you at all and you were only a child. So vulnerable."

"Looking back, Grandfather, I think I should have known better."

"It is impossible for a child to make adult decisions. And you needed love. If anyone was to blame for your situation, it was Franz. Though in the beginning he did good things for you, Franz was the one who came to help you when your father died. He offered his aid when you were so young and hopeful. However, he was taking advantage of your youth. This is why it was Franz who was really guilty. I know I have not given my opinion before now, but that is what I think. So does your Grandmother. Then he made promises to you that he knew he would not be able to keep. He was fully aware of his mother's position. Still, he led you on, and he was the one who was responsible for you being with child. He is so much older than you. He was a man of the world, and you, just a child, were unknowingly led by him with visions of what could never be."

"I never thought of it like that," Annabelle said, beginning to cry.

"Then, when his mother inserted herself between the two of you, he did not take a stand or push back. He was more concerned about his inheritance than the child you were bearing. You were placed in an impossible situation. Think about how you had to attempt to travel to another country alone, and with no aid or protection. So many evils foisted on you, one on top of another. Thank God that Alfredo took pity on you and helped you. Otherwise, the authorities may have sent you back to Hungary."

"So I guess you think that Alfredo's offer is a good one?"

"I think you do not have many options, Annabelle. I believe you are a loving and giving woman who will do your best to make it work, and I believe, from what I have witnessed, that Alfredo is an honorable man."

Annabelle walked around the table to where Rudolf was sitting and hugged him appreciatively. "You have made me feel so much better."

Alfredo hesitantly walked up the steps to the church. He would talk to whichever priest was there at this time. He was going to leave it to God to tell him, through His priest, what he should do.

He found a young priest, Father Emilio, in the rectory and asked him if he would have a few minutes to talk to him. Alfredo wondered whether talking to this man was a good choice. After all, what would a young priest know about marriage? About as much as I know, he thought.

Alfredo proceeded to explain what had happened to his wife and that he now had a young child to care for. He also told Father Emilio that his marriage was arranged by the two sets of parents, and that he really never wanted to marry Lucia. He did not accuse her of tricking him; he knew it was his fault and that he should be the one to bear the responsibility for her and the child.

He talked about Annabelle and what he had experienced on the crossing, how she lost her daughter and how he felt she was sensitive and caring. This is the kind of woman he wanted for his wife and the mother of his children, he told Father.

When he had finished, Father Emilio asked Alfredo, “So you want me to tell you what to do and how to proceed? I cannot do that. You must decide if this woman will be your wife, not just until your little girl grows up. As a solemn vow of marriage requires, it will be as long as you both shall live. And does Annabelle want to commit to that too?”

Alfredo replied, “Father, I am so confused. I have set aside what I want, in order to consider what is best for all, and I can no longer separate the two in my mind. She is now thinking about these things as well.”

Father Emilio thought for a few moments. “For just a few minutes, forget that you have a child to care for. Forget that your wife died and your sister is now burdened with the care for your child. Think about how you as a man feel about this woman you say is so caring. Is she really caring, or is that your vision of what you want for your family and of what you hope she will be like? From what you say, you do not know her that long or even that well.”

Alfredo was quiet. He bowed his head in thoughtfulness. “I know, Father, that before I actually married Lucia, this woman was the one I wanted to marry. I cannot explain why. I felt it as soon as I started to observe her. This was before we got to Ellis Island; it was on the ship, even before her child died. It was an indescribable attraction for me. I knew that I had too many other problems to overcome with my parents and Lucia’s parents. So I just decided to do what everyone else wanted me to do. It was easier than fighting everyone.”

“Then you have your answer, but remember that vows are sacred, and you will be committed to each other without any consideration for separation or divorce. You cannot enter into this marriage thinking that, if it does not work out, you can leave."

Alfredo spent the rest of the afternoon thinking about how he would discuss all of his thoughts with Annabelle. He decided that when he got home tonight, he would make a list of the things they had to consider, so that he would cover all the potential problems that they might have to face. After all, he already knew that life had many challenges coming, many that a person had no idea about. However, at least he should be thinking about the ones he could foresee.

In the meantime, Annabelle was making her own list of questions for Alfredo.

The next day was Sunday, so Alfredo did not have to report to work with Luigi. He begged his sister's patience with caring for Christina while he went to talk to Annabelle. Both Luigi and Maria were understanding and supportive of him, in this process of making this life-critical decision. They wanted him to be certain, not to rush into anything, the way he had rushed into marrying Lucia.

He slowly approached Janos' apartment, hoping against hope that no one there would object to his taking Annabelle outside to have this discussion. When Janos came to the door, Alfredo offered his hand in greeting. Janos seemed accepting and extended his hand as well. Then Alfredo asked to see Annabelle.

Janos asked that he wait at the door for a moment. Shortly he returned to invite him inside, while Annabelle prepared herself to see him. Alfredo entered a warm and inviting kitchen with the rich smells of delicious food being prepared. At the window was Rudolf, who had been reading the newspaper. When he saw Alfredo, he stood and walked forward, greeting him warmly.

"I hope I am not imposing on your day. I really wanted to spend a little time with Annabelle talking about the things we would have to face together."

Rudolf replied quickly, "I am so glad you are giving this a very serious consideration. Annabelle is also doing the same. You both have a lot to gain and a lot to lose if things do not work out as planned."

Alfredo, as nervous as he was, grew red in the face. "I will promise you that, if Annabelle consents to be my wife, I will move heaven and earth to care for her. I will never let her down, nor will I ever disappoint you either, Rudolf."

"That sounds like a solid plan to me. Oh," turning at the sound of Annabelle approaching, Rudolf continued, "Here she is now. Please go out and talk about everything that worries you. I hope today you can decide what is best for all."

Annabelle shyly approached Alfredo. "Hello, Alfredo. I was hoping you would come here today so that we could talk about everything."

He offered his arm to her, "Yes, let's go now."

As they walked down the steps, Alfredo paused and turned to Annabelle, "I have not told you how lovely you look and how lucky I am to be here with you today, proposing what I hope will be acceptable to you. I thought we might walk to the park where we can sit undisturbed and discuss what is on both our minds. Nevertheless, this will be your decision. I promise not to pressure you."

Annabelle looked into his eyes. "I was hoping you would feel that way. And I am grateful to hear your feelings about everything. I want you to be honest, and not to worry about whether what you say to me might be hurtful to me. This is too important for both of us."

They proceeded slowly, taking in the sights around them …the hustle and bustle of the population as they rushed out to attend church services, children laughing and running, parents arm in arm, smiling at the prospect of some time together. The tantalizing smells of Sunday dinner, together with all the other sights, gave both Alfredo and Annabelle a sense of well-being. It also provided a distraction for both of them before they had to face this discussion.

When they had settled on a park bench, just distant enough to provide some privacy for them, Alfredo reached into his pocket, pulling out a long sheet of paper. Seeing it made Annabelle's heart stop. She was immediately fearful of a long list of requirements that she would have to meet. Her eyes filled with tears.

Alfredo immediately noticed the change in her demeanor, "Why are you upset, Annabelle? I just wanted to remember everything we should talk about, and so I wrote things down."

She took a deep breath. "I was afraid I was looking at a lot of things you wanted from me, and that I might not be able to deliver to you."

He put his head back and chuckled. "No, not at all. Marriage is a give and take, so there will be things for you and things for me. That is what we will have to agree upon. Shall we begin now to talk about everything?"

CHAPTER SIXTEEN: A DAY TO REMEMBER

Annabelle listened as Alfredo talked about what he called the Conditions of Acceptance. It sounded so legal. It was totally unlike any experience Annabelle had ever had or ever heard of anyone else having, yet she was totally mesmerized by his thinking. She had to admit that she liked how meticulous he was, how he had tried to think of things from both his point of view and from hers as well.

After spending hours discussing what their marriage would be like, Annabelle went back home to consider what she had consented to do for and with Alfredo.

Of course, they both agreed, the first primary consideration was Christina. Annabelle said she felt that she could function as the baby's mother, to love and protect her from harm, to give her a solid sense of what is right and what is wrong, and to teach her the skills she would need as a woman in the society in which they lived. Alfredo agreed that he would be a good and attentive father, that he would discuss with Annabelle the steps they would take together in raising this child, and that they would keep any disagreements they had about how to manage Christina between the two of them, out of the child's earshot. Under no circumstances would Christina know that she could pitch one parent against the other to get her own way.

They talked about the values they wanted to impart to the child and any other children, if they had any. They agreed that this would certainly be a matter of future discussion, since the terms of their marriage and their intimacy were still uncertain.

Alfredo agreed that he would work hard to provide the necessities of life for his family, that he would never overindulge in drink or gambling and that he would not consider having any engagements with other women.

Annabelle agreed that she would handle the household with a budget that they both thought would work, and that if needs came up over and above what they thought was necessary, they would talk about them before spending any additional money.

They also talked about intimacy. Since Alfredo wanted a mother for his child, but also admitted that he had fallen in love with Annabelle, it was important to set up some guidelines for their life together. Annabelle was not as certain as he was about wanting to be a wife in every sense of the word, though she did want to be a mother without any restrictions.

Because of her uncertainty, Alfredo agreed that they could live together and get to know each other better, before becoming romantically involved.

Annabelle had never heard of or thought that this kind of arrangement was ever made by anyone else, at least certainly not by anyone else she knew. Also she had never heard about such a thing happening anywhere. She had been raised to believe that the man had the final say. But Alfredo was willing to do whatever he could to make her happy and help her fall in love with him. She could not believe that such an arrangement could exist between two people and told Alfredo that she wanted to talk with her Grandmother about everything they had agreed upon. She continued to have trouble believing that all of this or any of this was real.

Alfredo had no misgivings. He felt he was a patient man and could wait for Annabelle to get used to him and to 'fall in love' with him, as he was certain she would do. He also thought that not rushing Annabelle into a marriage requiring intimacy was the best way to proceed, because he wanted a real commitment from her for his child. If things didn't work out as he hoped, he would keep his word. It was just what had to be done.

That night when he went home and faced Luigi and Maria who questioned him about the meeting, he only offered that Annabelle was still thinking about things and she would let him know soon. They seemed to understand the situation since this was not Annabelle's child and she would have to be there for Alfredo and Christina, as if they were her own family. They had no knowledge of Annabelle's past and, except for her child dying on the ship, they had no idea of any other traumatic experiences Annabelle might have had growing up.

Alfredo laid his head on his pillow and sighed in relief. He knew he was promising things that no other man would promise and that, if he revealed these things to Luigi, he would be thought to be "crazy."

That night he dreamed of Lucia. The dream was so real that he woke up and started searching the room for her presence. He decided she was trying to tell him something, so he went over the dream again and again, to try to figure out what it all meant.

He decided that Lucia seemed to be expecting him to be more forceful with Annabelle, because she kept saying that Christina's life was in jeopardy. When he awoke in the morning, he started to wonder if he had taken the right approach to the situation and worried all day about it. He knew he really had to make this decision himself, that he had no one to provide him with the correct answers, nor anyone who had the experience to see things in a more worldly way.

That same morning, Annabelle and Rudolf set out for her grandmother's home. Annabelle was intent on sharing with *Anyóka* all of the conditions that she and Alfredo agreed to follow.

They traveled in silence since Annabelle was so involved in her own thoughts. Rudolf would frequently ask her if she was all right and if she needed to stop along the way. She just shook her head no and continued to weigh things in her mind.

She knew she had to have a protector, and Alfredo seemed to be more than fair and accommodating. In fact, she worried that Alfredo could or would really adhere to his words. Yet, deep inside herself she trusted him.

She was deeply absorbed in considering how she would handle another woman's child. Since Christina was a baby, Annabelle would be the only one she would remember. She knew she would not have to fight the presence of another mother. She knew that she did not feel jealous because she was not in love with Alfredo and did not feel that another woman had stolen him from her. So, at least, she did not have to face that emotion. She was worried about bonding with the baby more than she worried about any other aspect of the arrangement.

She felt confused about Alfredo's ability to give her such a level of independence. Yes, he had told her that he expected a warm, loving and clean environment in his home. He said that he was not concerned about her being able to provide that for them, because he had seen and experienced her grandmother's home and how comfortable she was in that environment. He said it was a deep feeling that he had, that she would be just as wonderful as her grandmother. Annabelle kept wondering if he was being sincere, or if he was just trying to influence her without exerting extreme pressure, or if he was only deceiving himself.

She knew that *Anyóka* would have some thoughts about this and Annabelle was relying on her grandmother's ability to foresee things.

When they arrived at home, her grandmother was nowhere to be found. Annabelle found herself becoming more and more frustrated with her absence as the hours went by. Where could she be? Surely, she knew they were returning. She had to know because of the powers she had.

When dusk fell, they heard Margaret's footsteps. Annabelle ran to the door, throwing it open and nearly knocking her grandmother down. She raised her voice, "Where have you been? I have been waiting for you for hours."

Margaret replied, "I have been at a birth, Annabelle, and frankly I am very tired right now. It was a difficult time."

Annabelle pulled her emotions under control. "I am sorry. I know how important your work is. I am just being selfish because I have so much to talk about with you."

"I guess that means that you had a good meeting with Alfredo," Margaret replied.

"Yes, it was good, but so confusing. And I need to have your guidance. I have been so wrong at every turn. I have made so many poor decisions."

Grandmother responded, "Let's have some supper and then we can talk. We need to take care of our physical needs first. Then we can tackle the emotional and psychological needs."

Annabelle pulled on an apron and started to set the table for supper. Margaret produced some fresh bread she had baked that morning, some good cheese and some sausage. "We can feast on this, have some wine to drink and then talk over our food. I know Rudolf will be fine with the food we are preparing. Also, I am sure that he is also very tired from the long drive."

"Yes," Annabelle replied. "Please do not think that I am not appreciative of all that you have both done for me. I do want to be out of your home soon and in my own life, but I do not want to make a serious mistake."

Grandmother listened while Annabelle related what she and Alfredo had discussed. She said nothing, until Annabelle was finished.

Annabelle asked, "What do you think?"

Her grandmother said, "It is not what I think. Rather it is what you think and how you feel about everything."

Annabelle was startled, "I thought you would tell me what to do, *Anyóka*."

Margaret paused for a moment, "I never tell anyone what to do. I try to help them discover what they really want and start there. So what do you really want, Annabelle?"

Taking a deep breath, Annabelle said, "I guess I want security, a home of my own, someone to love and someone to love me. And I want children. But I don't know why I can't really feel anything right now. I feel empty inside and I am fearful it will always be that way."

"Annabelle, you have been through a lot. Think about it. You have lost the *love of your life* and the child you had with him. You saw him collapse under the will of his mother and experienced the disappointment that resulted from him not choosing you. You then experienced the powerful and uncompromising personality of Miklos, a man who at first made you believe that life would be different for you. You had to accept his anger and he made you fearful. Now you have to decide if you want to trust another man, if he is what he says he is, and if the life he promises is even possible for you. It is a lot to consider. On top of it all, you have to agree to be a mother to another woman's child."

"But what do you think, *Anyóka*? Do you think Alfredo is what he says he is? Do you think he is a trickster and a manipulator, like Miklos?"

Grandmother thought before answering. "When I consider Alfredo, I see a man who finds himself in a situation that he needs to resolve. He had a child and recognizes his responsibilities, now that the mother of the child is dead, a mother, by the way, that he was forced to marry and who he never really wanted to marry."

She continued, "He could just as easily give that child away, but he is not doing that. So that is a testament to his character, isn't it? And he seems gentle and yet strong. When he saw Miklos being abusive to you, he exerted his power to defend you. I think you could do worse, but I cannot tell you what to do. If money means a lot to you, this may not be the man who can provide that for you, Annabelle. You have all the pros and cons before you. Give it all a deep consideration."

"So I guess I have to decide for myself, anyway."

"Yes, I fear that is true."

"I feel I am back just where I started," Annabelle said as she climbed the stairs to her bedroom.

CHAPTER SEVENTEEN: ANOTHER CONFUSING DAY

When Alfredo came to see Annabelle, she was prepared with her questions. She found that he was also prepared with his thoughts. She now felt certain that they were both taking this arrangement very seriously.

They went outside in Grandmother's gardens and sat together on the bench in the quiet of the overhanging branches of the maple tree. The warm breeze enveloped them, leaving Annabelle with a feeling of peacefulness. Her nervousness seemed to disappear.

Annabelle asked, "Alfredo, if it is acceptable to you, I would like to start our discussion, because I have some questions that I need to have answered, before I can give you a commitment."

Alfredo took a moment, his heart beating wildly in his chest, and responded, "I am fine with that. I want you to be sure of your decision. What is it that you need to know?"

Annabelle hesitated a minute before responding. She seemed to be having trouble finding the right words, though she had rehearsed all of this many times, in front of her mirror and in front of *Anyóka,* who gave her the right English words to use. She cleared her throat and jumped in. "When you came to see me at my grandmother's, and I was having my engagement party, you defended me from Miklos. Why did you do that?"

Alfredo was taken back. Of all the things that he expected Annabelle to ask him, this was not one of them.

He thought for just a moment and began to stammer, "Annabelle, I had watched you on the journey to Ellis Island after your daughter died, and I saw a vulnerable young woman who had a lot of courage to undertake such a long voyage. I respected you for that, and I concluded that you had courage and the ability to survive against every challenge thrown before you. When I heard and saw Miklos talking to you without respect, I was appalled. I could never imagine speaking to you like that, and I despised him for his attitude. I just tried to protect you. I do not respect men who treat women badly. My mother always told me what I should do as a man, and I always felt she knew what she was saying was true. Then I realized, I had fallen in love with you on the ship, though I cannot explain why. We really had no time to get to know each other. But I had an instantaneous connection to you, like I had known you before. And I wanted to take care of you."

Annabelle took a deep breath before continuing, "So, I think you are telling me that if we got married, you would not view me as your possession?"

"Possession?" Alfredo responded. "No person is the possession of another. And I believe that marriage is between two people who want to be together and who will work together to create a family. When my parents disagreed, they argued, but in the end, they listened to each other and came to an agreement. That is what I want to do. I want to create a family like the one I came from and have a marriage like my parents have. They love each other, always listen to each other and are committed to doing the best for each other."

“That is all I wanted to know, Alfredo. I do want to tell you that, if we come together to build a family, as you put it, I will do my best to care for Christina, even though she is not mine. I will try to make her mine and to love her as if she were mine.”

“That is all I can ask for,” Alfredo smiled. “I had some of my own thoughts I wanted to share with you,” he continued. “When Lucia was alive, I was committed to her because I agreed to marry her. I planned to be faithful to her, even though I felt I was tricked into a union I didn't really want. I want you to know that, if you agree to marry me, I will be faithful to you, no matter what happens, and I hope you will give me that same commitment.”

Annabelle’s eyes filled with tears. “I promise that I will never stray. I am fearful of whether we can learn how to love each other, and want that to happen for both our sakes, as well as Christina’s.”

“I hope that you will find me to be a willing and gentle husband. I also think we should, right now, agree that we would discuss all the problems that might arise, just like my sister Maria and Luigi do. I have been watching them and I admire how they manage to work together.”

“What else would you expect of me?” asked Annabelle.

“I have been thinking a great deal about that, since my marriage to Lucia was such a failure, right from the beginning. I want to experience what I enjoyed in my parents’ home. It was a place where there was love and laughter, where the warmth of the surroundings made you say, ‘I am glad I am at home.’ And where the food that is served is good and hearty. Oh yes, and the home is clean, as is the clothing.”

Annabelle laughed. “Isn’t that what everyone wants?”

Alfredo hesitated. He did not want to speak against Lucia, even though she gave him none of those things. It was, after all, in the past.

Instead, he said, "One would hope so. Let's make sure those are all the biggest issues. What else do you need to hear?"

Annabelle continued, "I want you to understand that my grandmother and Rudolf are really important to me and that I want them to be part of our lives."

"Yes, I would want that too, as well as my family. If Lucia's parents change their minds and want to get to know Christina, I would want that to happen as well."

"So, it seems that we think the same way," Annabelle said.

"One more thing," Alfredo interrupted. "I will not expect you to be intimate with me until you are comfortable with that idea. Just because we are getting married, I do not expect you to be in my bed if you do not want to, though, of course, I hope you will want to."

Annabelle blushed and ventured, "When do you want to have the wedding and where?"

Alfredo looked at Annabelle and replied, "I guess that is a yes answer, you will marry me."

"I guess that is a yes," agreed Annabelle.

"Do you want to come back with me, and we can see the priest together?"

"Why don't you make the arrangements, and I will send a letter to Janos and Rowena to let them know that I might have to stay with them for a night or two?"

"Do you trust me to do that and to set up the apartment as well? I don't think I will do such a good job there, but you can make it as you like it when you arrive."

"Also, I have a little dog named Mez. I will leave her with my grandmother."

"All right, then. It is probably not a good idea to have a dog in the city. Let's share the news with Margaret and Rudolf." He reached for her hand, and she accepted his guidance back to the kitchen, where they replayed their conversation.

Margaret was thrilled that Annabelle had made a decision, and, in her heart of hearts, she thought this was the right path for her to take. It would give her a chance to get used to Alfredo and to being a mother again. Margaret felt that though this was in Annabelle's best interests, she also believed that Alfredo needed the arrangement as much, if not more, than Annabelle.

Alfredo decided on his way home that he would share his news with his sister and Luigi. He was not certain if they would be really happy about it, because they would understand that his decision was based more on what was good for Christina than on what would be good for him. He kept in the back of his heart and mind the feelings for Annabelle that he hoped would surface in her over time. He kept telling himself that he should not "dare" to hope to be happy. But he also was glad that he would have someone to love and to care for and that Annabelle would adequately care for his child.

Maria and Luigi agreed to help him ready his home for Annabelle and Christina. An air of 'happy anticipation' seemed to prevail, as they proceeded to clean all parts of his apartment. He wanted to remove any trace of Lucia that he could envision, thinking that her possessions would transfer a negativity to the new beginnings he was hoping to have. Scrubbed windows, curtains, bedding and kitchen surfaces did offer a welcoming appearance. Now, all he had to do was to see the priest and collect Annabelle from her grandmother's.

Annabelle was doing her own sorts of preparations for the move into Alfredo’s life. She went through Paula's possessions that she had carried from Hungary and discarded what was worn and unwelcoming.

She also reviewed her own wardrobe and, with her grandmother’s help, made repairs and adjustments so that her things did not look so ‘road weary.’

She folded the cleaned garments carefully, packing them into her valise, laying paper between garments to try to keep them fresh. She understood that the journey was short, but she wanted Alfredo to feel that she really cared about her appearance, and about this new life she was entering. She knew he was concerned that the home would be kept neatly, so she wanted to show him that she was indeed, fastidious.

While her grandmother was baking, she sat quietly at Margaret’s kitchen table, planning meals that she might be able to make that would be both nutritious and appealing. It gave her the opportunity to ask for instruction in those areas where she suffered from uncertainty. She knew that her grandmother had every recipe in her head. Confirming how many cups of flour were needed, whether butter or oil or lard was best to use in preparing some of the meat dishes she hoped to make, and many other small details that she needed to know to fortify her cooking skills were now all within reach.

Once, on her own, she would have to figure out the things she really did not know how to do, though she was certain that Janos would ask Rowena to help her. She also knew that Rowena was not a willing confidante for her. Annabelle felt that Rowena was not overly anxious to interface with her on a daily basis, so she was trying to be pretty self-reliant.

Alfredo was thinking about their day-to-day life as he took the steps to the entrance of the rectory. He hoped that Father Emilio would be available to speak with him and that he could arrange the marriage ceremony for the following week. It really required no preparation, since it would only involve the bride, groom and Alfredo's small family. He wondered if Margaret and Rudolf would bother to make the trip to witness the marriage but was glad that the whole event would not attract any undue attention. Maybe even Janos and Rowena would come? But perhaps not, if Janos would have to miss work.

As he sat in the vestibule of the rectory waiting for Father Emilio, he prayed that this would be the best course of action for both Annabelle and himself. That strange feeling of unrest seemed to creep up on him. In the past, before he had married Lucia, he was a man of unchallenged decision-making. What happened to that young man, he wondered. Why was he so worried about the future? When he had first seen Annabelle on the ship, he knew immediately that he was attracted to her. He could feel a chemistry between them. Did that still exist now, after Annabelle had lost her daughter and he, himself, lost a wife but gained a child? He tried to shake the cobwebs from his brain before Father Emilio arrived to meet with him.

When he heard the footsteps, he stood in respect, and offered his hand to his priest.

"Tell me, Alfredo, why are you here to see me?"

"As you know, Annabelle and I had a lot of things to work through. We have decided that, indeed, we would like you to marry us, and I am here to ask your help with that. Is there a time when we can set up that wedding ceremony? Can you officiate?"

"Let us go into the rectory and see what dates are available. I am sure we can work something out in the near future."

"Thank you, Father," replied Alfredo. We are very anxious to set up a time soon."

CHAPTER EIGHTEEN: FINALLY, THE WEDDING

Annabelle was overcome, even though only minor preparations were needed for such a small wedding. Indeed, the guest list was so limited that she wondered whether she could call it a real "celebration". There would be Grandfather Rudolf and Grandmother Margaret (of course), Janos and Rowena, Luigi and Maria, and the baby Christina. It would be a small ceremony on Friday night at the end of the work day. *Anyóka* and Grandfather would stay overnight with Janos, where both Annabelle and her grandmother would be working to prepare a simple repast. Rowena offered to make the cake, and Maria elected to take charge of Christina, since she had been caring for her all along.

Even with this simplistic approach, Annabelle was nervous. Would she behave properly? Would what she picked out to wear to the wedding really seem appropriate to all? Suppose she failed to make all the right responses? She was just learning English and was still not really fluid in the language. Suppose Alfredo changed his mind at the last minute?

The day of the wedding dawned with bright sunshine and a clear sky. It was believed by some that rain brought tears, so Annabelle reflected that this was a good sign. She put her apron on to help in the kitchen. All the food would be prepared in advance, and Annabelle was intent on creating some fine pastry to share, even though there would be a wedding cake. She wanted to show her enthusiasm and her desire to please, especially since Alfredo had always said that he looked forward to good meals and a comfortable, clean home. She knew they would retire to the apartment that night and leave Christina one more night with Maria, so that the child would not become fearful because of a drastic change so late at night. Then the next day they would arrive at Luigi and Maria's house for breakfast, gather the baby's things and start their new life together. Alfredo would not have to go into work, so it was a time of pleasant anticipation.

Annabelle woke early, having slept fitfully all night long. She dressed quickly, taking extra care to arrange her hair in an attractive way. Margaret had left some flowers for her to place in her hair, but Annabelle's hands were shaking so much that she was unable to add them into her bun. She quietly entered the kitchen, but everyone was already up and having their coffee. Rudolf was the first to greet her. "Annabelle, you look so lovely. This is a great day to be remembered forever."

Margaret turned from her cooking and smiled at her granddaughter. "May the Lord bring you many blessings on this day and all the days of your life!"

Rowena and Janos were quiet, so Annabelle feared their displeasure. But Janos cleared his throat and offered, "Rowena and I, as well, want to wish you happiness and plentiful blessings." Annabelle smiled graciously.

Rowena offered, "How about some breakfast?"

Annabelle said, "I am too nervous to eat anything, and I need some help putting the flowers in my hair. Would you help me, Rowena?"

Rowena smiled, "Yes, of course," while she deftly affixed the blossoms.

Margaret commented, “We only have about a half hour before we need to leave to walk to the nearby church.” So everyone began to gather their belongings as they readied to leave. Rowena tended to her baby, who was gurgling happily.

Annabelle took one last look around as she neared the doorway, thinking, this is the first day of the rest of my life. I will never stay here again, and I am committing myself to a whole new journey.

At Luigi and Maria’s house, Alfredo was also trying to calm his nerves. His heart was beating much too quickly as he watched his sister get Christina dressed for the church service. She looked so sweet; Alfredo hoped that Annabelle would think so, too.

He went back to his room to check over his jacket and to make sure it looked clean and pressed. As he paused to see himself in the small mirror on his dresser, he wondered who the person looking back at him really was. What a funny thought to have! Why such a lack of self-confidence? He was always the one who was sure of his next steps, until Lucia entered his life. She had turned him inside out, and he regretted that. He felt he would never find himself again.

He wondered if Annabelle really wanted to be with him, or if she only longed for a replacement for the child she had lost. Yet he had no intention of pressuring her or of forcing her to be someone or something she did not want to be. He would accept her on any terms; he only hoped that someday he would again experience that glimmer of excitement that accompanied happiness. When was he last happy, he wondered? Even when Annabelle agreed to the terms of marriage, he did not feel happiness. He did not feel her joy at the prospect of being his wife. He bowed his head in silent prayer to his patron saint. “Please,” he begged, “make this be the right decision, and put me on the path I need to be on." Then he joined Luigi and Maria. "Are we ready to make our way to the Church?"

The church bells rang a greeting as Alfredo stepped into the vestibule. There was no sign of Annabelle and her family yet, so he got his family settled in the front pews and went with Luigi to find the priest in the sacristy.

When Annabelle entered the church with her family, she could see Maria and the baby sitting at the front of the church. She did not walk down the aisle to speak to them but insisted that her family members, except for Rudolf, take a seat on the opposite side of the aisle, awaiting a sign from the priest. She stood in the back of the church just beyond the doors to the main part of the church, in the vestibule, but in direct line of sight to the altar. Father Emilio had said that he would beckon her forward when he wanted her to walk down the aisle with her grandfather. As she waited, she started to tremble. Rudolf grabbed her under her arm to steady her and whispered, "Annabelle, everything will be fine. Do not be scared. You are doing the right thing."

A tear escaped and trickled down her face. She wiped it, she hoped, secretly; she did not want Rudolf to see it. Suddenly Margaret was at her side. She took Annabelle in her arms and softly said, "I have such good feelings about this today. Do not be fearful. Put a smile on your face. This is the first day of the rest of your life."

Annabelle spotted the priest lifting his hand and beckoning her to come forward. Margaret rushed down the side aisle to reach her pew before Annabelle and Rudolf started forward. Elegantly, the two figures slowly proceeded in the quiet of the church, in the absence of music, to stand where Rudolf would deliver her to Alfredo.

Alfredo gazed at his bride, wondering how he could ever be blessed with such a beautiful and wonderful wife. He knew in his heart the beauty that Annabelle carried within her, even if she did not recognize what she had to offer. She was so unlike Lucia, who had been decked out with the utmost fanfare in finery that was beyond comparison. Though Lucia was beautiful, she did not possess Annabelle's inner beauty, and Alfredo had never felt his heart burst within his chest at the sight of her.

The new Mr. and Mrs. Alfredo Caruso left the church, holding hands as they slowly walked back to Janos' home for the modest reception. Behind them the rest of the two families proceeded, with Christina and Bartos (Rowena and Janos's son) capturing all the attention.

Annabelle, in her heart, could barely wait until the repast was done, so she and Alfredo could retire to his apartment ,and they could begin to learn about each other.

Later that night, settled into the new apartment, Annabelle and Alfredo rested side by side in the double bed, afraid to touch, fearful of rejection. After taking a deep breath, Alfredo ventured forth, "Annabelle, are you sleeping?"

"No," came the whispered reply. "I am thinking of our future and wondering how things will work out between us."

Alfredo responded, "Your thoughts are much the same as mine. I do want you to know that I think you were the most beautiful bride a man could ever hope for. You really make me stop and consider how fortunate I am to have met you, and that you have agreed to marry me. I also want to reassure you that I will stay true to my word. There are no conditions that you have to fulfill other than keeping the household and caring for Christina. It is my hope that over time you will find me acceptable as a husband and that you will come to learn to love me."

Annabelle said nothing. But the tears streamed down her cheeks.

Alfredo continued, "Do you want to say anything?"

"No, Alfredo. I am trusting that you will do what you have told me. But I do want you to know that, in a way, you are saving my life. Until I decided to accept your proposal, I really had nothing and no one. Now I am overcome with the thoughts of this family that I suddenly belong to, you and Christina, but also Luigi and Maria. Everyone is so accepting of me. I only wish that my family would reciprocate in kind."

"Annabelle, your grandmother and grandfather have been so kind and wonderful to me. Today was the first time they had even seen Christina, and they were accepting of her as well."

"Yes, but Rowena and Janos seem so distant. I worry about them and hope that we can become a whole, integrated family unit. I want Christina and Bartos to be friends, to play with each other and learn to love each other."

"Change does not come quickly," Alfredo continued. "Give it time and space for everyone to make adjustments. For your family, it was so sudden, for mine, not really. We have been talking about Christina's future since Lucia died. And both Luigi and Maria hoped that you would consider becoming my wife."

"Why was that?" Annabelle inquired.

"It was because they understood that I have been in love with you since I saw you on the ship, though they probably thought it was just an infatuation. I know everything will take time, but I want us to learn to cherish each other and to share all our concerns as they arise. Can we agree to do that?"

Annabelle shook her head yes and shyly reached across the covers to take Alfredo's hand. He gently and tenderly held it in his, closing his eyes and thanking God for the gifts he had received.

CHAPTER NINETEEN: SETTLING IN

Annabelle and Alfredo awoke early, rushed to dress and to prepare for the breakfast they would be having at Luigi and Maria's home. They were expecting to gather Christina's things and get her settled in their apartment, giving the baby time to get accustomed to the new routines and to Annabelle.

Annabelle was nervous, afraid that Christina would not be willing to accept her attention. As they approached Luigi's apartment, Annabelle began to tremble. Suddenly she was becoming overwhelmed with her decision.

Alfredo realized her fears and tried to calm her mind. "Don't worry, Annabelle. Christina is used to people. Maria has many friends, and she has taken Christina with her shopping and visiting others. She readily goes to others and is not fearful of anyone. She is a happy baby and has spent plenty of time in my arms, so I don't think you have anything to worry about. Just be yourself. How can she ever resist you?"

Annabelle smiled and vowed to be positive. When Maria opened the door and Annabelle heard the baby cooing, smelled the fresh baked bread and tantalizing breakfast fare, she said a silent prayer of thanks and prepared for her new life as Mrs. Caruso to Alfredo and Mama to Christina.

She was smiling at the baby and talking to her as they walked to their own apartment.

Luigi carried Christina so she could see Anabelle, and he encouraged the baby to interact with her. Annabelle felt pleased when Christina reached out to touch her face. She was hopeful but nervous. She still had not tried to pick her up.

When they returned to their home, Alfredo told Annabelle to be free to change the way things were set up, to rearrange the baby's room to her liking, so it would be easier to manage and even to make adjustments in their bedroom. He told her to do whatever she liked to make the place more cozy and comfortable. "It is your home now, Annabelle, and I want you to be happy here."

Annabelle offered a shy smile of acceptance and busied herself with straightening the apartment and with making dinner for them both. She prepared food for Christina, who seemed perfectly content in her father's arms.

When Annabelle reached out finally to pick her up to feed her, Christina was at first hesitant to respond, but Anabelle moved slowly and cautiously, smiling and talking soothingly. Alfredo watched carefully, holding his breath and hoping that the baby would accept Annabelle. He had to admit that things were going more smoothly than he had anticipated.

Dinner was a light fare for the first night. Alfredo asked what kind of things he should bring home to enable her to prepare the type of meals she liked. Annabelle gave him a list of vegetables and fruits that she always liked to have and that he could bring from his market.

"Tomorrow, before I leave for work, I will give you some money so you can procure whatever else you need from the corner grocer. Please set up an account with him so you can just get what you need when you need it and I will settle the bill each week." And so the first day passed without any crises.

At the end of the day, Annabelle, tired and tense, closed her eyes, falling asleep before Alfredo even changed his clothes. Christina was peacefully sleeping in the corner of their room.

As for Alfredo, he was pleased with the day and how things were developing between them. He had no idea of the challenges that lay ahead.

Margaret and Rudolf were surprised when they arrived at home. There was a note pinned to their door indicating that Miklos wanted to speak with them. Margaret immediately felt uneasy. This would not bode well, she knew. Miklos was one to be suspicious of, as she had learned from his behavior with Annabelle. She crumbled the note and tossed it into the trash. Yet all day long, Margaret could tell that trouble was brewing. She could foresee it.

The rest of the day went by without any complications. Rudolf tended to the garden, and Margaret spent the afternoon seeing her clients. She prepared an enticing supper for Rudolf with all his favorite dishes. As she was putting the meal on the table, she heard a knock at the door. Opening it, she found herself facing Miklos.

He greeted her affectionately, immediately putting her on guard. As tactfully as possible, Margaret inquired, "How can I help you Miklos? It is so nice to see you again."

"I wanted to see Annabelle. I have an apology to make to her."

"I am afraid she is not here anymore, and you will not be able to contact her."

"Surely you can provide me with her forwarding address. Where has she gone?"

Margaret hesitated for a moment, wondering just how much information she should share with Miklos. After considering she decided he would find out anyway, so she replied, "Annabelle has gotten married and moved away."

Miklos responded with fervor. "Got married? Who in the world would want to marry her anyway," he replied.

Margaret thought carefully. "She has married a young man that she has known for some time."

"Oh, you are talking about Alfredo, I am certain. I am not surprised at all. I can see that he was interested in her."

"The wedding has already taken place, and there is a child involved. Let things be. What is done is done."

"I suppose you are right," he replied, tipping his hat and quickly exiting the house.

When Rudolf entered the kitchen from his workshop, Margaret told him of the incident. He frowned, expressing great concern. "That man cannot be trusted, Margaret. I heard some talk of his connections, and none of them are good. I think we should warn Annabelle and Alfredo of his visit so they can be prepared, should he suddenly show up on their doorstep."

"Oh, I don't want to create undue concern for them. They are just now starting a new life with many hopes and dreams in front of them. Let's allow the newlyweds time to adjust. We can mention it casually when we next see them."

Rudolf considered for a moment. "I guess that you know best, Margaret. I will follow your advice."

Yet Margaret still had a heavy feeling in her heart. Rudolf might be right about everything. She knew that Miklos was the type of man who always had to have things his way. As she thought about the events that led up to his and Annabelle's break up, she became more certain that some difficulty was sure to arise. What could he do anyway? They were legally married, and everyone has a right to their own life.

Annabelle found the days flying by. She was investing so much time into making a home that was pleasing to Alfredo that she never had a spare moment from morning to night. At the end of the day, she was fatigued and fell asleep quickly, an experience that she had not had for several years.

Christina became responsive, a happy little girl who provided no trouble at all. Suffice to say, Annabelle was happier than she had been for a very long time. She loved the afternoon time with Christina, when after her lunch, Christina allowed Annabelle to cuddle with her in the rocking chair until she took her nap. When the baby was asleep, Annabelle would hug her and plant a kiss on her cheek, so happy to be holding a baby.

This particular morning Annabelle was intrigued with the smell of springtime. She looked outside and could see in the distance some greenery from the trees in the park. It was brisk, but she felt that she could take Christina out in the pram if she bundled her up well enough. She managed to get the pram down the stairs and set aside the blanket that she thought would provide adequate warmth. As she turned around to go back upstairs and get Christina from her crib, she noticed a man across the street, hovering about and watching what she was doing. She felt a strange fear creeping into her chest. Who could that be? Why was he there?

She had no way of reaching Alfredo or anyone else, for that matter, so she thought twice about bringing the baby outside. She also thought that perhaps she was making too much of this circumstance and tried to disregard her concerns. She left the pram on the stoop and went back inside. When she got into her apartment, she secured the lock and walked to look out the window. Fortunately, she had a view of the street in front of the house.

She watched as the man stepped off of the curb and walked over to the pram. He looked inside the buggy as if to see whether Christina was sleeping there. At that moment, Annabelle decided that they would not go out at all, and that she would risk leaving the buggy at the door until Alfredo returned from work, even with the possibility of it being stolen. She knew that she had not imagined the concern she felt. She remembered how her grandmother had told her, "Never ignore those instincts you have about danger."

This man, whoever he was, had some kind of plan to interfere or hurt them. And she was afraid she would not be able to protect herself and Christina. The rest of the day she worried and fretted about the incident, determined to let Alfredo know the details when he got home. Who could that person be? She did not recognize him, but perhaps it was someone that Alfredo knew. But why would he be snooping into their possessions?

She went over his appearance and admitted to herself that he had an intimidating manner. He was a large man with an unkempt appearance. His clothes were shopworn, and his shoes were muddy. She could see him well enough to be able to identify him, if she and Alfredo went out together and came across him. He had a threatening air about him, making her feel really uneasy. She prayed that the rest of the day would pass without incident, and could not wait for Alfredo to arrive home at the end of his work day.

She tried to deflect her attention to tasks at hand and was determined to make a cake for dessert to take up the time that needed to be spent. Worrying was tiring, and fear was creeping into her mind, making her feel paralyzed.

At about five o'clock she started to pace, hoping that Alfredo would not be late today. She knew it would be another hour before he got home, so she prepared Christina's bath early and got her daughter ready for bed. She fed her and held her, rocking her in the chair until she heard the key in the lock.

As soon as she saw Alfredo she started to cry. "What's wrong, Annabelle?" he questioned, kneeling before her as she clasped the baby to her bosom.

She blurted out, “There was a man lurking outside today. I wanted to take Christina for a walk to the park, but when I brought the buggy downstairs, he was across the street staring at me. I got frightened and left the pram at the door. Is it still there?”

“Yes, it is. I wondered why it was still on the landing but thought perhaps it was too heavy for you to get it back upstairs. I will go down and get it for you. I don’t like what you are telling me. Let me bring up the pram, and then we can talk some more.”

“All right, Alfredo. I will put the baby in the crib and wait for you to come back upstairs.” When Alfredo returned, he sat down on the sofa with Annabelle, turned her towards him and said, “Tell me everything you can remember about what happened and what this person looked like.”

Annabelle repeated the things she had gone over in her head, again and again, until she was certain that she had provided Alfredo with every small detail around the event. At the end of her explanation, she started to cry again. “Alfredo, I did not want anything to happen to Christina. I do not know this person and why he would be here, but I am afraid for us both, and for you as well.”

Alfredo reached out and pulled her to him, wrapping his arms around her. She put her head on his shoulder, feeling the protection he offered and thanking God that he had managed to get home without incident. She was glad, at that moment, that he was her husband.

For Alfredo, it was a moment of anger and of fear combined in an effort to remain calm. He wanted to be sure that he did not cause Annabelle to become even more fearful, but he also did not want to take this incident too lightly. Something was not right about this. Why would someone be watching them, and why would they be looking into the baby buggy? Who could it be? Was there someone he had offended? Surely, it could not be Annabelle who offended anyone. No one knew her in this neighborhood, not even the other families in the building. Annabelle, he realized, had such a friendly and accepting manner that she would never be able to hurt anyone's feelings. He would make it his business to make acquaintance with everyone so that she could have someone to go to, should something else happen.

Could it have to do with Lucia's parents, he wondered? However, they had made it clear that they wanted nothing to do with him and his family. They claimed they did not want to ever see the baby, so it could not be them.

Tomorrow, he would talk it over with Luigi, who was such a clear thinker. He would be better able to analyze the situation and to make suggestions about what could be going on. But he also did not want to leave Annabelle alone tomorrow. They would leave early and go to Luigi's, where he would lay out the incident, and Annabelle could spend the day with his sister, Maria. He felt resolved. Yet, he was unable to sleep, concerned about his child and his new wife. What would he do next?

After talking with Luigi and Maria, Alfredo decided that Annabelle would go with him to Luigi's every morning until they could figure out who the mysterious person was, watching their premises. Annabelle felt comfortable with that decision, though she was worried about taking advantage of Maria's good graces. She offered to cook dinners for all of them, and Alfredo agreed that was a fair exchange, but he would leave it to the women to work out the details.

Between the two men, it was determined that Alfredo would leave at lunch and see if anyone was loitering around the apartment building. In the morning, he would take the pram and set it outside the entrance to the building to ensure that it looked like Annabelle was readying herself to leave with the baby.

The first day that they set this plan in place, everything was quiet, and no one was around. Alfredo wondered if Annabelle had imagined the whole thing in her efforts to take care of and protect Christina.

At lunchtime on the third day, when Alfredo began to approach the building, he saw the man that Annabelle had described standing on the other side of the street, watching their doorway. Anger welled up inside him, and he began to seethe. Trying to control his temper, he kept himself somewhat distant to observe the man's next movements. As predicted by Annabelle, he crossed the street, peering into the baby buggy. Alfredo came up behind him, grabbing him by the collar and throwing him around to come face to face with him. "Who are you, and what do you want?" he yelled. The man showed no fear and shoved Alfredo backwards, causing him to hit the back of his head on the wall.

"Who do you think you are, grabbing me like that?" he screamed.

"I think I am the owner of this buggy and the child that would go in it. Why are you here, and who sent you?"

Cowering somewhat, he replied, "I have a message for you. Watch yourself and your family. You may be sorry that you have taken the steps you did."

With that, Alfredo struck him, knocking him out cold. Where were the foot police when needed? He wanted to run and fetch help but was fearful of leaving the man alone, lest he get himself up and run away. Instead, he decided to search his pockets to see if he could find his name and any other information indicating why he was stalking them.

When he pulled the papers from inside the man's jacket, he saw a note from Miklos, Annabelle's old fiancé, directing the man to frighten her and to warn Alfredo that he would pay for his actions.

Alfredo kept the note and the man's identity papers, leaving him on the street. He proceeded to the local police station where he provided this evidence to the constable in charge.

They promised to investigate, but Alfredo still feared that more was to come. When he returned to work and shared the events with Luigi, the two men decided to form a local citizens troop of residents to patrol the streets, watching for people who looked suspicious and were seeking to commit crimes.

That night, they began their efforts to protect their homes from these unwanted criminal types. Annabelle and Maria were confused about whether they felt safer or more at risk under these circumstances.

Annabelle was shocked at Miklos' involvement, so on the following Sunday, they proceeded to her grandmother's to talk about the events with Margaret and Rudolf. When they arrived, unannounced, Margaret knew something bad had happened. She revealed to them the visit from Miklos and the fact that she had informed him of their marriage. Alfredo decided that it would be safer for Annabelle and Christina to remain with Margaret and Rudolf until the investigation was concluded, and he could secure a more safe and controlled environment for his family. Annabelle consented because she needed the comfort of her grandmother and knew that Rudolf could offer sufficient protection for her and the baby. She was too alone in the city without any male protection during the day, and she certainly did not want to put Maria at risk, especially now that she learned that Maria was expecting a baby. Maria did not need to have Annabelle and Christina invading her home daily.

Alfredo returned home that night, stopping to inform Luigi of his decision to leave Annabelle and Christina with her family. Then he paid a visit to Janos, knowing that Annabelle's cousin would have some worthwhile advice.

Janos was taken aback by the information that Alfredo shared and promised to use his contacts to make some inquiries about Miklos' background. He already knew that Miklos was a powerful adversary, having learned of the altercation that took place between him and Alfredo. But he found it hard to imagine that anyone would go to such great lengths to bring harm to another man's family. Janos promised to contact Alfredo when he had more details to share. Alfredo left Janos' home, feeling lonely and frightened for the well-being of those he loved. Arriving at his home after dark, he did not see the figure lurking in the doorway and never knew what hit him, as he fell to the ground.

No one was coming and going at this hour, and so he laid there all night in the bad weather, bleeding and unconscious. In the morning, his neighbor found him when he left for work, was able to arouse him and took him into his own home, where his neighbor's wife started to administer first aid.

After the woman finished bandaging Alfredo and providing him with breakfast, Alfredo said that he felt well enough to go to work. When he arrived at the market, Luigi was stunned to see his brother-in-law in this condition. He immediately left for the police station to get some help around the incident. Luigi and Alfredo decided that Annabelle should remain at her Grandmother's house at this time. They also decided that Alfredo should stay with them, so Maria could monitor his condition and administer to his needs.

Annabelle and Christina were peacefully sitting in the front yard, enjoying the fresh air and sunshine, when she heard the horses' hooves. Shielding her eyes from the sun, she recognized Miklos' cart. Now why, she wondered, is he coming here today? *Anyóka* had let her know about his inquiries about her, and she felt uncomfortable and uncertain about having another encounter with him. She quickly picked the baby up from her buggy and went inside the house.

Margaret was in the kitchen baking an apple pie for lunch. She said, "Miklos is on his way. I am going upstairs with the baby, and I do not want to see him. Please send him away."

"Go quickly," Margaret warned, "and lock the door upstairs. Rudolf just went into town for some supplies. I would feel much better if he were here."

Annabelle ran up to the second floor, securing the bedroom door and pushing a chair under the doorknob for some extra protection. Her heart was beating so fast that she was finding difficulty breathing. She clutched Christina to her breast. The baby seemed to sense her fear and started to cry. Annabelle was soothing her when she heard the pounding on the front door. Pressing her ear to the door, she could just decipher Margaret's words.

"Miklos, what are you doing here?"

"I have come to see Annabelle and speak with her."

"I am afraid she is not interested in speaking with you, Miklos. Her life is settled, and she is happy with her choices. You need to follow your own pathway and forget about her completely."

"Margaret, I always get what I want, one way or another. So this is not over. You can let Annabelle know that. I wanted her for my wife, and I will have her, whether or not she wants to cooperate."

"Those are foolish words, Miklos. You are not in control of the world or of her life. You can only set your own direction in life. Go home and forget this nonsense."

"Don't think you can tell me what to do. I intend to continue with my plans until I get what I want."

“Well then,” Margaret continued, “let me inform you that you are no longer welcome here. I will not be responding to your visits.”

Miklos pulled his hat down over his eyes. “As I warned, you have not seen the end of me yet. Be wary of what you say and do, and so should Annabelle.”

He turned on his heel and climbed onto his buggy, taking off in a flash. Margaret felt her skin crawl, wondering how they could handle this situation. She paced the floor, anticipating Rudolf’s return. When time had passed, Annabelle crept down the stairs to speak with her grandmother.

“What can we do about Miklos?” she asked.

“I wish I knew,” Margaret replied. “When your grandfather returns, we will talk about it with him.”

On Sunday, Alfredo prepared to visit Annabelle and Christina. Throughout the trip, he kept going over in his mind what he would tell Annabelle and how he was going to approach the next steps they would have to take. As he pulled up to the house, he paused and took a deep breath, saying a silent prayer for guidance.

Margaret heard his arrival and opened the door in welcoming enthusiasm. Alfredo jumped down and greeted her enthusiastically.

“How is Annabelle and the baby?” he asked.

“They are upstairs now and will be coming down soon to see you. Annabelle cannot wait for you to arrive. She has been getting Christina dressed to see her father.”

As she spoke, Alfredo could hear Annabelle’s footsteps and, turning, he was overtaken with joy to see her and his daughter. Since Annabelle and Christina were staying here with her grandmother, he had become so much more aware of the blessings he had received when Annabelle consented to marry him. He sorely missed her presence, and he knew he would have to tell her about the events that followed her departure.

She rushed forward, hugging him and planting a kiss on his cheek. It was the first time she had expressed any visible affection for Alfredo, so he was taken aback by her actions.

“I have missed you and our home. I really want to go back with you, Alfredo. I do not want to be separated from you anymore. I am more afraid now than ever before. There is nowhere safe for me, not here and not at home. I would rather be with you than anywhere else.”

Alfredo carefully embraced Annabelle, holding her close as she continued to talk about her fears. When she paused, he suggested, ‘Let’s sit down in the kitchen, all of us, because I have a lot to tell you.”

Rudolf came in from the barn where he had been doing morning chores. “Alfredo, so good to see you,” he stated, offering his hand in greeting.

Margaret, standing apart, noticed the strained look on Alfredo’s face. “Let me get some coffee for you and give you a little something to eat while we talk.” When Alfredo removed his hat, Annabelle gasped, seeing the wound on the back of his head.

“What happened to you?” she cried.

“That is what I want to talk to you about,” Alfredo began.

CHAPTER TWENTY: NEXT STEPS

A silence overtook the family, as they realized that something frightening had occurred.

Margaret served Alfredo a piece of her apple pie and a steaming coffee. He pushed the fork around on the plate, looking for a way to begin.

Annabelle stepped forward. "I am glad that Christina fell asleep just before you arrived, so we have some time to talk. Please tell me how you got hurt."

When Alfredo began to relate the details of the attack he had endured, Annabelle shed silent tears. She quietly listened, fear building inside her.

"This is all my fault," she said." I only bring sadness to others, no matter what I try to do."

"Annabelle, don't be silly," Margaret countered. "This is not caused by you. It is Miklos. I am sure of that right now."

Alfredo began, "I am afraid Grandmother is correct. We found a note from Miklos on the person of the attacker, instructing him to take vengeance on me. So, clearly, he was behind the scheme. I am only glad that you were not there. It would have placed you in danger, as well as Christina."

"Alfredo, what can we do now?" Annabelle cried, tears streaming down her face. "I am really scared that I will not be able to protect the baby or myself, if someone comes while I am alone."

“I understand, and you are correct, Annabelle. That is why Luigi and I have formed a neighborhood watch group to protect all of you women who are at home while the men are working. Those who have late shifts will volunteer some hours during the day. Those with early shifts will volunteer hours later in the day, and together the community will keep everyone safe.”

“I guess that means you will agree that I can return home with you now?”

“Yes, that is true. But to be extra careful, we are going to have you and Maria remain together during the day while we are at the market, at least for the next few weeks.”

Margaret interceded, “Did you make a complaint with the local police station? And does Janos know?”

Alfredo smiled, “You are thinking just like I am, Grandmother. I did speak to the constable at the station, and he assured me that a patrol will now frequent our neighborhood. He also knows about the residents who were offering to keep a watchful eye on things and agrees that it is a good idea. But he warns that we should not get into a physical conflict with whoever is behind this effort. It is too dangerous.”

‘I would agree with that,” Rudolf jumped in. “Also, another option is this: since Margaret is safe here, I am able to come and stay with Annabelle for a couple of weeks, just to ensure that things will go well. Would you like that to happen? In that way, Annabelle can stay in your home and, if you decide it is better, Maria can come and stay with us during the day as well.”

“The sleeping arrangements will not be very comfortable, but we can get a cot for you, though you would have to be sleeping in the living room at night. Would that be a problem?”

"That is fine with me," replied Rudolf. He then turned to Margaret. "I know I did not ask you about this in advance. I really just thought of the idea. How do you feel about that suggestion?"

"I like it very much. It puts me at ease. Even if Miklos comes by here again, I will not open the door for him. He is not interested in me. I have already told him that he is no longer welcome here, though I don't think that anything will stop him from doing whatever he wants to do. He is used to getting his own way. I am so disappointed in him."

"As for Janos," Alfredo continued. "I did stop by his home and speak to him about Miklos. He offered to make some inquiries into Miklos' background; he has a lot of people he knows that come from Miklos' area in Hungary. I hope he will have some beneficial information to offer and some suggestions about how to effectively deal with Miklos."

Annabelle offered, "Then I guess, Alfredo, it is settled. Grandfather, Christina and I will return home with you this afternoon."

"Yes, that is what we will do," Alfredo agreed.

Margaret, now more relaxed, smiled and said, "Let's sit down together and have something to eat."

Annabelle set the table while Alfredo held his daughter, rocking her in the chair. Annabelle watched him from the corner of her eye, knowing in her heart that he was much different from any of the other men she had known, including Franz. Her heart swelled with joy at the prospect of her future. Now it would be up to her to make him feel appreciated.

Meanwhile, Miklos was plotting his next steps. He already had engaged a more ferocious opponent to tackle Alfredo. The plan was not to injure, but to kill, making it appear to be an accident.

He thought back to the engagement party, angered by the remembrance of Alfredo's sudden appearance and of Annabelle's rejection of him. How could she have done that when he had done so much to help her? He believed that she owed him, not just for the jewels he had offered, but for the prospect of a life of luxury. Certainly, she would have to follow his directives. After all, he was the man and had the final say in everything. He was even willing, now, to assume responsibility for the child after the father was gone.

He smiled to himself at his own cleverness and how he had mapped out the attack. It was going to be so easy. This time a bash on the head would not be sufficient, but it still would have to appear to be an accident.

Perhaps he would take a drive to Margaret and Rudolf's today, while Rudolf was there, just to further intimidate them. They could then relate the threats to Annabelle, whose heart would fill with fear. She would be so much more willing to cooperate, especially with the baby to consider. Yes, Miklos thought, *I am really brilliant, and I will have my way.*

Janos, meanwhile, after making his inquiries, had learned that Miklos was much more dangerous than anyone ever guessed. He had a history of violent behavior in Hungary, but because of his family and the fortune they had, no one had attempted to bring any actions against him. It was the way it was. The powerful get to run the show and the rest of the community has to comply. He could only wonder how Franz had allowed this man into his personal life. How did he ever take the chance of exposing Annabelle to his personality?

He would make it his business to see Alfredo after work on Monday and inform him, not only of Miklos' reputation but of the types of activities he had been involved in back in Hungary.

Rowena was anxious too, not wanting to bring attention to their family. After all, they also had a baby and, for the couple, Bartos was the center of their lives. Janos must think about them first; she vowed to remind him of that obligation.

The ride home for Annabelle, Alfredo, Rudolf and Christina was uneventful. Annabelle could not believe how happy she was to be returning to her own place. She had come to cherish the apartment and the home she was attempting to create for her new little family.

Once Christina was in bed and Rudolf was settled on the couch for the night, Annabelle and Alfredo had the first block of time for themselves. She needed to get all the details on the attack. When she heard what had occurred and how injured Alfredo actually was, lying on the street all night long, she began to tremble.

"I am so fearful for us," she told Alfredo. "I don't know what I would do if faced with this kind of situation again. I am so glad that Rudolf is going to be here for a while, and I am so proud of you and Luigi for forging such cooperation in our community, so there will be men to watch us and take care of all of us who are alone most of the time."

When she offered to change the bandage on Alfredo's wound, she did not expect to have the reaction that she did. The wound was deep and, though it did not look infected, it was a serious injury. She carefully removed the old bandage and replaced it with a clean one. Thinking of the suffering her husband had endured made her that much more appreciative of him. She sat opposite him on the bed and told him of her feelings.

"I really want to share with you what I am feeling, Alfredo." He looked at her and recognized the sincere emotional response she was having. Her eyes were welling up with tears, and she seemed unsure of how to proceed with him.

She reached out to touch his cheek. "You are a good man, and I am fortunate to have met you. I really do appreciate what you have done for me, and I intend to make you as happy as I possibly can. I also want you to know that I am coming to love Christina as if she were my own child. Please take heart, and do not worry about the future between us. It is going to take me a little time to really become your wife in the full sense of the word, but it is my intention to learn to love you physically as well as emotionally."

Alfredo gently took her hand in his. "Annabelle, when I first saw you on the ship, I knew that there was something very special about you. I immediately wanted to get to know you more. When your loss occurred, I only wanted to make you stop hurting. I have never felt that way with another human being, with another woman. I am glad that you allowed me to help you."

Annabelle responded," We may not have a long history between us, but we certainly have a complicated set of circumstances to overcome together. Everything you endured with Lucia, the birth of your child, the death of your wife, the rejection by your in-laws"...one thing after another. And now this nonsense with Miklos. I feel I should apologize, but I do not know what I could have done differently or how I could have managed to make this last attack not happen. I did not want to marry Miklos as soon as I realized what kind of a man he is. I also did not want to over impose on you, Alfredo."

Alfredo reached out and tenderly pulled Annabelle to him, gently hugging her and wiping her tears. "Things will work out as they should. I am certain of that," he whispered.

Annabelle put her arms around Alfredo's neck in a tender embrace. She kissed him on the cheek as she caressed the side of his face. He moved closer to her, pressing his lips against hers. The intensity of their kiss was like an electrical jolt through both of them. Annabelle gasped in surprise. She had not expected that kind of a response to his kiss and found difficulty catching her breath. Maybe, she thought, he is the man of my dreams after all. Maybe the soothsayer on the ship was right. Only time would tell.

Climbing into bed, Annabelle lay on her side, facing away from Alfredo. She did not want him to see the level of emotion she was experiencing; she needed to figure out how she would be able to cope with all of these developments.

Alfredo, on the other hand, closed his eyes and sighed. It was the first time, since he had proposed, that he felt any measure of peacefulness. In spite of the threats and the dangers that lurked, Alfredo admitted to himself that he was actually happy. Happy to have Annabelle; happy to have a little daughter; happy to be working with Luigi; happy to be part of Annabelle's family, too. So many blessings to consider.

CHAPTER TWENTY-ONE: LIFE BEGINS

Annabelle felt that she had finally settled into a routine, the kind of lifestyle she had always wished for. She had a husband who respected her and was tolerant of her thoughts and ideas. He never made her feel inferior and was open to her suggestions about changes in their lives. She wondered how he had ever come to be like that. Men in this world that she had known growing up, except for Rudolf, were not that understanding of their wives. In fact, in most cases, wives were not informed of what was going to happen and were not part of discussion around changes taking place.

She had watched Rowena with a sense of awe. There was a woman who adored her husband, but she never felt that Janos had the same level of feelings for his wife. He took her for granted, expecting her to be there all the time, providing him with anything he needed or wanted. Rowena did not seem to mind either. She seemed to know that this was what was expected of her.

Maria and Luigi, on the other hand, had a more give and take relationship. He clearly loved her, and she was ready for anything he would expect, but they had known each other for a lifetime. Annabelle had always realized that people who knew each other from childhood had a deeper understanding of who they were and of each other, There were seldom surprises in behavior, because the couple had seen it all, had lived with the ups and downs of maturing, of adolescence, of struggling to figure out who you are as a person. Annabelle knew she had never experienced anything like that and tried to learn what she had to do to become more accepting of others in general.

Christina was no problem at all. She was a good baby, undemanding and happy, so unlike Lucia, as Alfredo had described her. Annabelle tried not to think about Lucia, but concentrated on the characteristics that Christina exhibited that were like Alfredo. Through her efforts, Annabelle tried to make the baby accept love, content with what life had to offer and open to all kinds of new experiences. She knew that was what she had tried to do with Paula, for the little bit of time that she was blessed to have her.

On this particular day, Annabelle was set on making a special meal for Alfredo. She had learned from Maria how to prepare his favorite pasta and was careful to take notes as Maria gave her instructions. She wanted to show Alfredo how much she appreciated him, how much she valued how he treated her and Christina and how she was trying to be a better wife to him. She felt disappointed that she was so shy about fully connecting physically with Alfredo, but she also realized, as *Anyóka* had explained, that she had been under a lot of stress. Grandmother told her that the kind of stress and fears that she had endured will desensitize a person. Now that everything seemed to be calmer, Annabelle was trying to move forward and felt more emotionally stable.

Suddenly she thought again of Miklos. Margaret had not said that he had been around again, so Annabelle hoped he had finally accepted the status of things and that he was concentrating on his own future and not on hers. Nevertheless, a nagging fear presented itself in her heart and mind.

Alfredo and Luigi were exceptionally busy on this day. People were out and about and anxious to shop. Their produce was excellent, and their prices were competitive. They felt it was an honor to offer good food without trying to gouge others. They also liked the interchanges they had with their customers; the customers obviously reciprocated by returning again and again.

Little old lady Filomena came into the market, smiling and bringing them each a home baked donut. She wanted them to know how much she enjoyed shopping at their market and how she appreciated the cleanliness and the condition of the produce they offered.

When Pietro, their favorite 5-year-old, came in with his mother that afternoon, they happily presented him with a beautiful red apple that he was so excited to receive. He told them, "You are my favorite place to come with my Mamma."

All in all, it had been a great day. The people continued to frequent the market, even though they were at closing time. Neither man wanted to rush their customers; they wanted them to understand that they were there to serve them and to meet their special needs, that, as customers, they were more important than the time of day.

As they finally closed up and started to clean up, they realized that it was starting to get dark and that their wives probably were wondering what had happened to them. Luigi was the first to leave, "I promised Maria that I would be home on time for supper, and I am already late. Do you mind if I sneak out now?"

"Not at all," Alfredo replied, knowing that Annabelle would never make a fuss, even if he was late in returning home. He finished sweeping the floor, checked the bins to be sure that everything looked fresh and up-to-date, took his hat and coat from the rack and turned to lock the front door when he received the first blow.

He gasped, reaching out to grab the assailant, thinking that Miklos had finally struck again, but ready to take on the challenge. He was turning to grab the attacker when he felt the knife penetrate his shoulder. The blood came gushing out, and the pain grabbed him, making him feel paralyzed for a moment. Anger kicked in, and Alfredo thought, "He will not get the best of me. I have to protect "Annabelle" and Christina and be there for them." He failed to see the second attacker come from the left side. By now, the streets were empty, as everyone had headed home for the evening.

The second stabbing pain was in his side, and he suddenly blacked out. The two men ran, knowing that the job was done and that Alfredo would probably bleed to death on the ground in front of his stand. What they did not realize was that the police station had initiated a late patrol after the last attack on Alfredo, keeping their promise to the community to be more watchful. Luckily, they were on their way now, as part of the regular patrol route.

It took several minutes before the officer got to Alfredo's location, but he spotted him immediately. Using his whistle as an alert, he gave notice that he needed help. Finally, the wagon came to take Alfredo to the hospital.

At home, Annabelle was putting the finishing touches on the meal. She had soft candlelight; the baby was asleep and the cooking smells were intoxicating. Alfredo would really be surprised and happy. But as time passed, she started to become uneasy. She understood that the business sometimes required later than usual attention, but now it was getting so late that she really started to worry.

She paced back and forth, trying to figure out what to do. Rudolf had gone over to Janos and Rowena's for the evening to be able to provide Annabelle and Alfredo with a little private time to themselves. The time passed by, her uneasiness mounting by the minute. She sat in the rocking chair, praying that Alfredo would be fine when she heard the key in the lock. Unfortunately, it was Rudolf, not Alfredo.

"It really smells great in here," he called out as he pulled off his outerwear.

"Grandfather," Annabelle called. "Alfredo has not come home. I know something has happened to him, and it cannot be good."

Rudolf grabbed his jacket and said, "I will run to the market and see if he is there. Don't worry, Annabelle, I am sure something routine has detained him."

Annabelle nodded yes and settled back in the rocker, continuing to pray for the husband that she suddenly realized she was beginning to love. The presence of her grandfather seemed to calm her nerves as she anxiously awaited his return, hoping that Alfredo would be with him.

Rudolf got to the market quickly, but saw nothing or no one around. When he stopped to think, he saw the blood on the ground, pooling in front of the entrance. He was stunned, trying to figure out what to do next. He saw a shopkeeper down the street just closing up and asked him if he had seen anything unusual. When he learned that Alfredo had been taken to the hospital, he immediately started to go there, knowing that he would have to search for Alfredo once he got there.

When he arrived at the hospital, he was taken into the waiting area, where a doctor greeted him.

"Sir, how are you related to the injured man?" the doctor inquired. "My granddaughter is his wife, and I was trying to see what delayed him from work when I learned that he had been attacked."

"I am sorry to tell you, sir, that these injuries are very serious. The gentleman who you are asking about has not gained consciousness yet, and we are not certain that he will." Rudolf stood up, saying, "I am going to get his wife and sister and will return as quickly as I can."

Taking a deep breath, Rudolf tried to recall where Luigi lived. He knew he was somewhat confused about it, but after a few minutes recalled some landmarks. He rushed there first because he realized that someone would have to stay with the baby so he could get Annabelle to the hospital. When he reached Luigi's home, he pounded on the door, frantically calling his name. Luigi came rushing out to discover Rudolf in a frenzy. Explaining what had happened, he begged Luigi's help, telling him how he wanted to go back and get Annabelle.

Luigi cut him off. "Let me get Maria. She will come with us to Annabelle's, and she can stay with the baby until we figure out how badly injured Alfredo is and decide what to do for him and for Annabelle."

The three set out for Annabelle's, arriving as Annabelle was staring out the window, hoping for a sign of Rudolf and Alfredo returning. When she saw Luigi, Maria and Rudolf, she was already putting on her coat to leave. Her face was a pasty white, fear emanating from her eyes. She gave some short instructions to Maria for Christina's care, and was down the stairs to head for the hospital before anyone had a chance to give her any details. As she ran, Annabelle called out, "Where in the hospital is he, Grandfather?"

Rudolf, right behind her, responded," Ask the woman at the desk when you get there, but the doctor told me that it doesn't look good, Annabelle."

She darted ahead. "I have to get to him."

By the time that Rudolf arrived at the hospital, Annabelle was sitting next to Alfredo, who was unconscious. She was crying, holding his hand and whispering to him, "Alfredo, we need you. Please come back to us." It seemed fruitless to her, but she continued her prayers. Finally, the doctor arrived to re-check Alfredo. "Are you the wife?" he asked.

"Yes," whispered Annabelle.

"Your husband has a chance of survival, but until he opens his eyes, we will not know if he can talk, or even the full extent of his injuries."

"When do you think that he will wake up?" she asked.

"It is hard to tell. We have repaired the physical damage, as far as we can see, but there is still a lot to learn about these injuries."

"I will be here until he opens his eyes," Annabelle promised.

As time went by, she laid her head on the corner of the bed, still holding Alfredo's hand. Rudolf witnessed this pathetic scene when he decided that he would go back to the apartment and talk to Luigi, seeing if he could help him at the market.

Time crawled along, and it was not until the next afternoon that Alfredo's eyelids started to flutter. Annabelle reached out to caress his face, speaking softly to him.

"Alfredo, thank God you are coming awake. I have been waiting here with you. Maria has Christina, and Rudolf is helping Luigi. You have nothing to worry about, just get well."

Though his eyes opened and closed, Alfredo did not make any other response. Annabelle left his bedside to find the nurse, so she could tell her that he was beginning to respond. When they returned to his room, he was awake, looking totally confused and mumbling, "Where am I? Someone help me, please. Where am I?"

As soon as he spotted Annabelle, he calmed down. "What happened? Please help me, Annabelle. I don't know what happened."

"No one is clear about just what happened to you, but someone attacked you when you were getting ready to leave work at the end of the day. It was so late; I was worried that you had not come home yet. When Rudolf came home from being at Janos' house, and you weren't home yet, he went to look for you and found you here in the hospital. Then Rudolf came to get me and brought me here and I have been here with you for the past two days. Maria is with Christina and Rudolf is helping Luigi at the market."

Confusion took over his features. "I remember getting ready to go home, but I cannot remember anything after that."

"I hope in time you will be able to tell us who attacked you. For now, just concentrate on getting well."

When Alfredo was released from the hospital, Rudolf stayed with Annabelle. They had several meetings with the constable, but as hard as Alfredo tried, he had no information to offer that would provide a clue to the attack. He just could not remember exactly what had occurred.

In the meantime, Janos put his unnamed supporters to work to see if they could shed any light on this situation. After two weeks of investigating, he learned that Miklos had ordered this attack, hoping for Alfredo's demise. But the informer would not agree to be named for fear of harm to his own family.

Janos took it upon himself to pay Miklos a visit. When Janos arrived at Miklos' home, he was greeted with suspicion.

"What brings you here now?" asked Miklos, standing at his door and not inviting Janos to come in.

"Do you recognize me?" asked Janos.

"Of course, you are Annabelle's cousin. I met you at Margaret's home."

"Yes, that is true. If you have a moment, I would like to speak with you."

"We are speaking now. Just say what you have come to say," Miklos replied, standing firmly on his threshold.

"Can I come in for a moment? I really do not want to have this conversation on your doorstep."

Miklos stepped back reluctantly to allow Janos entrance. He directed him to the parlor to take a seat there.

Janos began, “This will not take long, I am certain.”

“And what is this all about?” asked Miklos, feigning ignorance.

“We have reason to believe that you are behind a recent attack upon Alfredo, Annabelle’s husband. I would like to talk about that with you. I would prefer that we come to an agreement here, so that I will not be forced to bring my evidence to the police.”

“Are you out of your mind?” Miklos responded, raising his voice. “Why would I care about Alfredo or Annabelle? She wholeheartedly rejected me.”

“Exactly,” said Janos. “Yet I am familiar with your tactics and know that you are out for revenge because she did reject you.”

“No, you are crazy. Just get out of here.”

“I think you would do well to discuss this with me. You have seriously injured Alfredo, and he is just out of the hospital now.”

“You can’t prove anything. I have been here at my home for months and have not traveled anywhere.”

“Of course, that’s the case. Because you hired others to do your dirty work. I have *proof* of that.”

“What kind of proof? What is it you want from me?” Miklos asked.

“I want your word that you will leave this family alone. And if you do not, I will bring charges against you. It is your choice.”

“I think you can go now, Janos. I have nothing more to say to you.”

“I would advise you not to tempt me or to push me to take steps that do not need to be taken. Let Annabelle have the life she wants. There are plenty of women out there who would be happy to be married to you.”

Janos turned and put his hat back on his head, pushing through the outside door. As he rode away, Miklos stood at the door, considering. Janos had an upstanding reputation, so he was likely to be believed; he was no pushover, and Miklos needed to think about what he was going to do.

The days seemed to pass so slowly. Margaret came to help Annabelle in her home as Rudolf spent the days at the market, working with Luigi. It was quiet, and no threats were forthcoming. Janos came to report to Annabelle, Alfredo, Margaret and Rudolf the result of his meeting with Miklos.

"One wrong move and we take the evidence to the police. We will press charges against Miklos, and he knows it. I think you will be safe for now."

Annabelle was still fearful. "I do not know how I can defend us? Alfredo is incapacitated, and Rudolf and my grandmother cannot be here forever. I am afraid to go out by myself and to even take Christina to the park by myself. I feel like a prisoner in my own home."

Janos was more confident, "You still have the neighborhood watch group in place. You should be fine," he continued.

Margaret stepped up to say, "I will meditate on this situation and let you know what I see and what might be next." And so, the day ended with as much confusion as it had started. Later, Annabelle, in her time alone with Alfredo, told him about the conversations.

He shared his feelings as well. "I am afraid, not for myself, but for you and the baby."

"I know," she replied." As you have been recuperating, I have come to realize just how much you mean to me and how much I need you in my life. I am afraid I am falling in love with you."

"Then this has happened for good, not for bad," Alfredo replied, taking her hand to his lips. "I do love you, Annabelle, just because of who you are. We can make it through this together. We have a beautiful life in front of us."

CHAPTER TWENTY-TWO: WHAT TO EXPECT

For two months things were quiet and Annabelle started to feel like she had a life of her own. Alfredo went back to work, using a cane to support himself in his walk back and forth from the apartment. Rudolf returned home with Margaret, and Annabelle settled into a routine. She watched Christina grow into a toddler, taking little steps while holding on. She began to try to say words, and her first "Da, Da" was a thrill for Alfredo. As Christina advanced in growth and ability, Annabelle felt pleased with her own performance as a mother. She had formed great affection for this little girl who responded in kind. They spent many afternoons walking in the park and playing games together at home. Christina was even beginning to watch Annabelle as she was preparing their meals and wanted to help, too. Things could not be better between the mother and child.

The most important change for the couple was the blossoming, loving relationship they were experiencing. Annabelle came to cherish Alfredo in his ways and in his values. Alfredo learned that Annabelle was all he had hoped she would be, and he loved having her as his wife. He did not push intimacy on her, but slowly and surely she warmed up to him. At night, when Christina was sound asleep, she snuggled into him, putting her head on his shoulder. She kissed him good night. Linking her arm across his chest, she slept soundly, and he waited patiently for signs of her acceptance of him as her husband. Eventually, the bond they were fusing brought them together. Alfredo would close his eyes, drifting into prayerful mode and thanking God for his good fortune. He was almost panicky about being so happy. How was this possible, and what would happen if he lost Annabelle or Christina?

Annabelle decided that she needed to take more control over stabilizing the family situation. She spent a lot of time trying to figure out what she could do that would make a difference. As a youngster, she never really experienced family solidity, so it was hard for her to come to any conclusions. She decided to ask Alfredo what he thought about her ideas.

She suggested they all get together at a park, midway between them and where Margaret and Rudolf lived. Alfredo liked the proposal and told Annabelle to move ahead with it. She assured him that Janos, Rowena and Bartos would be invited, as would Luigi and Maria. She knew that her grandmother and grandfather would come if they were able to do so; Margaret loved gatherings.

Annabelle talked to both Rowena and Maria. They thought it would be a fine celebration of family connection and talked about preparing food for the outing. They decided that they would cook some of each family's favorites, provide fresh bread and lots of water and wines for the men. Annabelle wanted to concentrate on pastries and Margaret would surely bring some pies – that was her specialty. She asked Janos to help locate just the right spot; he found a nice park that was easy to get to. And so the preparations went on.

When the time finally arrived, the weekend day was clear and crisp, not too cold or too warm, delightful for a gathering. The breeze was gently caressing their faces and everyone was smiling.

It was a real opportunity for the family members to get to know each other better. Rudolf brought his guitar and played some Italian favorites as well as some Hungarian tunes. Everyone sang while Luigi and Maria danced their tarantella.

For once, no one felt that they had to be on guard. The babies were playful; Christina and Bartos were sitting on blankets on the grass. They were taken with each other, laughing and playing with their toys. It was the first restful and non-stressful time the family members had experienced since before Alfredo and Annabelle's wedding. The best part of the day was Grandma Margaret's tale of how she had lived as a little girl in Hungary.

"I remember well how happy I was then," Margaret continued. "I would awake in the morning and rush downstairs to see what my mother was cooking for breakfast. Since I lived on a farm, I knew we would have some fresh eggs, and I usually went out to the coop to gather them. Some of the chickens were not so willing to give up the eggs they had laid, so I had to be careful of how I gathered them. Often, I would have a handful of grain that I could tempt them with, and they would then move away from the coop to eat. That let me reach in and take the eggs that were there, ready to be gathered up. In the summer, I would stop next at the garden and see if there were any strawberries that I could pick and bring in for a special treat. Meanwhile, my Mother had fresh bread baking, and we had butter that we churned from the cow's milk. I loved the warm cow's milk that Mom gave me from the recent milking. That, together with the fresh bread and butter, was a real treat. If she also gave me an egg to eat, it would make such a special day. This, of course, only happened on weekends. During the week, we had school and no time for big breakfasts. Maybe some cheese and oatmeal would suffice."

"Did you have brothers and sisters?" Alfredo inquired.

"Just one sister," said Margaret, "and she has now passed ten years ago. She was my best friend, and I miss her very much and think of her every day. She never married or had children, so our family was really very small."

Alfredo answered her, "Perhaps there is value in a smaller family. We had so many children running around, six of us, that it was often bedlam at home. It is a wonder that my mother could remain so calm." Annabelle turned to her husband. "Tell us more about your parents, please." Alfredo began, "My mother is a loving and giving woman who works really hard to make a comfortable and inviting home. She made most of the household curtains, blankets, pillows and clothing that we wore. She delighted in seeing us pleased with what she created for us. Of course, with such a large family, there were hand-me-downs that we all used, but they were always kept fresh and clean and mended. She did her best to adjust the sizing so we did not look like urchins. She was an amazing cook and knew just how to manage the food so we had enough to eat. My Dad was proud of her."

"What about your father?" Annabelle asked.

"He was a disciplinarian, never lost his temper, but only had to give you a look to make you behave. He loved us all, told us stories at bedtime every night and tucked us in. He worked really hard to provide for us as a family and always made us feel that he was planning ahead."

"Why did he encourage you to come to America?"

"He felt that I would have a better chance for a good life here, that I would be able to make a family and work hard with no concerns about having to do without. Of course, a lot of what he believed was born from tales that he heard from others. I can see that no matter where you are, life is a bit of a struggle, and you always have to work hard, no matter who you are or where you live."

"Is that why he tried to arrange a marriage for you?" Annabelle asked. She worried about asking the question, but she felt she had to know what Alfredo's family had expected. Alfredo hesitated a moment before answering her. "I guess he felt that he had known Lucia's family for so long that it was a good choice for me. What he did not understand was that Lucia was not who he thought she was. If he had truly understood her, he never would have made that arrangement. But let's not talk about that anymore."

Luigi jumped in to divert the conversation, talking about the produce business and how he thought it could grow to help both families. Janos quietly listened, taking everything in. In the back of his mind, he still worried about Miklos and what he might try to do next. However, he never mentioned his concerns to the family, not wishing to spoil a perfect day. They had had so few together. He and Rowena both really cherished this outing, hoping to be able to meet more frequently, allowing the children to have more solid relationships with each other.

When the afternoon wore on and the air cooled a little, Annabelle and Alfredo decided they would accompany Margaret and Rudolf back home. Janos and his family followed Luigi and Maria to New York, since they did not live so far apart. Alfredo agreed to return to New York by Tuesday morning, since Luigi had assured him that he could manage without him on Monday, though that was the most difficult day at the market. After the weekend, families needed to replenish their food supply. Yet he had managed alone before Alfredo arrived. Surely he could manage one day without difficulty. And so, the party broke up, each group going their separate ways.

Janos decided that he would continue his watchful connections, keeping his ears open about Miklos' activities. He did not fully trust the man, knowing that his reputation allowed him to appear to be one way, while actually acting another way. His reputation was to wait patiently until he could get what he wanted. Janos was hoping that some other woman would attract his attention and that he would forget about Annabelle. Janos' network was faithful and on watch for any indicators of new threatening behavior.

Margaret, with the powers she had, would meditate faithfully, daily, to see if she could detect any warning signals. She never felt entirely comfortable, but would not allow herself to think for one moment that Miklos had given up. Her friends kept track of him as well, so, though he did not realize it, Miklos was the target of constant surveillance.

Yet Miklos was clever. He distanced himself from the contacts he had used before. He was plotting in his mind how he could set up a situation that would appear to be an accident and focused on all kinds of options that might open up to him. He remained determined to have Annabelle as his own, one way or another.

The neighborhood group of watchful immigrants were faithful to their task and continued to offer a constant and careful agenda for tracking and trailing any unknown visitors to their residents. Miklos, assessing that situation, could sense that he had to be extra careful and extra clever.

Miklos finally engaged a local man who desperately needed money to keep tabs on Alfredo and Annabelle. He got up-to-date information about their habits and their comings and goings. He was patient and decided to wait it out until he felt they would abandon their guard. He knew that as time passed and they did not feel threatened, they would relax and be less cautious.

He followed Alfredo's work schedule faithfully, learning that on Thursday evenings he was the one left behind to close the business. It was the market's late night to remain open, and the streets were fairly empty after the 8 pm closing time. For some time, Luigi stayed late as well, not allowing Alfredo to become exposed to danger. As Alfredo healed and became stronger, Luigi began to back off, just what Miklos was hoping for. This time, there would not be an attack at the marketplace. Still, it would have to look like an accident, and he worked out the details carefully.

He waited patiently, letting the time go by and allowing Annabelle and Alfredo to build their self-confidence. Additionally, he would make sure that he hired someone without a record, someone who really needed the money. On his walk home, he planned that Alfredo would get pushed in front of a passing carriage, hopefully under the horses' feet and the carriage wheels. This time there would be no saving him, and Miklos would get what he wanted.

Then he would pose as an apologetic and concerned old friend who would step in and help out the poor widow. No one would suspect that he was guilty, because he was intent on forging a better relationship with Margaret and Rudolf, long before this accident would occur.

Dominick was only a teenager, but he really studied Luigi and Alfredo. He went to the market regularly to make purchases for his family. Living in Alfredo's neighborhood and becoming friends with Alfredo and Luigi had become one of the most important aspects of his life. He admired these men and wanted to be like them. He wanted to have the discipline, energy and foresight that enabled them to start their own business and succeed in it. And then he got drawn into something he never expected.

This particular day, he scratched his head trying to figure out what he should do with the information he had just heard. He was standing on the corner across from the market, about to go in to make the daily purchases for his mother, when he realized the two men talking near him were referring to Alfredo and Luigi's business. At first he could not make out exactly what they were saying. Yet he knew he had to pause to listen. As he concentrated more on their words, pretending to be waiting for someone, looking down the street as if he was anxious for someone's arrival, he realized that they were referring to Alfredo's last injury. He heard them admit that they were responsible for what had happened to Alfredo and that they were being paid to "take care of him," which he realized meant to "eliminate him." The men gave no thought to a teenager standing nearby and continued their discussions with abandon.

Dominick, at only seventeen years old, was frightened by the information he had overheard. He knew he would do anything he could to protect his friends, but he also knew that no one would believe a seventeen-year-old who claimed to know about an upcoming "hit" job. He decided that every night when the men were ready to close up the business for the day, Dominick would be there watching out for these troublemakers. He would then intercede and warn Alfredo and/or Luigi of the impending danger. A poor plan, he agreed, but all he could think of to do. At least he would be watching and be able to warn them, if nothing else.

Should he go directly to Alfredo and Luigi with the information he had? Probably not.

They did not know him well enough to trust him. After all, he was only a young man who dropped into the market to purchase produce for his mother. Maybe, he thought, they would consider giving him a part-time job. He would request afternoons, after school, so he would be around at the end of the day. After all, that was the time these men were talking about. Then he could try to help to prevent another incident. And it would allow him to learn more about the business that he was so interested in becoming a part of. He decided that there is no time like the present, so he walked into the market, waited for a lull in the customer load and asked to speak to Luigi.

"Hello. My name is Dominick Stattone. I know you recognize me from coming in every day to shop for my family. I would like to know if you would consider hiring me in the afternoons to help out? I see how busy you are, and I really want to learn how to be a businessman like you."

Luigi smiled, shaking his head. "I admire an ambitious young man. As a matter of fact, it is funny that you should ask about this. We are getting busier every week, and I was actually thinking that we could use some additional help. Let me ask Alfredo what he thinks."

"*Grazie*, thank you," Dominick stumbled over his words. Luigi called Alfredo over to meet Dominick. "Alfredo, this is Dominick, and he is looking for part time work. Do you agree that we could use some additional help in the afternoons?"

"Va bene. That's great," Alfredo agreed. "When can he start?"

"Dominick?" Luigi turned to the young man. "How about tomorrow? Be here around 3:30 pm, and we will start to teach you what you need to do. We have a lot of cleaning up, refreshing the produce and re-arranging the vegetables after they have been picked over." Dominick smiled, happy with the outcome. "I will be here, on time. Thank you for this chance." To himself he thought, and now I can also watch for trouble that might happen.

The next day dawned, bright and clear. Alfredo felt so much more at ease at the prospect of having a strong young man to help out in the market. After all, he was still limited in what he was able to do, and Luigi was bearing the brunt of the responsibilities, especially when it came to lifting the product. Dominick starts today. What a big help he will be, he thought to himself!

Annabelle was joyful to learn that there would be some extra help for Alfredo and Luigi. Maybe it would allow Alfredo to get home at a more decent hour and have some time to rest before dinner? He was really run down and not fully recovered after that last physical attack. She had a funny feeling in the back of her mind that this was an important change that was taking place.

The next morning, she smiled, kissed him goodbye, tucking his lunch pail under his arm and bringing Christina to him for the morning good-bye kiss. Alfredo smiled, his heart heavy with happiness, and started on his way to work.

It turned out to be a very demanding day. The brisk pace of the shoppers gave the men barely enough time to eat some lunch. Before they realized it, Dominick was standing in front of them, reporting in and waiting for instructions.

As it turned out, they were even more thrilled to have Dominick as their new employee than they thought they would be. He was eager to learn and accepted every challenge with grace and enthusiasm. He stocked and restocked, cleaned the floors, straightened up the mishandled fruit and vegetables, and worked happily, bearing a smile for customers and employers. They could see that not only was he quick to learn, but that he had a sincere interest in the business as well.

Alfredo thought to himself that Dominick reminded him of himself at that age. So anxious to do well; so happy to be part of an enterprise with dreams and aspirations of his own. He was having so much trouble with the tiredness he was experiencing after his injuries, so having a young and energetic person on board was really helping him feel better and more hopeful. He worried that something else might happen to him, because, in the back of his mind, he attributed the accidents to Miklos and the band of thugs he associated with, and he was fearful of trusting that it was all over. He could not accept that Miklos was the kind of person that would let things go. He knew, inside his heart, that Miklos was determined to have his way, so he silently feared for himself and for Annabelle.

The day went quickly, and at closing time, Dominick asked Alfredo if it would be all right for him to walk with him as they left for home. Alfredo commented, “I did not know you lived in my direction.”

Dominick replied, “Actually, I don’t, but I have to stop at my aunt’s for my mother, and so I would love the company on the way.”

Dominick smiled, accepting the conversation and comradery. “I would enjoy that, too,” he said. “Sometimes it feels like a lonely walk at the end of the day.”

When they started out together, Dominick surreptitiously kept checking to see if anyone was lingering on the streets. Alfredo thought it strange that he kept checking behind them and asked if anything was wrong. “No, I always have had the habit of paying attention to what is going on around me. My Dad taught me to do that. *Stai Attenti* (pay attention). One can never be too careful.”

Alfredo smiled, “Such wisdom in such a young person.”

When Dominick saw that Alfredo entered his building, he continued on his way. Every night after that, they started out together because Dominick claimed that he had to stop at his aunt’s every day. Alfredo accepted it as fact and thought no more about it.

After three weeks of this habit, Alfredo commented, “Dominick, I feel like you are walking with me because you think I won’t make it home without help. Really, I am fine.”

“No, Alfredo, that is not the case. I enjoy your company and have this chore to do for my mother every day. I learn so much from you and appreciate the advice and guidance you provide me as we talk.”

‘Well, tonight, I am not going directly home. I am on my way to Luigi’s, and he and I will go together.”

Dominick felt a fear grip his heart as he replied, “Have a great dinner, and I will see you tomorrow.” To himself he said a prayer of supplication to the saints for the protection of his boss. As he hesitated on the street, he decided to discreetly follow them. He kept back about half a block. He enjoyed watching Luigi and Alfredo chat and laugh along their pathway. Suddenly, a carriage came thundering by. Dominick knew at once that this was the threat. He began to run alongside the vehicle and screamed out to Alfredo to move away. The horse and carriage just missed Alfredo as the two men, hearing Dominick’s warning, bounded off to the left. Another incident, thought Alfredo. Another attack averted, thanks to Dominick.

As Dominick caught up with them, Alfredo yelled at him, “Dominick, why were you behind us?” Dominick then admitted that he had overheard a man telling another that this would happen soon. He did not know when, but he wanted to be sure he was watching for the incident that he knew would occur.

Luigi replied, “I guess we got a lot more than an employee. We got a loyal friend, just like a family member. Thank you, Dominick, we really appreciate what you have done for us.” Luigi jumped in. “Now, what do we do about these repeated attacks?”

“Let’s talk to Janos,” suggested Alfredo, whose fear at the possibility of being run over had gripped his heart. Yet, he knew that he had to use his intellect to solve this problem and that he would need some help in making decisions.

Janos was surprised when, unannounced, Alfredo suddenly appeared on his doorstep.

"I am not sure if I should be talking about this with you, Janos, but I have nowhere else to turn."

"What happened, Alfredo?" Janos asked, his forehead wrinkled with worry. "Oh, please, forgive me, come in and have something to drink while we talk." Rowena stood in the shadows fingering the edges of her apron. She thought to herself. Now there is more trouble. Anytime Annabelle or her family member comes by, it means trouble.

"Shall I make some coffee?" Rowena inquired.

"Yes, please, Janos replied."

"It will just take a few minutes." She hurried into the kitchen, checking first on the baby who was sleeping nearby. "Let me first move the baby to his crib."

Janos led Alfredo to the cozy kitchen, the smell of bread freshly baked, filling the air.

Alfredo stretched out his injured leg and awkwardly shifted in the chair. "I really do not know where to begin, Janos. There has been another attempt on my life since we last talked. Just last night, a horse and carriage came careening along the street as Luigi and I were walking to his home. It was aimed directly for me, but a warning call from our employee, Dominick, saved me from being trampled. Of course, I have no definite proof about who is behind this plot, nor can I prove that the driver was really heading for me, but I thought perhaps you, in your wisdom, would have some ideas about what to do and how to proceed. Dominick, our part time employee, overheard some men on the street across from the market talking about a plot to injure me. But we do not know who they are or how to find these men."

Janos cleared his throat, trying to catch his breath. “I thought perhaps I had taken care of this. Although I never mentioned it to you, I paid Miklos a visit and warned him that if these attempts did not stop, we would take further action.”

“How did he take that warning?” asked Alfredo.

“He denied any culpability and acted like he had nothing to do with this. However, we do have evidence of his involvement in the other incidents, and I told him that we did. He obviously did not believe me, or did not care.”

Rowena interrupted them, asking if Alfredo wanted cream and sugar for his coffee. She also served some slices of the freshly baked bread that made Alfredo’s heart beat faster.

“Rowena, thank you for your hospitality,” Alfredo offered. “The fresh baked bread brings memories of my mother’s kitchen to my mind, and I am really taken aback by this wonderful offering. “

She nodded and left the men alone to discuss the problem, but stood behind the door listening for what Janos would say. She had a deep-seated fear that if he got involved in this, something would happen to him, as well as to her and the baby.

“Well, what do I do now?” Alfredo questioned.

“Let’s take a walk to the police station and consult with the officers there. See what they have to say. Can you meet tomorrow after work?”

“Yes,” Alfredo agreed. “And I will ask Dominick to come with us, since he actually heard the men plotting against me. Perhaps his presence there will provide more of a convincing argument for the police. “

“Good idea,” Janos said.

As he made his way home that evening, Alfredo kept turning things over and over in his mind. What would become of Annabelle and Christina if something happened to him, and what would Miklos do to retaliate when they visited the law enforcement authorities? He decided that he would take his family to Margaret's home on the weekend and see what she and Rudolf would suggest. He would like to resolve this quietly, but he feared that Miklos was set upon inflicting harm, no matter what they decided to do or how they might go about it.

The visit to the police station did not really resolve anything. The evidence, as they saw it, was circumstantial. The local police chalked it up to an immigrant squabble that did not need too much attention. Even when Janos pointed out that Alfredo had been hospitalized previously for serious injuries after the last attack and that he had almost lost his life, the police did not offer any help at all. Dominick's retelling of the conversation he overheard did not seem to make much difference since he was unable to identify the men he had heard talking.

When they left the station, Janos decided, "We may have to take this into our own hands and bring it to a conclusion that way."

Alfredo inquired, "Then the law would take an interest, wouldn't it?"

Janos agreed but thought that things might not go in their favor in any case.

When Alfredo related these discussions to his brother-in-law, Luigi decided to reach out to his community contacts. After all, he had been in business more than five years and was respected among the population. He had friends in high places. He would talk to them and see what could be done to end this conflict. One of his contacts suggested that they hire a private detective and was even able to furnish a reliable name. Yet Luigi and Alfredo looked at each other, trying to figure out how they could ever afford such a move.

CHAPTER TWENTY-THREE: ONE FAMILY

Alfredo and Luigi met without their wives to further discuss the idea of employing a private detective. There was no sense in getting the women any more agitated than they already were. After going over the financial records for the produce market, they decided that there was no possibility of being able to afford such a plan. Although they did not have any referrals to reliable sources, they also knew that whatever the cost, it would be way beyond any discretionary income that the two men had. They finally decided to see what Janos thought about the possibility. Was it a good idea at all? And would it be only wasted money?

After work that evening, the two partners took a walk to see Janos. He was somewhat surprised when they arrived at his doorstep, but, though he had no idea when or if they would come to see him, Janos had a feeling that they would be visiting him.

Janos was equipped with more information about Miklos. It seemed as though, as time passed, Miklos was getting more and more out of control. He was maddened by the concept that he could not control the world around him and that he was unable to achieve what he wanted. There were tales of him harassing his neighbors, of offending some of his business contacts and of becoming more associated with the unsavory element of their society. Janos feared another attempt at an attack on Alfredo, or even on Annabelle.

When Alfredo and Luigi explained that they had been seriously considering finding a private detective, Janos agreed that it was a good idea. In fact, there was a fellow who had done some work for Janos' boss; he vowed to get the man's information from his boss and to get in touch with him to see what kind of services he might offer and how much he would charge them.

That night Alfredo actually got a little sleep. He kept waking up to make sure that Christina and Annabelle were safe and sound, but he felt that, at least, he had some direction. It was better to be working towards a plan than to be wondering what to do next.

When 5:00 pm arrived the next day, both Luigi and Alfredo were exhausted. It was not so much that the trade was so brisk, as that they were emotionally spent. They knew that they still had an hour to go before quitting time and started their clean up chores a little earlier as they continued to help customers.

When Alfredo turned around, he saw Janos standing at the back of the store. He anxiously approached him, never expecting to have any information so quickly. Janos explained that the detective, John Connors, was willing to work with them and that he would even consent to take payments over time, after he learned that attacks had already taken place and the amount of physical damage that Alfredo had already endured. Still the cost was steep for Alfredo, even though Luigi was prepared to help out.

Detective Connors agreed to tail Miklos, tracking who he was communicating with and, if he could arrange to overhear conversations, what was being discussed. Janos explained that the detective estimated the value of two week's pay for this effort. Alfredo's face dropped. He did not have enough savings to cover even one week of pay, and he knew that Luigi did not have any more money set aside than Alfredo had.

Janos said he had been giving this a lot of thought and wanted everyone to meet at Margaret and Rudolph's house the following Sunday to further discuss strategy. Alfredo agreed and was able to get Luigi's consent as well. And so another day went by. Extreme caution around every move they made was a requirement for both Alfredo and Luigi.

When Alfredo got home and revealed to Annabelle what he had learned, she was dubious. What good would it be to get her grandmother and grandfather involved any further in this mess that enveloped them. Alfredo told her, "Janos said that Rudolf is a man of the world, and we need to get his opinion before taking any further steps. And we need your grandmother's feedback, too." When he stated the reason for involving them in this way, Annabelle had to agree that it was advisable.

Sunday was cold but sunny. They dressed Christina warmly, agreeing to meet Luigi and Janos at Margaret's home. Of course, when they arrived, Margaret had planned a wonderful dinner for all. They decided to enjoy the company and wait until after dinner for the discussion. Moving into the parlor, Rudolf brought out an aperitif, and they settled comfortably in front of the banked fire. The room was cozy, not too warm, but welcoming.

Janos started the discussion explaining the role of Detective John Connors and the estimated cost of his services. Alfredo questioned if this was a good idea. What would happen if Connors could not gather any information? How would they make the police buy into the possible guilt of Miklos, even if the detective did manage to come up with some kind of solid proof. The police had not really been helpful up to this point. Silence overcame the room.

Then Margaret spoke up, "We are one family. We are all responsible for each other, and therefore we should be armed with defenses for each other." She addressed her husband, "Rudolf, I know we have not discussed this at all, but be open and honest if you do not agree. No one will take offense."

“What are you trying to say, Margaret?” Rudolf responded.

“I have some money set aside from my practice, and I would like to contribute to the cause. We need to ensure safety for Annabelle, Christina, Alfredo, Luigi and Maria as well.”

Without hesitation, Rudolf responded, “I agree.”

At that point Janos interjected, “Rowena and I will also help out. After all, it could implicate us as well, if Miklos loses his mind.”

“All right then, it is settled. Janos, Alfredo and Luigi, meet with the detective and have him start his investigation. There is nothing more important than this family. We are one unit and will stand by each other, no matter what happens.”

It was decided that Janos would make arrangements on Monday for the meeting with Detective Connors, and the men would go over the details of the investigation and what would be expected from both sides.

Annabelle, Maria and Rowena worried about the men and how much danger they were in. They vowed to make sure they would get word to each other if anything worrisome happened.

On Monday evening, the men met with John Connors at the appointed time. He listened to the evidence against Miklos and learned about the response from the head of the local police station. He wondered if anyone was being paid off.

John promised to initiate his efforts the following day and to keep in touch. He would investigate carefully all of the events that had taken place. He wondered why the police did not give this case more consideration, especially since Alfredo was hospitalized, and multiple attempts had been made on his life. John Connors vowed to himself to see if there was any shady connection with the law and to update Alfredo and Luigi on a regular basis. And so the plan was laid and put into action.

CHAPTER TWENTY-FOUR:
THE BEST LAID PLANS

Alfredo opened his eyes to the bright sunshine filtering through the curtains. He shook himself to activate his senses and then remembered that John Connor was about to begin this much needed investigation today. He turned to look at Annabelle, so peacefully sleeping, and at Christina who was still quietly sucking her thumb. But there was no time to waste. He gently shook Annabelle's shoulder, saying, "We have to get up right now in order to get Christina ready to go with you to Maria's. Luigi and I have decided we want you to be together. In that way, we can get to both of you at the same time should anything more occur."

"Please, Alfredo, don't say that. We want to be safe, but not to have to worry every minute."

"Unfortunately, Annabelle, until we get Miklos in control, I am not taking any chances."

"I understand, I will get ready now."

John Connor immediately started his investigation, searching through records to see if Miklos had any recorded violations of any kind. It was a tedious job, and the day's work did not reveal anything. So he decided to interview neighbors and anyone that Miklos seemed to be communicating with. He continued to tail him and saw that, on a regular basis, he seemed to get into verbal arguments easily. Clearly, John thought, Miklos liked to have things his way.

At the end of the first week of following Miklos, John got his initial break. As he lounged against the wall outside the coffee shop near Miklos' house, he heard two of Miklos' neighbors talking about a conflict that Miklos had with an antique dealer who refused to give Miklos the discount he wanted in purchasing a Queen Anne chair. Apparently, Miklos had made some threats against the man and his business. John decided to talk to the Caroni Antique Shop's owner and see if he could get more information. When he arrived at the location, the store was closed for the day, so he vowed to revisit it on the next day.

When he arrived the following morning, he found Severino Caroni in a frantic state. He was afraid something would happen to him, he stated, because of Miklos' aggression. John Connor advised Mr. Caroni to seek the aid of the police to resolve the situation. However, he now knew that Miklos, at least, was on the record with threats against someone who would not cooperate with him.

At the next meeting Janos, Alfredo and Luigi seemed to feel that John Connor had demonstrated a fruitless effort so far, and the men were discouraged. In the next week, Severino Caroni closed up early to make his way home before dark. He felt anxious about his safety and wanted to be in his house where he felt more secure. He and his family had a pleasant dinner, and Severino began to relax, thinking that his imagination was getting the best of him. His family went to sleep early and, for the first time in weeks, Severino was enjoying a blissful night of rest.

Then he heard the knocking on his door. He looked at the clock—3:00 AM. His stomach turned over when he saw the police officer standing there, a troubled expression on his face.

"Mr. Severino, come quickly," the police officer stated. "Your antique store is on fire."

The insurance company investigation showed that the fire was not an accident. They found evidence that pointed to Miklos. After securing positive proof of his involvement, Miklos was arrested. He had finally made a serious error. In his passionate pursuit of power, he had failed to realize that he had left his gloves behind, alongside the gasoline can he had purchased locally that was used to start the fire.

A trial was held, and Miklos was convicted and sentenced to seven years in prison. Severino Caroni had won the case. The insurance company provided him with funds to rebuild the store and monies against his lost inventory. Everyone prayed that this would be the end of Miklos' attempts to threaten Annabelle and attack Alfredo.

Maybe now, life could go on for Alfredo and Annabelle.

EPILOGUE

As with all facets of life, there are many ups and downs each and every week. Annabelle was learning how to cope with change and found herself happier than she ever expected to be.

She watched Christina grow into a smart and curious little girl who seemed happy with her parents and who was looking forward to going to school. Annabelle realized that her loving care had contributed to this young girl's approach to life and she was proud of her accomplishments. Alfredo wanted to ensure that Christina would have enough knowledge to take care of herself in life, should anything happen to require that. So he began to put aside funds for her to continue learning. It was an unusual strategy for an immigrant father to take, yet Annabelle secretly hoped that her influence on Alfredo had some effect on his decisions. She had spoken so many times of her plight in life, abandoned by her parents and by Franz and her inability to survive. Had it not been for her grandparents, Janos and, of course, for Alfredo who virtually saved her life, she would have been lost.

Margaret passed away the year after Christina started school and Rudolf died six months after her. Their home was sold as they had directed, the proceeds split between Janos and Anabelle. This act of generosity was what enabled Alfredo to set a new direction for his family. Once again, Annabelle thanked God for the blessings he had bestowed on her and Alfredo. Somehow, it looked as though things would work out, after all.

After having finally overcome his disabilities as a result of the physical attacks he received, Alfredo, with Annabelle's blessing to use the money she had inherited, bought a share of the produce business from Luigi and together they expanded the enterprise, making it profitable enough to support both families in a manner that enabled the men to buy houses for their families, to secure a second location and to hire additional help. Of course, it took a lot of hard work and determination, but Luigi and Alfredo only knew how to work hard.

Dominick still worked part time for them on weekends, though he had full-time employment in a manufacturing facility and was well on his way to becoming a manager. They did not want to part company with Dominick, and he wanted to retain the wonderful working relationship he had with the men. When Alfredo and Luigi opened the second market about 20 minutes away, Dominick became their manager. He invested his learning in keeping books for them, researching how to purchase produce more efficiently without sacrificing quality and implementing much needed changes, including a delivery service.

Annabelle was finally content. She had come to fully appreciate her husband and family and became involved in a community-based program to help other immigrant women to become more versed in the English language. She also undertook visiting new residents in their neighborhood, acquainting the women with the services available and helping them find whatever they would need to make their families more comfortable. She was surprised at how much she enjoyed this interaction with others and how she was able to overcome her shyness.

Alfredo and Annabelle were blessed with a baby boy, Antonio, and planned to have more children together. Luigi and Maria had a little baby girl, Anna, who became a steadfast friend to Christina and Antonio. The

Caruso family was growing, just like the psychic had predicted. Often Annabelle thought back to the wise old woman who had foretold so much that was actually happening.

Of all the people she had come to love, Annabelle most missed her grandmother, *Anyóka*. She would often speak to her in whispers, hoping that she would send some sign of acknowledgement and asking her for guidance in her life.

Annabelle and Alfredo made regular visits to her grandparents' grave site to pay their respects to the wonderful couple. Annabelle vowed never to forget the woman who had done so much to save her life, caring for her as a child and taking her through the really rough times after Paula died. Without her grandmother, Annabelle would never have made it through the challenges she faced.

Miklos met his fate in prison. His aggressive personality got him into a scuffle with another prisoner who was bigger and stronger than he was. The conflict continued until one day the other prisoner pulled a knife on Miklos and ended his life.

When Alfredo and Annabelle learned about it, they faced a challenge, sadness for the events that led up to Miklos' death and happiness from realizing they had nothing more to fear from him.

Janos and Rowena had a second child, a little girl that they named Melody in honor of Rowena's mother, who loved music and was always singing and dancing to her native songs. In time, Annabelle and Rowena forged a solid friendship and managed to create a circle of loving family members that included Janos' family, Luigi and Maria's family, Alfredo and Annabelle and all the children. It was an accepting and loving community of extended family members that brought joy and understanding to adults and children alike.

Annabelle would tell her husband how much she appreciated him and reminded him that she had agreed to marry him for better or worse, in sickness and in health, until death. She also reminded him that she was totally unable to offer him complete obedience and he assured her that he wanted his wife to be an equal to him; they were partners, a team. As Magyar had predicted, Annabelle grew in love and devotion to Alfredo and together they continued to grow their own family, enjoying a sense of stability and unconditional love.

ABOUT THE AUTHOR

Born and raised in New York City, Charlotte Caminos attended Mother Cabrini School, where she served as Editor of the school newspaper. Graduating with honors, she progressed to Fordham University where she secured a BS in Education. She taught high school for four years before transitioning to the corporate world, working first as a Healthcare Manager, then taking on the roles of Facilities Manager and Human Resources Manager in a commercial real estate firm. After receiving a Master's of Arts in Organizational Management (MAOM), she took on senior leadership roles for two Financial Services companies. During this time, she also functioned as an adjunct professor at Villanova University in the Graduate Human Resources Department, in Radnor, PA for five years.

Community service has always been an integral part of Charlotte's professional life. A longtime Rotarian, she has led numerous service projects, which include raising funds for a child undergoing open heart surgery, forming a Literacy Program, and organizing a blood drive for the North Jersey Blood Center bringing in 350 pints of blood in three days. Today she makes Angel Gowns for stillborn infants from discarded wedding gowns, as well as caps for premature infants in intensive care.

Charlotte is a writer at heart. Her articles have appeared in various outlets. She self-published a children's book (***We Have A New Baby At Our House)*** and recently completed her first novel, an immigration story (***New***

Beginnings: Annabelle's Story). More of Charlotte's work can be found on her blog (afteriretireiwill.com).

ACKNOWLEDGEMENTS

Writing has always been an integral part of my being. I have been writing since my teenage years but had never tackled a novel before this one.

The inspiration for this book came when I learned about my grandmother's struggles in her immigration experience. This is not about her personal life, but the main character mirrors her personality, dedication and loving perspective on living.

I want to acknowledge all the help I experienced in creating this story. I had the dedicated efforts and feedback from several peers, all of them qualified professionals. Some were educators, some were coaches; all were brilliant in their own right. So thank you Genevieve Kuhar, Nancy Brown, Stephanie Brown, Su Ellis and Lisa Penn. Your suggestions helped to make this a more cohesive undertaking and certainly a much more exciting tale.

Christy Mahon created the design for the book cover. It really reflects the feeling of family, and how all the members work together to provide a sturdy shelter for each and every person in their struggles through life. Thank you, Christy, for a beautiful representation of Annabelle's Story.

Thanks also to my publisher, HPN Books, and the efforts of Daphne Fletcher. Her patience in fielding my constant barrage of questions was remarkable. Also, thanks to Kevin Kern for guiding me through the process of editing and for his valuable input.

If my cousin, Frank Scotti, had not connected me to Daphne Fletcher, then this book might not exist today. So, my thanks go out to him.

Finally, deepest gratitude to my husband and children who have always believed in me and have encouraged me every step of the way.

www.ingramcontent.com/pod-product-compliance
Lightning Source LLC
Chambersburg PA
CBHW022248020325
22839CB00019B/203
* 9 7 8 1 9 4 4 8 9 1 8 7 9 *